SERIOUSLY FLAWED

A NOVEL

To Larry,

Best Wishes

R. T. Wiley

SERIOUSLY FLAWED

A NOVEL

R. T. WILEY

SERIOUSLY FLAWED, a novel

Copyright ©2014, 2016 R. T. Wiley
Printed in the United States of America

ISBN-13: 978-1532895111
ISBN-10: 1532895119

Credits: Cover design: @NewGalleryPublishing.com
Cover photo courtesy: ©Morguefile.com
Editing: @NewGalleryPublishing.com
Book design: @NewGalleryPublishing.com
Author photo courtesy R. T. Wiley

Interior text is set in Palatino with headers set in COPPERPLATE GOTHIC LIGHT. Title pages are set in Felix Titling.

Seriously Flawed, a novel, is also available for immediate download as an eBook from Kobo through independent book retailers and on Amazon.com (for Kindle e-readers) and from Smashwords.com for all other e-readers.

1

Colombia 2006

Today, as he had for every two weeks for as long as he could remember, Miguel Martinez would travel with his father to the nearest village to sell the family's harvest of fruit and vegetables. Miguel was of average size for a seventeen-year-old, a lean five feet six, but he had grown strong working his father's farm. The Martinez family dated back many generations; they had all been farmers who barely eked out a living for their families. Señor Martinez was already harnessing the donkey to the cart while Miguel loaded the bags filled with vegetables. Today would be just another day, like so many others he spent with his father.

The sky was blue and cloudless, and the heat beat down on them until they reached the jungle, where the long walk through its high trees provided some shade. It was a roughly worn trail, wide enough for only a donkey-drawn cart. Miguel always enjoyed the trip. He found the jungle a beautiful place filled with its wild exotic birds and stunning flowers. On the way home, he'd always gather a bouquet for his mother and sister.

He and his father dressed alike: open sandals and full, white cotton pants and loose, flowing shirts. The pants were a bit too short, as if they had outgrown them by at least two inches. His father walked slower than Miguel, stooped from many years of hard work in the fields. His face and arms, dark and leathered from the sun, made him appear much older than his fifty years. They had made this trip together often; Miguel knew every inch of the trail and could have navigated it in the dark if he'd needed to.

Approaching the other village, the trail widened into narrow dirt street lined with small adobe houses. Several children were watching them as they made their way up the street; soon the children were running beside the cart, their hands outstretched and begging. That was something Miguel's father would never permit his children to do. The Martinez family had been raised to work hard for everything they received.

The village was small, barely two blocks long. In its center was a water fountain, and a well that had long ago gone dry. Two men were sitting at the base of the fountain, drinking what was probably warm beer and shouting drunkenly at each other. Miguel and his father ignored them and continued to the general store.

Miguel tied the donkey to the rail outside, and he and his father hefted the large sacks of vegetables, tossing them onto their backs. Señor Martinez groaned from the weight and walked slowly up the steps to the porch. As he reached for the door, it crashed open, nearly knocking itself from its hinges.

Pedro Gonzales stepped out of the store. He was a big hulk of a man, known throughout the area as a low-life thug, whose main activities in life were drinking, fighting, and abusing women, married or single. If anyone crossed his path, that person was in for trouble. Pedro was the village bully, and he was glad everyone feared him.

He faced Señor Martinez who was waiting before him. "Get the hell out of my way, you dried-up piece of burro shit!" he shouted. Drool was running from the corners of his mouth and into his stubble of unkempt beard. He glared at the older man through narrowed eyes.

Señor Martinez had always been a proud man who did not feel he needed to step aside for someone such as Pedro. Without warning, Pedro struck the old man across the face, lifting him off his feet and sending him crashing over the rail into the pile of rocks below.

Miguel ran to the edge of the porch and stared down at his father's twisted body. A small stream of blood was running from his father's left ear and down his cheek; it was drying almost instantly in the hot sun. Miguel stood for what seemed like a lifetime, watching for any movement from his father.

Pedro's two friends followed him out of the store, but they did not even glance at the Miguel or his father.

They were laughing and joking as they walked down the steps to the Martinez's vegetable cart. The three men grabbed the lower edge of the cart and turned it over with ease; the vegetables spilled out, rolling in all directions. They began kicking and throwing them about randomly, at whatever target they could find.

The village peasants were collecting the squash and fruit and potatoes like it was a treasure hunt and then running away with their arms full. They didn't want any part of Pedro and his friends either.

"Please!" Miguel cried. "Somebody please help my father!" There was no response. Not even the shop owner, who had known Señor Martinez for most of his life, would step outside. The townspeople feared they might become Pedro's next victims. The three men continued down the street until they stepped into the local cantina.

Miguel crouched over his father, grasping his head in his hands, and sobbed. He gently lifted his father's lifeless body and carried him to the old church a half block away. He knocked, and someone inside opened the door.

An elderly nun greeted him. "I'm so very sorry about your father." Her voice was soft and kind. "Is there anything I can do?"

Miguel didn't answer. He was confused and could not speak. He laid his father down on the cool marble floor and stared helplessly at his body. After checking for any signs of life, the nun called for the parish priest;

kneeling together the three of them prayed. Miguel's grief was turning slowly to rage, something he had never felt before; his heart was pounding wildly. He stood, continuing to stare at the floor but seeing nothing.

"Muchas gracias, padre," he said and then left them abruptly, returning to the street and their overturned cart. He grabbed the machete his father had used on the trail to cut through the jungle. Everyone still seemed to be in hiding, as if the population of the village no longer existed. Miguel started toward the cantina, his right arm held close to his side and gripping the machete so tightly his knuckles were white, his anger building with every step. He reached the cantina and waited, poised like a snake ready to strike, behind the pile of boxes stacked by the doorway.

"Hey, Pedro!" he called, his voice trembling and breaking. "Come out and face Miguel!"

Raucous laughter poured from the cantina.

Pedro answered him, his voice high and mocking. "Well, I guess you're not old enough to come in, little Miguel. I'll come out and teach you a lesson." There was more laughter, and at last Pedro came outside.

Miguel stepped from behind the boxes, the machete gripped in both hands, and swung at the big man who had killed his father and who was now taunting him. His move must have caught Pedro by surprise: the village bully did not have time to even raise his arms. The blade struck with such force that it severed Pedro's head from his body. The body remained standing for a moment, spewing blood in all directions, before it crumpled to the steps. Pedro's bloody head rolled back into the cantina, stopping at the feet of Pedro's two *compadres*. Without him for protection, they jumped up and dashed out screaming through the back door of the cantina.

Miguel's anger changed to fear: he couldn't believe what had just happened. Overcome with grief, he dropped the machete as if it had suddenly grown hot, like when it was left too long in the afternoon sun. A dog barked somewhere, as if from far away, but it was only outside the cantina, jolting Miguel from his trance. Slowly and cautiously, the townsfolk began coming from their homes again; a few approached the cantina.

Arms outstretched, he started toward the oncoming peasants. He wanted to speak to them, but couldn't say anything. The words were trapped inside him. "Please forgive me," he longed to say, although the villagers ought to be glad Pedro was dead. Miguel feared what would happen to him if the authorities found out he had killed someone.

His day that had begun like every other day he spent with his father had changed in an instant.

Frightened and disoriented, he realized he would never be able to return to his family again. He turned and started running, faster and faster, headed back into the jungle. After what seemed like hours, he stumbled across a stream that led to a river. His father had told him once that the big river would lead to Colombia's largest city, Bogotá, and so he kept following the stream.

How would he survive? He had no food and no money. Running through the jungle had exhausted him. Branches would snap across his face and thick leaves cut through his shirt, leaving welts all over his arms and chest. He was not following any trail now but trying to stay close to the river. Finally he came upon a small house in a clearing.

Miguel stretched out flat on his belly, hiding in the thick undergrowth and waiting to see whether anyone was around. He was out of breath, his throat was so dry it was difficult to swallow, and the fear of being caught was making him sick to his stomach. After he gauged that at least twenty minutes had passed, he decided it was safe to enter the house. Quickly gathering up what little food he found there, he wrapped everything in his bandanna. There were a few coins in a tin cup on the table; he grabbed them too and stuffed them into his pocket. He had never stolen anything in his life: he knew it was wrong but must keep going.

Behind him the door opened inward slowly, groaning on its hinges and startling Miguel. An old woman began to yell and wave her arms about. He ran to the door, accidentally knocking her to the floor as he passed. *What have I become?* he agonized. *I'm a killer and now a thief? Have I turned into another Pedro?*

Miguel reached Bogotá after three days. The big city overwhelmed him, crowded with people, tall buildings, and noisy traffic. Confused and worried, he was uncertain what to do next. He was hungry and needed clothes. What he had been wearing the day he left home was torn and dirty. He passed a crowded, busy bakery where people were waiting to buy bread and pastries. Ignoring the stares of the customers, the aroma of baking bread tempted him, and he circled around to the back door that was standing open and slipped inside unnoticed. While the owner was waiting on customers in the front, he filled an empty flour sack with bread. It looked like stealing was going to be a way of life for him.

"*Madre de Dios!* How I miss my family and home! I don't want to go to prison!" He was living in an alley behind a heap of trash. Nights were so cold, and he longed for his mother and sister and the warm comfort of their small house.

2

COLOMBIA

Life alone in Bogotá was not easy. Miguel endured a nightmarish existence living on the streets. Nights were cold; many days it rained heavily. Miguel sought shelter anywhere it could to be found, in abandoned school buses or cardboard boxes. He huddled in the hall-ways of run-down buildings and under railroad bridges. When the weather turned colder, he would seek out the warmth of a mission, and he often resorted to begging on the sidewalks. He was arrested for fighting and spent several nights in the city jail. Life was tough-ening him, and he became hardened and streetwise. He claimed his last name was Vargas, hoping to avoid the law.

One day after he had turned eighteen, Miguel was huddling in the doorway of an older, two-story house in the suburbs. He had been spending the night in the shelter of its outbuilding for a week when one of the women who lived in the big house called out to him.

"*Hola! Bonito!*" she called in his direction.

Confused that this attractive woman was calling for someone "good-looking," he craned around, looking behind him, and tried to hide in the evening shadows.

"I'm talking to you, silly." She stepped down into the back courtyard. "What's your name?"

"Miguel," he stammered and faced her. Wide dark eyes, outlined with makeup such as he'd never seen before, looked back into his, and lips colored with bright red lipstick smiled back at him. *Oh, Dios! What a beautiful woman,* he thought. There were no women like this in his village of San Colón.

"Miguel," she murmured his name softly, in a way he'd never heard it spoken before. "You look like a good boy. Would you like to work for us? It's not much, a few chores here and there." She waved her hand, red nail polish glinting in the dim light.

Miguel gulped and nodded. "*Gracias.*"

"I'm Miss Cherry."

The English words sounded strange to Miguel, but he practiced the pronunciation in his head: *Meez Cherrie.*

Gradually, Miguel learned that he was working for one of the most notorious whorehouses in the city and that Miss Cherry was its Madame. After he finished some basic work repairing the old house, she seemed to find other excuses to keep him there. She must have taken a liking to him.

"You're a hard worker," Miss Cherry said one day. "You need a proper place to stay." She set about rearranging a small room at the rear of the house.

"*Gracias,*" Miguel murmured, too happy to say anything more. He had never had his own room before.

Miss Cherry's house was a large, sprawling home with many rooms and an adjoining vacant lot that was used for parking. Music was always playing on the radio, adding to the light-hearted atmosphere. It was not long before he knew all the girls by name and was hustling business for them. He was good at it, and he doubled the business of the house in less than a year.

The girls were also getting to know Miguel. He would often overhear their chatter when they thought he wasn't listening: "Look at his body," one of them would whisper. Another would say, "I want him for *me!*" They were actually making bets as to who would take him first.

Miss Cherry silenced all of them. "That boy's a virgin. The pleasure's going to be mine, when the time's right." She was silent for a moment and looked thoughtful. "I will take my time and teach him all the fine points of making love."

Sometimes Miguel would study the Madame, when he thought she wasn't looking, and wondered what it would be like. She might have been twice his age, but she didn't look much older than him. Maybe a bit harder than the girls he had known back in San Colón. She was tall too and voluptuous, but she wasn't fat, like other older women he'd known in his village. She wore her long, black hair pulled into a ponytail; her eyes seemed black as coal and very mysterious. She sometimes passed by him when he was at work and hugged him against her breasts, which took his breath away. At other times, she would simply grab his ass or reach through his legs and grab his *cajones.* When he jumped, startled, she would laugh and giggle at his innocence.

Some of Miguel's duties included general cleaning around the house. Miss Cherry started asking him to work extra in her upstairs suite, shampooing the carpet, polishing the furniture, and making her bed. She would often leave her bathroom door ajar, just enough so that he could catch a glimpse of her in the shower while he worked.

Thursday was the day Miguel was always scheduled to clean her room, and he knocked on her door.

"Come in, Miguel," she called. "I've just started my bath."

He entered and began his regular chores and dusting. Cherry had drawn a tub of hot bathwater and added bubble bath and sweet-smelling bath oils. She hadn't bothered to pull the door closed at all this time. Nervously, he kept glancing back into the bathroom as often as he could.

"We've sure been busy lately," he said. "That's good for the house, isn't it?" *How stupid that sounded,* he thought. He couldn't think of anything else to say.

"Miguel, would you do me a favor?" Miss Cherry's voice was low and sultry. "Help wash my back. Here's the washcloth and soap."

Miguel set down his dust cloth and came into the bathroom, trying to approach her from the back. The bubbles were almost up to her shoulders and partially covered her breasts. Even with that much exposure, Miguel could feel his excitement starting to rise, his body responding to a beautiful naked woman. He thought his heart might burst through his chest.

"Miss Cherry?" Miguel's voice cracked, high and uncertain. "I've never done this before... I don't know what to do."

"Don't be silly, Miguel. Put some soap on the cloth and gently wash my back. That's good," she said, encouraging him. "Now, reach down. Yes, deep into the tub—down to my ass and around to each side."

Miguel followed her instructions. He was sweating in the heat of the room and feeling breathless. Her breasts glistened through layers of soap bubbles, the dark, round areolas and thick nipples inviting him to touch them. The pulsing he had felt before now throbbed in his crotch: he'd grown hard as a rock. *Dios! She was beautiful, with the soap cascading over those wonderful breasts.* He longed to touch them, but refrained and resumed washing her neck and her back.

Cherry stood up in the tub, water dripping off her, and faced him. She took Miguel's hands in hers, urging him to stand up, and whispered in his ear, "My sweet boy, I want you to wash all of my body. But you should take your clothes off first. We don't want your clothes getting wet, now do we?" She smiled at him. "You can leave your undershorts on if you want to," she added casually, as an afterthought, and eased back into the water.

Miguel began removing his clothes, carefully folded and placed them on a chair, and returned to the tub. With the soapy washcloth in one hand he started at her shoulders, drinking in the color of her skin. It was like milk with coffee, and it was soft like silk. He continued down her back to her buttocks and then stopped. He started again nervously at her ankles and legs.

"Miguel?" Cherry grasped him and tried to guide his hand between her legs, but he was trying to turn away from the tub. She held onto him firmly. "Don't stop now."

Miguel's penis was straining at the confines of his shorts, as if it had a life and will of its own. He seemed to have no more control over his body, and his mind was racing wildly.

She touched him, caressing his erection through the thin cotton fabric. "*Sí, el grande,*" she whispered. "Yes, the big one... what I've been waiting for." Then, as if remembering the bath once more, she motioned to her breasts. "But you haven't finished washing these."

Miguel picked up the washcloth, but his hands were shaking and he dropped it. Awkwardly he started rubbing her breasts with his bare hands.

"No, no, no…," she murmured gently. She pulled his face down close and placed one nipple in his mouth. "This way is much better, no?"

Her nipples were almost as hard as Miguel was. He tasted one, and then the other, amazed at how each would respond to his tongue. He was certain he would burst at any moment—his head, his heart, or his hard-on.

Miguel picked up the cloth, again rubbing her flat smooth stomach. His hand strayed lower, and he discovered that she was clean shaven. He had never seen that before. All the pictures the younger boys shared were of women with crotch hair. Her being hairless aroused him even further. Cherry helped push his fingers down further, up to the spot that seemed to make her moan with pleasure. He hoped that was what it was. When he tried to stop, she made him continue. He was soaking through his shorts, but his penis was staying full and erect. *Dios! What's happening to me?* he thought.

"Now, sweetheart, it's your turn." Cherry was always in control. One minute driving him mad and another minute focusing on the bath. She pulled his shorts down, and he stepped out of them unresisting and into the tub. He was standing calf-deep in the bubbles while Cherry washed him, stopping every few minutes to take his *pene* in her mouth, teasing him with little flicks of her tongue.

At first he was embarrassed, but he loved the way her hands glided over his body.

"Now, for you, *el grande*," She caressed his swollen erection tenderly, "something very nice for your big boy, *no?* There are some special oils that will make you tingle with delight."

Miguel couldn't imagine anything feeling better than what she'd already done.

"I want you to remember this for the rest of your life," she whispered. "Now, make love to me."

"Oh, Dios! I can't wait any longer!" he would remember calling out at times.

"Yes, yes. You can!" She breathed against his ear and whispered a word. "Wait. Just see... like when I touch you there?"

She would bring him to the brink, nearly driving him crazy, and then cool him down until she had climaxed again and again. They spent the afternoon entangled in the hottest, steamiest love-making that Miguel could have ever imagined, trying all the things she had promised and what Miguel could never have dreamed possible.

That was the only time he had sex with Miss Cherry. She was right: he would remember everything she taught him and for the rest of his life. Curiously, they remained good friends. On occasion, Miguel would have sex with the other girls at the house, but it was never the same as his first time. Whatever he did with them was all right with Miss Cherry, as long as it didn't interfere with their regular work.

Miguel worked at Miss Cherry's for another year, but his comfortable and satisfying life would end one fateful night when the house caught fire. Most of the girls escaped from the flames, but Miss Cherry and two other girls were trapped upstairs.

He couldn't find her, and he rushed back into the house, but the stairway was fully engulfed in flames. There was no way anyone could get up or down. "Miss Cherry!" he called. He heard their screams of panic, but was unable to help them. The fire was too intense and he ran from the house again.

Outside on the sidewalk, he huddled with the other the girls, watching the flames consume the house until all that remained was a pile of smoldering ash. The fire department, in the poorer section of the city, arrived too late and was not able to save anything. Miguel had lost his new home and a special friend.

Miguel wandered off into the night, not sure what to do or where to go, back on the streets once more. He had managed to grab some clothes and the money he'd saved before escaping into the parking lot. This time he at least knew his way around. He slept in an abandoned car that night.

The following day, Miguel began making inquiries. He had never needed to join any of the local gangs, but he had a few friends in them. Keeping on their good side had been helpful from time to time.

Soon, an acquaintance in one of the gangs had news.

"There's this religious nut who's been bragging about torching an old whorehouse."

Miguel could feel rage building, but forced himself to remain calm. "Tell me about him, *amigo*. You know where I could find him?"

His friend gave Miguel the information he needed. "He's not hard to spot. He's *loco*, you know. Has a large, religious cross tattooed on both sides of his neck. You want help finding this *pendejo?*"

"No. *Muchas gracias.*" Miguel smiled and exchanged the special handshake his gang member friends thought necessary. He didn't want any help finding this particular *pendejo*, the asshole that killed Miss Cherry. That was going to be his pleasure. He searched the streets and finally found a car that someone had left with the keys still in the ignition. Several hours passed while he watched to see whether anyone would return for the automobile.

He opened the door on the driver's side and slid in. He had little experience driving, but luckily the car was automatic. Miguel started the engine, slipped it into gear, and drove slowly away. The police would be looking for the stolen car soon, so he would have to act quickly.

The address where the religious fanatic was staying wasn't far away, but he noticed the car needed gas and headed for a nearby station. A young boy helped him.

"How much do you need?" the boy asked.

"About 5000 pesos should be enough," Miguel answered. While the boy was servicing the car, Miguel found a discarded 40-liter can and asked him to fill it too. The can was missing a cap, so they stuffed in a rag.

He found the address he'd been given and parked in an alley behind the building. Two guys stood by the back door smoking weed; they didn't seem to notice the car. Miguel approached them. "You know some guy who has a cross tattooed on his neck?"

The two smokers burst out laughing. "Yeah, that's Jesús!" one of them said. "He's inside sleeping off a hangover," the other added. Both were having difficulty keeping their balance and staggered down the alley and away from him.

Miguel cautiously pushed open the door and saw a young man passed out on a cot, the distinctive tattoos vivid on his neck. He tried to shake him awake, but there was no response. Miguel pulled the fellow to his feet, propped him briefly against a wall, then lifted him and slung him over his shoulder. Jarred by the sudden movement, Jesús vomited down the back of Miguel's shirt.

"Fuck!" Miguel muttered. He stepped to the doorway and searched up and down the alley: no one was in sight. He carried the young man to the car, placed him in the backseat, and secured his hands with a belt. Jesús was still so drunk that he seemed to have no clue what was happening.

Miguel drove his unconscious passenger to an area used as an illegal dump on the edge of town. There were always old cars, broken furniture, appliances, rags, garbage, and smoldering tires strewn around the treeless landscape.

He parked between two mountainous piles of trash and searched for what he would need while Jesús snored in the backseat. He found an open 200-liter barrel and collected some loose wire that would also be useful. Miguel rolled the barrel close to the car and left it turned on its side. He pulled Jesús from the car, bound him tightly with the wire, and dragged him over to the barrel. After shoving him into it feet first, he stood the barrel up. Satisfied, Miguel lifted the gas can and poured it slowly over the young man.

"Now, you bastard, you're going to get what you deserve," Miguel said.

Jesús was waking up and started to scream. Miguel stuffed the gas-soaked rag in his mouth, lit a match, and touched it to the rag. The inside of the barrel erupted in flames. Miguel watched the skin peel from Jesús's face and smelled his burning flesh.

"Jesús, now go meet Jesus." Miguel turned and walked away. He drove the car back to where he'd found it. It seemed no one realized it had been missing.

"*Dios!* Two men murdered now by my own hands," he said. "But they both needed killing." Speaking the words somehow helped to lessen the anger within him.

3

Riverside, California

Today was a special occasion for Officer BJ Taylor, a day he had been anticipating for years. He pulled into a parking spot at the corner of Eleventh Street and Orange, directly in front of the Riverside Police Department.

Normally he would have parked his police cruiser at the rear of the building, but today he was driving his private vehicle, the pickup he had purchased last year. The new F-450 was as heavy-duty they come. BJ had ordered every extra the dealer offered: four-wheel drive, dual batteries, a winch on the front bumper, the sturdiest shocks available, an extra-large radiator, and super-sized, off-road tires. The high-clearance vehicle had a step and a handle he could grip to pull up into the driver's seat. He'd bought the truck with Oregon and their retirement—days filled with hiking and fishing—in mind.

BJ briefly studied his reflection in the gleaming black paint. He stood straight, at six foot two, pleased that none of his 195 pounds had turned to fat with middle age. His hair was neatly combed and not thinning, although some gray was showing here and there and around the temples; his eyes were still clear and very dark. Some folks told him that his intense, deep brown eyes made him seem harder than he really was. Bobby Jo was his given name but somewhere along the line he had picked up the initials BJ, and they had stuck.

Continuing up the walkway, he glanced at the bronze statue of a police officer holding a child. He remembered well the day it had been dedicated, the same day two officers had been ambushed by four Latino gang members. The officers had never had a chance. Their murders were never solved but were never forgotten, cold cases that remained very much on the books.

Walking up the steps to the police station it occurred to him that he hadn't come through the main entrance for a very long time. He pushed open the double doors made of heavy glass and entered the barren lobby. There were no chairs or windows, and voices echoed off the walls. Clear plastic boxes, holding a selection of report forms, were hung along the wall for the public. At one end of the room there was a bulletproof glass window protecting a uniformed staff member at the desk behind. Wall phones connected the lobby to the main desk and allowed visitors to state their business while three remote cameras monitored the room. To the left was a metal door leading directly into the heart of the police station; it could be opened only from the inside.

He picked up one of the phones, waiting until a female voice answered. "May I help you?" Her words crackled through the glass barricade, further muffled by the phone connection.

He looked up directly at one of the cameras and displayed his badge. "Buzz me in, please. BJ Taylor, Badge 14."

A squawking buzz filled the lobby, and the lock on the heavy door clicked. He pulled it open, stepped in, and let the door slam shut behind him. BJ liked repeating his badge number, because it outranked everyone else by seniority. Every year the department reorganized the order, but tomorrow he would turn in his badge. His Badge 14 would be replaced with a detective's gold shield, a symbol of his retirement and his service. He had been a cop in Riverside for thirty years.

BJ could have done almost anything on his last day before retiring. Had he wanted to, he could have stayed home. However, he had chosen to spend a ten-hour shift as a ride-along on patrol, back on the streets again.

While he waited in the squad room for his assignment, tapping a pencil on the desk, he thought back over his many years with the department. As a rookie patrolman his first beat had been downtown on foot patrol, working the bars, alleys, bus station, and the adult theaters. Shortly after the next new rookie took over the foot beat, BJ was assigned a regular beat.

When he first joined RPD, it was a much smaller department, and the city's population was about fifty thousand. Over the years Riverside had grown to three hundred thousand; the Department had grown larger too. The police had nineteen car patrol beats, one foot patrol, and a helicopter beat every day, requiring a force of three hundred regular officers and thirty sworn reserves.

After two years on a car beat BJ made rookie sergeant. It was back to the graveyard shift to work his way up again. He was well-liked by his men. He'd overheard some of the junior officers talking about him. "BJ's one damn good guy," one of them had commented. "He always has your back." "Yeah," another young cop had said. "But just don't try anything really stupid, like stopping at your girlfriend's place for a quickie while you're on duty. You'll get caught."

His next move had been to Vice and Narcotics, a position he'd held for seven years. Working that area could create havoc with any officer's marriage. All things considered, he had been lucky, but he could write a book about the stories he'd gathered.

BJ had been fortunate on the Vice and Narcotics beat until one night when some hooker's pimp attacked him in the neck with an ice pick. The wound had caused serious nerve damage. After he completed the prescribed course of physical therapy, his doctors had recommended six weeks more medical leave. During his recovery, he had traveled with his family to Oregon; that was when he had started to dream about retirement.

BJ's wife Carol was slender and blond and had the prettiest, sparkling blue eyes that he had ever seen. Born and raised in Riverside, she had been crowned Miss Riverside in her senior year of high school. After graduation, Carol pursued a medical career in college and became a registered nurse.

BJ met Carol in the ER; it was her first week working as a nurse. He had brought in a drunk who had just caused a three-car accident. The drunk had broken his nose on the steering wheel and was spurting blood everywhere. Carol and the ER doctor were tending to the driver when he vomited onto her, the sheets, and the floor. She stepped back, slipping in the puddles of blood and vomit, and BJ had caught her in his arms. Grinning as he told the story, he would say that it was love at first sight. Six months later, they were married. Several years later their first son Dane was born, and then Carson came a year later. *Damn, where had the time gone?* he wondered. *Their sons were young men now.*

BJ contacted the Chambers of Commerce in several cities researching places for them to settle after he retired. He was seeking information about each city— its weather, crime rate, cost of living, and, of course, opportunities for fishing. He and Carol finally settled on Grants Pass, Oregon, a small city of about 16,000 located in the southern part of the state that had won national recognition in 1986 as an All-American City. The picturesque Rogue River ran through the center of town, adding to its character and beauty. It was also noted for its Steelhead trout fishing and river rafting.

BJ checked out the crime rate: it was almost non-existent. After spending his entire career in law enforcement, he would appreciate that. Carol and the boys liked the small community too. They decided that when BJ retired, this was where they would set down roots.

The family drove to Grants Pass to spend a week looking for property for their retirement home. He bought the local paper and searched through the real estate classified section; quite a few listings looked promising. They were interested in unimproved land located outside the city limits and within the county.

On the fifth day, they found twenty acres of forested land along the river. There was a high-producing well and a standard septic system already in place. Most of the land was heavily treed, except for a few back acres that included a suitable area for a building pad. It would provide a prime location for their future home. A paved road ran up to the property, and there was an electrical transformer at the driveway entrance.

The owner Mr. Sullivan was offering the property for sale on a land contract. He had started to develop the property for him and his wife, but she had become ill and died. Sullivan was selling the land himself and had priced it reasonably. BJ handed the owner a personal check as down payment, and the two men worked out a payment plan that was agreeable to both.

Carol listened as BJ and Sullivan worked on the contract. "Make sure you keep the payments within our budget," she reminded him.

Sullivan nodded and smiled. "You still have those two boys to raise and get through school."

BJ had studied the agreement. "Hon, we'll have this paid off before I retire! Thanks, Mr. Sullivan." The men had shaken hands. That was less than *twenty* years ago, and their land was paid for.

He was called back to work two weeks after they returned from Oregon. BJ was assigned to the front desk for almost ten months—seated behind that bullet-proof glass—until the doctors allowed him back on full duty. The front desk, with all its Mickey Mouse problems, was not something he enjoyed: people whined about their neighbor's tree dropping leaves on their side of the fence, someone's dog barked too much, too many cars were parked in a neighbor's yard, and the list went on and on. He longed to get back into real police work.

Finally BJ requested and received an assignment in the detective division, in the crimes against persons unit, a department within the detective bureau. Reams of paperwork in this position seemed to take most of his time, and he would have preferred field work. However, the job served as a stepping stone to where he really wanted to be. After eighteen months, he transferred to Homicide, received his gold shield, and settled in for the rest of his career with RPD.

"You ready, BJ?" Ryan Bradley called, bringing him back from his reveries.

"Sure am!" BJ pushed to his feet. Funny, he had come full circle. Today he was partnering with a rookie who had just finished his phase training and was ready to hit the streets on his own. Furthermore he knew the kid, his old partner Jack Bradley's son Ryan.

BJ and Jack Bradley had gone through the academy together, what seemed like a lifetime ago. He and Jack had experienced some great times as partners and helped each other through many a rough spot. One of the worst was when Jack's wife was killed by a drunk driver. On her way to pick up Ryan after a school function, she had never had a chance, because the asshole crashed into her head-on. Then Jack was a single father, raising Ryan the best he could. With the help of Jack's folks, his wife's family, and his friends at the department, Jack had succeeded. Ryan was a police officer with RPD: the kid turned out pretty damn good.

BJ followed Ryan out back to the squad room, still thinking.

A while ago Jack, BJ, and four other officers went to the Colorado River in Parker, Arizona, for the weekend. One of them had a ski boat, and they'd decided that the river was a great place to release some of the pent-up tension that came naturally with their work. "You can only deal with shit and the seamy side of life for so long," one of the guys said. "Then you got to get the hell away from it." The others heartily agreed with him.

They set up camp on the beach, off-loaded the boat, and found some shade for the coolers and blankets. The river was busy with campers, boaters, and teen-aged girls flaunting their bodies in thong bikinis. Around them young guys hid behind dark sun glasses and ogled the girls.

On their second day, Jack planned to have them pull him behind the boat in their inner tube. While he was still tying the rope around the tube, someone yelled, "Hit it!" The boat surged forward, snapping the rope tight and wrapping it around his hand.

The second finger on his gun hand was gone before he felt it. They rushed Jack to the nearest hospital; that ended their weekend camping trip. Back in Riverside, the doctors decided to remove the remaining part of the bone up in his hand and thus bring his remaining fingers closer together. He would spend three months in therapy before he was released for full duty.

Jack walked into the squad room for roll call his first day back. One of the cops jumped up and called to him,

"Hey, Jack! Welcome back, buddy! Give me a high-four!"

The squad room had exploded in laughter. Nothing was sacred among cops.

4

Riverside, California

Even if it was for only a ten-hour shift, it would be great working the streets again, BJ thought. He'd always loved patrol. A cop never knew what was heading his way; each call was different and yet somehow the same. Maybe he could give his friend's son a few pointers: thirty years of experience should be worth something. The truth was that all rookies would gain experience one day at a time.

As the city grew the department had added two additional sub stations, and BJ had worked them all. The squad rooms all looked the same: battleship gray walls; high, narrow, bare windows that offered little ventilation; asphalt tile floors; rows of old school desks; and a few file cabinets. There was usually a bulletin board where cops offered various items for sale, from vehicles to guns, and *Wanted* posters letting them know who was back out on the streets. At the front of the squad room were regular desks for the watch commander and shift sergeant.

Today BJ glanced around the room: the building might be newer, the desks were larger—computers were everywhere—but little had actually changed. Roll call had begun.

The sergeant called out their names. "Bradley, you and BJ are R-13 tonight. Miller is attending some damn training school. Let your heart not be troubled—Sherman and Reed will be R-13A for backup. It's been kind of hot in there lately, so watch your butts."

R-13 was a beat called Casablanca, a Latino barrio, where two extended families that hated each other with a vengeance were engaged in an ongoing war. Cops were never welcome, so it was important to be familiar with the beat. Getting trapped in a dead end alley could be a setup for ambush. Casablanca covered about one square mile.

BJ thought back to the first time he'd worked R-13, when he'd come to know Casablanca. The shift was short staffed, but they had sent BJ in as a one-man unit to cover the beat. Not long after he arrived, dispatch had radioed that a call had come in reporting a woman screaming.

"The screams are coming from the playground in Rosetta Park," the caller had said.

BJ was familiar with the area in the heart of the barrio. It was still early evening, not quite yet dark, and he decided to go in alone and had not requested any backup. He arrived at the playground equipment near the southeast end of the park and saw what looked like a body sprawled at the edge, where the sand met the grass.

The person appeared to be female, lying face down in the sand. She had long, dark hair and was wearing a dress but no shoes. After notifying dispatch, BJ got out of the unit and approached on foot. There was no one else in the immediate vicinity; no one had come to check on the screams.

He walked through the sand toward the female, sinking into the soft ground, and was glad he was wearing combat boots. Trees and bushes grew throughout the park, while the open areas were reserved for picnics, ball games, biking, and walking trails. The park had several restrooms. It was a very nice place for the barrio's residents.

One glaring blight was the amount of gang graffiti on everything from the teeter-totters to the restroom walls. The gangs were making certain their presence was known. Just as BJ reached the person on the ground, he noticed a figure step from behind a tree a few feet away. It was a young man, smaller than BJ, with gang tattoos covering his bare chest and arms. His head was wrapped in a do-rag, and he was carrying a baseball bat.

He advanced toward BJ as if he were stepping up to the plate for his turn at bat. The person on the ground rolled over: it was not a woman, but a man with a moustache and goatee. He grinned up at BJ. "Pig, you are so fucked!"

He was also holding a bat and leapt to his feet in one fluid movement. BJ's heart was pounding, adrenalin rushing to his head. He was in trouble, but there was no one to help him. He was automatically reaching for his service revolver when the man from behind the tree swung at him. The bat hit his wrist, sending the gun flying.

Losing his balance, BJ crashed to the ground. He was reaching for the backup weapon in his ankle holster, but the second gang member swung his bat, hitting him across the butt and sending him sprawling again. He hit the ground with a thud, knocking the wind from him. During the tumble, he'd lost his backup weapon too. For a moment, he lay on the ground feeling disoriented and trying to catch his breath. He rolled onto his back and faced the two gang members that had attacked him. They had dropped their bats and were aiming his weapons directly at him.

Oh, God, I don't want to die, he'd thought. Random thoughts raced through his mind, like missing his son's graduation from grade school. Then he heard the clicks: the punks were pulling the triggers, and he wondered what it would feel like being shot. Then he realized they didn't know how to take off the safeties to fire weapons. He did have his mace and baton, which were not a match against two firearms. If he could reach them before the two gang members figured out why the guns weren't working, perhaps he had a chance.

Another unit rolled up. The two cops came over to where he was lying. He had managed to get onto his elbows and was sitting up halfway.

"What the hell happened to you? We thought we'd cruise over and see how your call was going." Vic laughed. "Guess we're just in fucking time, I'd say."

"Those two bangers," BJ said shakily and pointed. "They're taking off like a couple of scared rabbits. And they've got my guns." BJ started to shake uncontrollably and pissed his pants.

"Damn!" Vic helped him stand. "I'll get you over to Emergency right away. My partner can take your unit and follow us. He'll clear the call with dispatch and bring the watch commander up to speed."

BJ didn't know Vic's partner well; the other cop had recently transferred in from another department in Orange County. "Vic, those sons of bitches tried to kill me with my own guns. How in the world can I ever explain losing both my weapons?" It sickened him to think that someday in the future another cop or innocent citizen might be injured or killed with one of them.

Flashes from a camera were going off in his face as he waited in the ER at Riverside General Hospital. The two cops who had brought him in were taking a full-length picture of him. He was wearing a silly expression, his face was dirty, his uniform was grass-stained, and it clearly showed he had pissed himself.

Now that his fellow cops knew he was safe and in good hands, they wouldn't let this chance get away. The men were laughing.

"Oh shit," he muttered. He was certain the picture would end up on the squad room bulletin board. The ER doc had given him something to calm his nerves, and it had already started to take effect. The doc wanted to keep him overnight for observation. He expected a lot of ribbing for quite a while afterwards. Even after the picture came off the bulletin board, he had kept the photo in his locker.

Three months later, a raid on a house in the barrio netted key pieces of evidence that brought closure to several other cases; in addition, both BJ's handguns were recovered. When he was informed that they'd been found, he sighed with relief: at least those particular weapons wouldn't harm another cop or anyone else.

Ryan nudged BJ and brought him back to the world of today. "Hey, detective, you can hang around and swap lies with these jokers for a while. I'll go down to the pit and check out our unit." Ryan headed out the squad room door.

BJ smiled. "Go ahead."

Mentioning the pit, the secure area with gas pumps, wash racks, and the radio cars, brought back other memories. When he checked out his unit, he would inspect each item of safety equipment and make certain everything was working properly. He'd pull out the back seat to see whether any contraband or weapons had been left by someone being transported on a previous shift. Even when he would pat down a suspect before putting him in the unit, occasionally something mysteriously would appear, stuffed in the crack of the seat or under a floor mat. It was best to be more than careful; he wondered how Ryan would do tonight.

BJ joined Ryan, and they headed to US 91 at the Brockton on-ramp and headed south. The city was laid out like the letter *L*, and it was often easier, saved time, and was more economical for the Department's gas budget to use the freeway. Casablanca, R-13, would be their beat for the next ten hours.

5

RIVERSIDE, CALIFORNIA

It seemed there were always some people with a disdain for all law enforcement agencies. They showed it in little ways, like an icy glare or flipping off a cop. Others must have believed that the freeway was a hallowed ground that belonged exclusively to the California Highway Patrol; they didn't realize that local agencies also had jurisdiction.

A low-rider passed by them, still barely under the speed limit, and the punk driving leaned out the window and gave Ryan and BJ a three-finger salute.

"Nothing much has changed, has it?" BJ said quietly. "I remember when a jerky asshole like that would pull a stunt—riding my bumper or smirking as he was speeding past me. Then it was my turn. I'd light 'em up and pull the guy over."

Ryan chuckled. "Yes. I know the script. 'You can't do this because we're on a California state highway.'"

"You got it," BJ said. "Are they still shocked out of their minds when you tell them that our authority extends far beyond the city streets of Riverside? All while we're scratching out the citation, of course, and handing it to them for a signature."

Ryan grinned. "Yes, of course. Then I have to say, 'This is not an admission of guilt but a promise to appear. Thank you, sir. Have a nice day.'"

BJ nodded. How well he remembered. "And isn't it an even bigger kick in the ass—while I'm running their plates, they usually come back dirty with one or more warrants." He glanced back down at the new copy of *Field and Stream* he'd brought along, in case it proved to be a slow night.

"Hey! Look at that!" Ryan pointed ahead toward the highway shoulder. There was a man standing on the edge of the freeway, waving his arms wildly and jumping about. "What the hell?"

"Pull over. Let's check him out. He looks drunk as a skunk."

Ryan eased to a stop on the shoulder of the freeway and turned on his flashers and overheads.

The man looked to be in his fifties, rather short, and round in the middle. He was wearing a blue suit and tie. His clothes looked to be of decent quality, not the average loner alongside the road.

"There's no car in sight," BJ said, "so what's this guy doing out here on the edge of busy highway?"

The man raced up to Ryan's side of the unit, yelling

and pointing to an area of vegetation and trees near where a block wall separated a housing tract from the freeway. It was at least ten feet lower than the road. "There's a body down there!" he screamed. "A body!"

"Go around to the other side of the car, sir, out of the line of traffic. I'll talk with you there," Ryan said.

BJ nodded. The guy could become a traffic fatality at any minute; that was one report he didn't want to write. It took them several minutes to calm the man down.

"I was driving southbound when my hubcap rolled off the road into that ditch," the man finally explained as he leaned against their unit. "I drove to the next exit ramp and parked my car. Then I walked back here to find it." He paused for a minute and gulped. "That's when I spotted the body. At first I thought it was a couple of trash bags, but then I saw the hands and feet."

BJ thought the fellow looked like he was about ready to hurl. He stopped talking and turned away for a minute.

"My hubcap is lying right next to the person's left leg."

Ryan nodded. "Could I have your name first, sir?"

The man was too excited. He had grabbed BJ's arm and was pulling at him. The last thing they needed was for some civilian to go charging down the hillside and foul up what might be a crime scene.

"Come on! I'll show you!" he insisted.

"We'll handle it, sir," BJ said calmly. "You need to relax."

"Officer, will one of you retrieve my hubcap so I can get the hell out of here?" the motorist demanded.

BJ didn't answer him, but walked over to Ryan. "Let's have dispatch call CHP and turn it over to them. In the mean time I'll get this guy's information." Even if this was his last shift, he was the senior officer.

"Glad to oblige, buddy," Ryan said and reached into the unit for the mike. "Just as glad that CHP can do the report too!"

When BJ was still on the beat, all reports were hand-written and had to be cleared by the duty sergeant before he left the station at the end of his shift. Now, cars were equipped with electronics and computers, so that everything was recorded. Back in his early days, if he had had a busy shift, he could easily be down several reports. He shook his head at the memory and how things had changed. The public once made fun of cops and their romance with doughnut shops, but those friendly spots had served as a great place to write up reports while enjoying a hot cup of coffee.

A few minutes later, two CHP units rolled up, one officer on a motorcycle and one in a brand new Pontiac Firebird. The unit looked as though it could keep up with anything on four wheels.

"Give you guys a hand?" the female officer asked as she walked up to them.

"You bet." BJ grinned at the attractive younger officer. "I'll bring you up to speed, we'll exchange information, then we'll get the hell off your turf. And

Mr. Blue-suit over there wants his hubcap back." In less than five minutes, Ryan and BJ were on their way to R-13.

Ryan broke the comfortable silence of the past five miles. "I saw the invite to your retirement party on the squad room board."

"Are you going to make it?" BJ asked.

"You can count on me and my dad. He's dying to tell some of those wild stories about when you guys were partners. It'll be one hell of an evening, don't you think?" Ryan said.

"I can just imagine. Cops love to rag on each other." BJ was just as guilty as the next guy.

"R-13, see the woman at 2017 West Adams, domestic disturbance. A female will be at curbside wearing a red and white dress," dispatch continued.

"R-13 copy." Ryan placed the mike back in its holder, made a U-turn, and headed back to Adams Boulevard. The traffic was light and, it was still awhile before dusk. "Don't think we need a Code 3."

"There'll be time enough later for red lights and sirens," BJ agreed. Ryan had already turned off Van Buren onto Adams.

The address was a large apartment complex, a few blocks outside the barrio. An older woman in a red and white dress was seated at the curbside, holding her head in her hands, almost as if she were a sleep. She was crying. "I didn't mean to kill him! I really didn't mean to kill Henry," she sobbed.

Ryan's voice was soft and soothing. "Slow down and start at the beginning, ma'am."

She gulped. "I was doing the laundry in the garage, and he must have gotten into the dryer when I went to answer the phone. When the buzzer went off I went back to the garage to fold the clothes, and there he was—dead!"

"Who's Henry?" BJ asked reasonably.

"He's been our family cat for the past twelve years. He and my husband are the best of friends." Then she added, "He loved that damn cat more than he loves me."

Ryan shook his head and refrained from smiling. "About the cat, ma'am, you really need to handle that yourself. The police can't help with that."

"That's not why I called you," she said. "My husband's locked me out of the apartment. He's angry. He has a drinking problem too." Tears were rolling down her cheeks.

"Are there any guns in the house, ma'am?" Ryan asked.

"I don't think so." She shrugged. "But I really don't know."

They started for the front door. "How do you want to handle this?" BJ asked.

Ryan drew his weapon. "He's been drinking, and you can't be too careful."

BJ nodded. He took a position to the left while Ryan moved to the right of the door.

Ryan gently tried the handle: it wasn't locked. He cautiously pushed the door open, and together he and BJ peered in. An older man was sitting in a chair near the entry, a twelve-gauge shotgun across his lap. His head was down, his chin resting on his chest, and he was snoring loudly. Ryan eased in and carefully removed the shotgun.

While BJ covered him, Ryan inspected the firearm. "It's not even loaded," he said.

BJ glanced around the room. There was a cleaning kit on the floor beside an end table. They were all fortunate that the man didn't awaken to find two police officers aiming at him. He would have died on the spot had he moved the shotgun even an inch. It would have been a tragedy: he was cleaning his shotgun and fell asleep.

Ryan gently shook him. "Sir, wake up please."

He woke up, spluttering and angry. "She killed my Henry!"

"Now, sir, it sounds like that was an accident. Your wife didn't mean to kill your cat, right?" Ryan skillfully tried to diffuse the suspect's anger. "Can we have your assurance that your wife will be safe, if she comes back into the apartment?" He delivered a short lecture on proper cleaning of guns and storage of the dangerous chemicals used. Ryan cleared the call with dispatch, and they were on their way.

The rest of the night was fairly quiet. They stopped for a dinner break at a pizza place near the barrio. Ryan excused himself and spent most of the time on his cell phone, talking with his new girl friend about how much he wanted to spend the night with her.

BJ let the young folks talk, thinking about the future and the plans his family had made. The last thirty years had been a great ride for him, but it was time to move on. Their land in Oregon was paid for, theirs free and clear. He and Carol had saved enough to build their new home and the boys were already accepted at the University of Oregon. *Damn, it would to be nice to relax and do some great fishing.*

Next there would be his send-off party at the Fraternal Order of Police. The FOP's lodge was not big, but it served the off-duty officers well. There was a full bar, two pool tables, a kitchen, a separate meeting room, two restrooms, and tables and chairs arranged around the main room.

The ladies restroom had only one stall. In the front corner, directly beside the door to the stall, stood a four-foot, white marble statue of a Greek god, a hinged fig leaf covering his genitals. When a wife or a girl-friend visited for the first time and used the ladies' room, she usually couldn't resist peeking under the leaf. When it was lifted, bells and whistles would sound at the bar. The embarrassed lady would emerge later, red-faced, to loud, raucous applause. It was always good for a laugh.

The evening of his farewell party BJ and Carol parked in the FOP fenced parking lot, walked over to the cinder-block building, and rang the buzzer to the electronically controlled metal door. Inside, the bartender would check the surveillance monitor that allowed him to see who was requesting entry. The door buzzed, releasing the lock, and they stepped in.

"It's BJ and Carol!" the bartender called to the crowd. Everyone was standing, clapping and shouting. It seemed everyone was there: retired cops, cops from each station BJ had worked, cops he'd trained, and of course, the wives and girlfriends.

BJ's former partner Jack Bradley was the master of ceremonies. When BJ noticed Jack carrying a legal pad, he realized that tonight would not be a simple retirement party; it would be an honest-to-goodness, old-fashioned roast.

The party lasted far into the night. The cops shared many humorous anecdotes, some so funny that many in the crowd laughed until their eyes filled with tears. Jack Bradley had decorated the room with a three-by-four foot poster, an enlarged photograph of the time BJ had wet his pants, on the night he was nearly killed.

For those who didn't know the story, it looked like a cop with a dirty face, unruly hair, a grass-stained uniform, and a large wet spot on the front of his pants. The caption read: "I'm Just Here to Protect and Serve." The Department presented BJ a handsome plaque and his retirement shield. The rest of the cops had chipped in and given him an expensive fishing rod and reel.

Accepting the gifts, BJ fought back tears. "Guys, everyone," he started and swallowed with difficulty before he continued. "Thanks. It's a great day for me, but sad too. I'll miss this way of life and most of all, I'll miss you—my friends."

"You all right, dear?" Carol asked as they walked back to the truck. "It's hard leaving all of them. They're good people."

He squeezed her hand. "Yep. I'll be okay. There's a new journey ahead for all of us."

6

COLOMBIA

Since he had arrived in Bogotá Miguel had grown into a man. He was nearly five inches taller, over six feet tall; he'd gained forty pounds of muscle in the five years after he fled his old village. His hair was shiny black, with a luster that many women envied. He always wore his hair pulled back, tight against his head, gathered into a neat pony tail at the base of his neck. Miguel was a good-looking man with sharp features, dark eyes, and a clear olive complexion that was marred with only one scar, a broad cut near his throat, the result of a street fight shortly after he arrived in the big city.

An older man named Rafael had come to his aid then. He had personally stitched up the gaping wound without taking him to a hospital. Miguel and Rafael had become close friends. Rafael protected him and taught him the ways of the underworld in Bogotá. Over the next few years, together they began to take control of most of the drugs, gambling, and prostitution for most of the city.

Miguel was likeable and he knew it. He used his charm to gradually enter the inner circles of the elite and powerful. Soon he had become the most powerful of all and was on almost everyone's social list. Not to include him could prove dangerous. They knew the business he was in, and many were also his customers. He kept detailed notes on these people: names, dates, places, and what they did not want others to know. No one would ever again put anything over on him. Sometimes he would imagine he could hear the terrified screams of Miss Cherry and her girls as they died in the fire, and his determination only grew stronger. If anyone ever tried to cross him, he would show no mercy. There were times when one person or another would oddly disappear. He had an image to uphold and showing any weakness whatsoever would encourage others to challenge his position as the city's *numero uno,* its boss of the underworld.

There were few people Miguel trusted, but Rafael was at the top of that list. He had saved Miguel's ass on more than one occasion over the years.

Miguel never contacted his family again, out of fear for their safety. He would never put them in harm's way. An envelope would mysteriously arrive on his mother's doorstep once every few months; it would contain cash in small denominations. He never wrote a message to her or his younger sister. He would send a trusted messenger to deliver the envelope during the night. "It's for one of my charities," he would tell the boy he chose for the errand.

Miguel and Rafael were having coffee at one of the city's finest restaurants. The owner Señor Diaz would arrange to have them in a separate room where they could have total privacy. Miguel's bodyguards were stationed between them and the other customers.

"Here're the payments." Miguel handed Rafael several envelopes bulging with cash.

Rafael slipped them into his jacket pockets. He would make his rounds and deliver the bribes to the politicians and police officials Miguel controlled.

"This is just the beginning, isn't it?" Miguel smiled slowly. "I have bigger plans for us... much bigger."

Rafael's expression didn't change at first, then a faint smile appeared as his lips tightened. He knew what Miguel was referring to; they had spent many hours discussing what the future might hold, and the older man listened intently when Miguel spoke. Miguel had been Rafael's mentor, but he had quickly surpassed anything Rafael could teach him. Rafael was a much larger man than his protégé and fifteen years older than him. Although he carried himself well, women did not find him attractive, and most men fearfully avoided eye contact him.

Rafael excused himself and left to start on his rounds. At first, those taking bribes were happy and excited to see him. However, over time the payoffs had become expected, and occasionally one of the officials would get greedy and treat Rafael with disrespect and demand a larger share for himself. Rafael knew he had Miguel's permission to handle the situation or replace these troublemakers altogether, and he often took pleasure carrying out Miguel's wishes.

There were several gangs in the city, and each had carved out a territory for itself. Miguel supplied the narcotics to all of them, but there were three rules they must follow: never cross into the other gang's territory for selling dope; never talk to the police or any government agent; and never, ever show disrespect to Miguel or his men. Any violation of his rules would be dealt with cruel and deadly force.

The gangs were more than happy to comply, since it kept order throughout the city, and they were making vast amounts of money. When a problem arose, it was handled by Rafael in a way that made a lasting impression.

It was one thing to be in charge of the city's drug trade but quite another to run the whole country, Miguel was realizing. Becoming the drug czar of Colombia was a lofty goal, but he was certain he could do a much better job than the current leader.

There was already one man in that position, Hector

Campos. Just being in the same room with Campos could give the average person goose bumps. Hector was powerful, dangerous, and violent, but not especially clever. At five feet nine and two hundred pounds, his stocky frame made him look more menacing. He had broad shoulders, a barrel chest, and a narrow waist, but his legs were quite short. His hair was black and curly. He wore a thick moustache, and his sweaty face always seemed to have an ill-kempt stubble of beard. When Hector spoke, he usually mumbled, unless he became angry, and then he would bellow until the veins in his neck bulged. His face would turn blue, and he had a nervous habit of thumping his chest, like an ape trying to declare himself the alpha male. His rise to leadership of the powerful cartel was not through the ranks, but by ambushing and murdering the previous leader and then assassinating all who had been close to him.

After he assumed control of Bogotá's drug trade, Miguel had been to Hector's compound to introduce himself and establish business contacts. Hector had bragged that his compound was virtually impenetrable. The compound consisted of several buildings at the edge of a river. The main house was Señor Campos's personal quarters that he had decorated like a low class whorehouse—gaudy furniture, mirrors, and crude, nude art on the walls. He had the latest in security equipment and was rightfully paranoid that someone would try to kill him. His bar was stocked with liquor; there was a constant turnover of women from around the country. There were drugs available for his visitors' personal use. Hector's wife and children had left him years ago.

The jungle and the camouflage concealed his base well. It was nearly impossible to detect the compound from the air. The river ran along its western edge, while the airstrip was about a mile to the north. According to rumors, he had the makings of a small army, in addition to a force of twenty personal bodyguards who were by his side at all times. His field troops, as he referred to them, numbered over two hundred. They guarded the outposts of his compound and patrolled the coca fields on foot and on horseback. Hector employed many other professionals: radar operators, pilots, chemists, and accountants. He was not certain he could trust any of them completely. He even employed a food taster, fearing someone might try to poison him. Hector had named his little slice of heaven Rio Vista.

7

COLOMBIA

Jake Zapata was waiting inside the iron gates at the entrance to Miguel's courtyard and home. He was an extremely big man with massive arms that probably could have crushed anyone with little effort. Jake had been Miguel's personal bodyguard for over three years and lived in an apartment over the garage to the main house. He was a devoted employee and would challenge anyone, at anytime, to protect Miguel.

The gate was electronically controlled and could withstand the direct impact of a heavy truck. The walls surrounding the courtyard were eight feet high, topped with razor wire hidden among the ivy. Surveillance cameras were mounted throughout the area and were monitored around the clock.

"Open the gate!" Jake relayed the order to the man in the guardhouse further up the drive. "Señor Vargas is coming!"

The gate swung open as the limo passed through and then closed behind it. "Good afternoon, boss." Jake smiled as the dark-tinted car passed him. He waved with one hand but gripped a machine gun in the other. The car continued on fifty yards and came to a stop at the entrance to the main house.

The driver opened the car door, and Miguel stepped out and called down to Jake. "Have one of the others guard the gate for a few minutes. I need to speak with you. Will you come up to my study?"

Respectfully, Jake nodded and switched on his radio. "*Hola!* I need another staff member to report to me at the front gate. *Sí! Pronto!*"

Miguel smiled, waiting for his trusted guard to arrive. Jake had been inside the main house—a lavish hacienda—only a few times, but never seemed comfortable there. He was a man of simple tastes and modest means. When he was not directly serving Miguel, Jake's recreation was hand-carving small animal figures from wood that he would give to poor children in the city.

Miguel was seated behind an imported, Italian, intricately inlaid desk, the high-backed leather chair wrapping around him and making him feel even more important. He stared down at the top of the desk, deep in thought, as if the desktop would reveal an answer to what was on his mind. Jake's footsteps sounded loud and heavy on the terrazzo tile of the entry. A servant closed the front door behind him. The sounds faded away as he stepped onto the plush carpet leading to the study. Jake stopped in front of him, and Miguel glanced up.

"Please sit down, *mi amigo.*"

Jake selected one of the chairs across from Miguel and perched on the edge of the chair, as if he weren't planning to stay.

"Relax, *mi amigo,*" Miguel said, his tone reassuring. "I'm not chewing your ass out. But there's something I need you to do—for me." Miguel knew he could trust Jake with his life. They had formed a tight bond over the years.

"How can I help, boss?" Jake's deep bass voice resounded in Miguel's study.

Miguel hesitated for a moment. "Would you like to work for Hector Campos?" Jake's eyes widened, revealing his shock at the question.

"No, boss, that man's a pig. He is the lowest of all things! I'd never work for such a person." Jake paused, then continued in a rush. "Please, boss, I like my job here."

Miguel could hear the fear in Jake's voice. "Relax, Jake. I'm not firing you. I have a plan and, if you're willing, you'll be a big part of it."

Jake leaned forward in his chair. "I will do anything to help you, boss. Just name it!"

Miguel had saved Jake's life. A thug named Angel Sago had taken a bullwhip to Jake, tearing the flesh off his back; some of the strikes had wrapped around his face, raising welts and causing deep cuts. Jake was a powerful man, but he had been no match for someone with a bullwhip. He was near death when Miguel rushed to his aid.

Miguel had jumped out of his car and charged the man wielding the bull whip. Using the edge of his hand, he dealt a crushing blow across Angel's throat. The man had fallen to his knees. Angel grabbed at his throat, gasping for air.

Miguel helped Jake into his car and drove him to the compound. After the staff had tended to his wounds, he slept for the next two days. When Jake was feeling better, Miguel asked, "Why was that man beating you so savagely?

"In the part of town I live in, it is known that Angel Sago has a fondness for very young girls. One day my twelve-year-old sister came home bruised and bleeding. She finally told us Angel had raped her." Jake had vowed he would find this molester someday, and he would teach him a lesson.

"Señor Vargas, I'm forever in your debt," Jake had said.

Miguel had asked, "Would you like to stay here and work for me?"

"That would be wonderful," Jake said that day. *"Muchas gracias, Señor."*

Miguel had committed many crimes, but never had he committed any crime against children or ever allowed one of his men to violate a child. Miguel summoned several of his henchmen and sent them to find and punish Angel Sago.

The men had followed Jake's directions. They located Señor Sago, asleep on his porch. They easily subdued him, duct-taped his hands behind his back, and taped his mouth and eyes. He struggled and kicked, until one of the men struck him across the shins with a tire iron. They dumped him into their car and drove across the city to an abandoned salvage yard. At the yard, they pulled him from the car and dragged him to a stack of crushed vehicles. On the bottom was what was left of a pickup, its front bumper made of steel. Miguel's men propped Angel against the front of the truck, using more tape to lash his arms to the steel bumper. Finally they stripped him from the waist down.

Using a five-foot metal pole they spread Angel's legs apart, taping one leg to each end. With his bare ass in the dirt, trussed-up and unable to move, Angel tried calling to his captors through the tape on his mouth. "Who are you guys? Don't leave me here!"

One of the men had backed the car around within ten feet of Angel. Another was tying a length of nylon rope to the center of the car's rear bumper. He walked up to Angel. "You will never harm another child again." He knelt down and knotted the other end of the rope securely around Angel's balls and cock.

Ignoring Angel's muffled screams of panic, the two men walked back to the car, started the engine, threw it into first gear, and hit the gas. After thirty feet, they stopped. Miguel's men untied the rope and tossed aside their bloody trophy.

The men reported back to Miguel. The job had been taken care of just as he had wanted. Miguel told Jake what had happened, and they never spoke of the incident again.

8

Riverside, California

BJ and Carol listed their home with a realtor friend. Unfortunately, the market was slow; they were warned that it might take quite a while to sell.

BJ started work on some of the jobs Carol had been asking him to do for quite some time. Their realtor pointed out areas that needed a little improvement and would create more curb appeal. Their home was located in Canyon Crest, an affluent neighborhood of Riverside. When they'd purchased the house years ago, the area was just beginning to develop. Their lot overlooked the golf course of the Canyon Crest Country Club, and over time the area had become a sought after neighborhood.

Eventually they received an offer that was much lower than their asking price. After much bargaining, the buyer came up reasonably near the original price and they finalized the sale.

"Now what?" Carol laughed. She'd been prepared to wait even longer. "We have land but no place to live!"

BJ contacted a storage facility in Grants Pass and rented two of the larger units. They hired a professional moving company but decided to do their own packing. He loaded his truck with the family's personal items, what they would need until the van arrived in Oregon. Carol would drive the family car with Carson; BJ and Dane would follow in the truck. Stopping at Sacramento the first night was a logical place to break up the 750 mile trip.

They pulled off the highway at the exit for the motel where they had made reservations. BJ checked in with the desk clerk and drove around to the back, locating two parking spaces next to each other and close to their rooms. They were tired and hungry after a seven-hour drive. They walked to the adjacent restaurant, and by the time they'd finished dinner, it was after eight o'clock.

"Honey," he said to Carol as they headed back to their rooms. "I'll check the vehicles and make sure that they're ready for tomorrow."

By the time he reached the rear of the truck it had grown dark. He heard crashing sounds, one after another; they were getting closer by the second. He peered over the hood of his truck. Two young men or boys were coming toward him, smashing the windshields of each car with a crowbar as they passed.

BJ wasn't carrying any weapon; every firearm he owned was unloaded and safely packed away. He hoped he could bluff them. He stepped out from behind the truck, displaying his retirement badge in the dimly lit parking lot. "Freeze punks, you're under arrest. Drop those crowbars and get on your knees," he called. He kept his right hand at his back, as if there were a gun tucked in his belt.

"Fuck!" one of them said. "He's only a cracker rent-a-cop. Let's teach this asshole a lesson."

"He ain't got no gun," the other one added.

BJ could see them more clearly now. They were young blacks who were either drunk or high on drugs. His situation could go badly wrong in an instant. The two men glared at BJ, their tire irons raised high.

Shit, BJ thought, *they're going to pound me into the ground like a stake.* He didn't want to get trapped between the cars and darted out to the center of the drive.

The guys had separated, and it looked as if they were going to attack him from both sides. BJ charged one of them and buried his shoulder deep into the kid's rib cage, like a linebacker sacking a quarterback. The blow took them to the pavement, the black guy falling underneath him. He delivered two quick, hammer-fist strikes to the guy's face, and the kid dropped the tire iron. There was no time for anything more; the other one was right over him. BJ swung his body to the left just as the second guy swung to hit him. The tire iron barely grazed him on the leg.

"Dad!" It was Dane, with Carson right behind him. They must have heard the racket and come out to investigate. Without hesitating, Dane jumped on the first thug; Carson took the other one. BJ grabbed their weapons and tossed them out of reach. His sons were sitting on his attackers, holding them down.

Both Dane and Carson had been on high school wrestling teams, and each had won medals in his weight class. Still breathing heavily, BJ dialed 911 and reported the incident; within minutes a unit arrived at the motel's driveway. The officer stepped out of the unit and walked over to where they were waiting. He first shone his flashlight on BJ.

"I'll be damned, it's BJ Taylor! I haven't seen you for over ten years, back in Riverside."

BJ couldn't see the cop's face because of the light in his eyes. "Who the hell are you?"

"You were my first training officer," the cop said. He laughed and turned the light away. "Sorry. I'm Pete Peterson. I transferred to Sacramento four years ago. Who are those guys on top?"

"They're my sons, Pete." BJ blinked for a moment. "And I'm very proud of them. They came to my rescue when I was in a mighty bad way. Pete, that's Dane, over there." The boy raised one hand but kept the other on his father's attacker. "And meet Carson." The boy grinned in reply.

"Let 'em up, boys. I'll put the cuffs on them." Pete finished putting the punks into his unit and turned back to BJ. "What happened here tonight? I'll need a statement."

BJ described what had happened and showed Pete the broken windshields and the tire irons. They spent the next several minutes chatting about old times.

"Would you give me your cell number, BJ? I'll call if I need any additional info on this report, but mainly I'd like to keep in touch."

"Glad to, Pete," BJ said. "After we get settled in Oregon, I'll probably get a new phone."

Dane and Carson shook hands with the officer, and Pete and BJ said a long goodbye.

"Pete, we got a long trip tomorrow, so I'll need to hit the sack early. If you ever get up our way look me up."

The boys were giving their father high-fives and laughing about the events of the night.

Dane grinned. "Dad, we saved your ass tonight. Now you owe us big time." Everyone laughed. Carol had been watching TV and fallen asleep; she hadn't heard a thing.

The phone rang and BJ fumbled for the receiver. It was the front desk with his six o'clock wake-up call. The previous night he'd fallen asleep as soon as his head hit the pillow, and he could have easily slept for two more hours. He called the boys' room; they were already up and showered. Everyone was waiting on Carol. After finally telling her about last night's events, BJ stepped out into the parking lot.

A police unit was there, taking information from the owners of the cars damaged the night before. He checked on his and Carol's vehicles: they were exactly as he had left them.

After breakfast, they were on the road again. Traffic was light and the weather was cooperating. Traveling north, BJ stopped for gas in the Redding before heading over the Cascades. At the gas pumps he called over to Carol. "Hon, this is one beautiful drive, isn't it?"

"And just think—it'll be our home soon," Carol said.

BJ tried to get the boys' attention. "Hey, guys! Pay attention to the scenery. You've never even been north of Bakersfield."

About forty miles later there was pullout, and they stopped to enjoy the scenic view. To the east, Mt. Shasta loomed near, its 14,000-foot summit gleaming with snow. From the crest at the overlook the downgrade was six percent, continuing for the next ten miles until they arrived in Ashland, Oregon.

Ashland was one of the places he and Carol had considered years ago. It was college town, but it had seemed almost too small. The next city was Medford, population 45,000, thirty miles from their new home. Anything Grants Pass lacked, Medford would have. BJ glanced around at Oregon's scenic beauty—the mountains and majestic forests and wild rivers. He was determined to explore a large part of it. Furthermore, the area they had chosen in the southern part of the state received half the rainfall of the north. There was enough rain to keep everything green, but also adequate sunshine for an enjoyable summer.

Grants Pass lay within the boundaries of Josephine County in the Rogue Valley. Interstate 5 skirted the eastern side of the city and continued on north through Portland. They pulled over at one of the last rest areas to confer before driving into town.

"We'll need to find a place to stay while we prepare the land for our home," Carol said. "We can't stay at a motel for six months. At least I won't." She winked at him mischievously.

"I plan to stop at the police station. Don't worry, hon." He had given the matter more thought than Carol gave him credit for. "I've contacted them, and they've prepared a list of temporary housing." There were two agencies in town, the city police and the Sheriff's Office that covered the rest of Josephine County. BJ spotted the Sheriff's Office and pulled in the public parking area, chuckling. "It's funny how these buildings all look alike. They don't even need a sign."

"Do you think the same guys design all of them?" Dane asked.

"Who said anything about a design?" Father and son burst out laughing.

Inside, BJ stepped up to the glass window and spoke to a young lady at the desk. "My name is BJ Taylor," he showed his badge, "and I've been in contact with your Public Affairs deputy. I'm retired now, but my wife and I are moving to Grants Pass."

"One moment please, Mr. Taylor." She pushed a button on her desk phone. "Mr. Taylor to see you, sir."

A gentleman in civilian clothes stepped into the lobby, his hand extended in welcome. "Hello, Mr. Taylor? I'm Sergeant Cory Williams. Nice to meet you finally, after being in touch by email. You're looking for some temporary housing while you're in town?"

"BJ Taylor. Pleased to meet you." They shook hands. "We're moving here actually. We own a piece of land west of the city on the river and we're building on it. We need some place temporary to live during construction." He grinned. "My wife says she'll leave me if we have to stay in a motel much longer."

Cory Williams laughed. "A motel room gets old mighty quick. To keep your expenses down, I'd suggest renting a manufactured home in Rogue Lea Estates. Here's a county map... this is where their park is located." The deputy carefully marked the two locations. "They used to call them mobile home parks, but I'll be damned if I've ever seen one of those things move once they're mounted on a foundation."

"You're right about that." BJ liked this deputy. Maybe he just liked being around other cops.

"So, you're retired, right?" Williams folded the map and stapled his card to the back. "Any plans?"

"Yep. Once the house is finished, I plan to go fishing."

"Right. You're a California boy. You California boys all say the same thing, but if you're ever interested, the County could always use an experienced reserve deputy."

BJ shook his head. "Thanks anyway."

"Hope this helps. My personal cell number's on the card." Williams handed BJ the map. "Welcome to Grants Pass."

Back at the car BJ shared his news with Carol and the boys. "We'll still need to stay in a motel tonight. Then we can check out Rogue Lea Estates in the morning."

In the morning there was a crisp chill in the air when BJ stepped out into the parking lot. He was hoping the good weather would hold while they searched for their temporary new home. While waiting for the desk clerk, BJ chatted with another motel guest in the lobby.

The man extended his hand and introduced himself. "Jumpy Gonzalez."

BJ shook his hand but must have looked puzzled.

"I know the name sounds odd," Jumpy continued, "but I earned it many years ago, courtesy of my fellow officers in the Santa Ana PD." He was nice looking man about BJ's age. He was tall and lean, with wavy black hair, dark brown eyes, and a neatly trimmed mustache.

"I'll be damned!" BJ reached into his pocket and displayed his retirement badge.

Jumpy smiled broadly, a smile that lit up his face. "What are you doing in Grants Pass?"

"We're moving here and looking for a place to stay while we build our new home."

"And we're looking to buy one," Jumpy said.

"Would you and your family like to join us for

breakfast?" BJ asked. "By the way, I'm BJ, short for Bobby Jo."

The clerk recommended a restaurant less than a block away. "We'll meet you there in an hour. Now that my wife's retired too, she's a slow mover in the morning."

Jumpy nodded. "That'd be great."

BJ, Carol, and the boys arrived first. "We'd like a table for six," he said to the waitress.

"We'll slide two of them together." She ushered them in. "That should work for you."

It was an older restaurant that appeared clean and very popular. A sign over the counter listed the morning breakfast specials. They had arrived just in time; the locals had started coming in by the truckloads.

Jumpy and Sandy arrived on time, and, after everyone had been introduced, they sat down.

"Jumpy, you gotta tell me how you picked up your nickname. There must be a quite a story behind it."

"You're right, my man. When I was a rookie and working the barrio, I pulled over a car for expired plates. While I was talking to the driver, two young Latino punks came running around the corner—a bottle of booze in each hand. They damn near ran me over. There was a liquor store there, so I was pretty sure it was a stop and grab." Jumpy grinned and looked around the table.

"I was in pursuit immediately," Jumpy continued. "They were probably from the neighborhood, and they begin darting between houses and jumping the wooden fences. They had long since dropped the booze and were concentrating on losing me. After about six fences, they had trapped themselves at a dead end. When I caught up to them, they were standing there with their hands in the air."

BJ and the boys were laughing already.

"One of the punks said, 'With all that gear on, we didn't think you could make it over the fences.'"

BJ shook his head.

"I didn't tell them that I still hold the high jump record for Santa Ana High School. When I was writing up my report, I had to mention the detail about the fences. That's when the other cops started calling me Jumpy," he finished.

Now everyone at the table was laughing.

He grinned. "True story. I swear."

Carol turned to Sandy. "Do you and Jumpy have children?"

"Just one son," Sandy said softly. "He died of cancer at the age of three."

"Oh, Sandy, I'm so sorry." Carol reached across the table and rested her hand on Sandy's. "Please forgive me." The mood at the table had changed from laughter to silence.

Jumpy looked serious for a moment, but then began recounting some humorous anecdotes from his years as a cop. BJ added a few of his own, and soon the group around the table was laughing again.

"How long were you with Santa Ana?" BJ asked.

"Twenty-five long years," Jumpy said and leaned back in his chair. "I knew I was ready for retirement when the bad dreams started ruling my nights—and my life."

"Want to talk about it?" BJ asked softly. He stared into Jumpy's steady brown eyes.

"Yeah. Maybe… some other time."

BJ recognized when it was time to change the subject. "Jumpy, do you like fishing?"

"Yeah, but I haven't done any since I was a kid." Jumpy reached overhead and pretended like he was casting bait.

"Let's get together sometime and test some of the nearby lakes or even the mighty Rogue River."

"We have an appointment with our realtor at ten thirty, so we'd better get going," Jumpy answered.

"Are you guys staying at the motel again tonight?" Jumpy asked.

"I'm not sure at this point."

"Let's exchange cell numbers and keep in touch," BJ said. He felt sure this was going to be a great friendship. He knew too what it felt like: there were some stories that only another cop could understand.

They returned to the motel and booked their rooms for another two nights.

"Just two more nights?" Carol asked. "Then you promise that we'll be in someplace where there's a kitchen and a regular bedroom?"

"Promise." BJ drove their family car and followed the directions to Rogue Lea Estates. The vine-covered arch at the entrance was well manicured, and there was a small lake to the right where ducks paddled across the still water. The units all looked neat and maintained. A red and white sign identified the manager's office, and BJ pressed the buzzer by the door.

"May I help you?" A lady answered the door, speaking while brushing at her apron. "Excuse me. I've been working in the garden

"Were looking for a rental for a few months," BJ said.

"You're welcome to drive through the park and, if you see any rental signs, you may inquire by calling the listed number of the owner or the real estate company. They will have all the information." She brushed the hair away from her face. "We're an all adult community. I noticed a couple of young men in your car. Are they eighteen or older?"

"Yes, ma'am, they're both over nineteen. They'll be transferring in to OSU this semester. Dane's a junior and Carson's a sophomore," BJ added.

"That should be fine," the manager said.

"Thanks for your help, ma'am."

After driving through the park, they had collected a list of four possible rentals. Carol was busy calling the contact numbers and making appointments. Their final choice was a three-bedroom home that backed up to the lake. It was furnished, vacant, and move-in ready. The lease was month-to-month, which would allow them enough time to build their own home.

Carol sighed. "That's one task crossed off the list."

"The next thing on my plate is to meet the moving van and guide them to the storage units."

"And then only 999 more things to do on the list!" Carol laughed.

BJ laughed with her. "Retirement is such a breeze!"

9

OREGON

It was early afternoon and the weather was holding. Carol wanted to drive out to their land to take pictures. She planned to create an album showing their home developing from start to finish.

Dane and Carson headed down to the river that bordered their property to the south. BJ and Carol traipsed around the land, selecting and marking some of the smaller trees that should be removed to open it up. The term the locals used was to "park it out." Selectively removing some trees would let more sunlight in and allow grass to grow, instead of the dense underbrush that could also become a fire hazard.

They arrived at the spot they'd selected for a building pad, a broad area with a gentle slope down to the river. Fortunately, not many trees would need to be removed in that area.

"Hon, what do you think? If we orient the pad from

about here—" he placed a rock to mark the spot, "to about down here. That'll give us the best view."

Carol snapped a few photos for reference. "Is this going to be the bedrooms?" She pointed to another spot. "I think it's nice to have morning sun for the kitchen and bedrooms."

Carson came running up the slope. "Dad! We found a school of fish swimming near the edge of the river. I don't know what kind they are, but they're big." He gestured, showing how long the fish were, and paused to catch his breath. "There were about six of them. Wow, wouldn't it be great if we had a boat dock to fish from?"

BJ's cell phone buzzed. He didn't recognize the number, but the prefix was from California. He took the call. "That's great," he said and switched off.

"Carol!" he called to her, and she trekked back from where she'd been photographing the land from different angles. "That was Carl from Capital Van Lines. They'll be arriving Sunday afternoon. They'll call us when they're thirty minutes out."

"Sometimes I can't believe this is really happening," Carol said. "It's beautiful up here."

They walked back to the car, his arm around her waist. The boys were waiting for them.

"We sure have a lot of work cut out for us, Dad," Dane said and wiped his hand across his forehead.

"You're right about that, son," BJ said. "When the moving van gets here, we'll grab the tools, rakes, and shovels. We need to buy a chainsaw to clear the smaller trees. We'll hire a cat operator to remove the stumps later."

It was two o'clock in the afternoon when they arrived back at the motel. As they drove in, BJ noticed Jumpy lounging by the pool. He grabbed a couple of beers from the small fridge and went out to join him. "How was your house search?" BJ twisted off the bottle caps and handed one to Jumpy.

"We looked at six more homes. I wasn't impressed with any of them," Jumpy said. He sounded weary already. "We're heading out again tomorrow at nine o'clock. Our realtor is picking us up, and I think she's selected some places outside the city." He took a long drink from his beer.

"What exactly are you guys looking for in a home?"

"Sandy and I think it'd be nice to have three bedrooms, two baths, a real dining room," Jumpy smiled sheepishly, "and a two- or maybe a three-car garage. Of course, I'd like a workshop, and she wants an area for her crafts—like sewing and other stuff."

BJ chuckled. "You're not asking for much, are you?" He raised the bottle and finished his beer. "God, I was thirsty. Today, when we were driving back from our property, I noticed a *For Sale* sign on a house that looked nice. Not too far from our place on Lower River Road."

Jumpy looked interested. "Do you have time to drive by so I can get the address?"

"Sure, no problem. I'll let Carol know and we'll take off," BJ said. Minutes later they were on the road.

"That's the one." BJ slowed down in front of the property and pointed to the sign.

"Dang! That place looks really sharp." Jumpy was scribbling down the address numbers on the mail box. "I wonder what they're asking for it."

"Call your agent and tell her the address. She should have all the information about the property. If you have a little time, I'll show you where our land is—it's just up the road."

While they were heading to BJ's acreage, Jumpy called his realtor Lori Hemmer at Red Ribbon Realty and gave her the information she would need. He listened for a few minutes and then turned off the cell phone.

"Well?" BJ asked.

"She said that she'll look it up and if it fits our price range, she'll set up an appointment for tomorrow."

"Let's hope you've found what you want."

"This sure is beautiful country, isn't it?" Jumpy said as they drove back to the motel.

The weather had stayed mild, in the mid-70s, with hardly any wind the entire week. The forecast was reassuringly for more of the same. BJ grinned and nodded. "It sure is." He felt happy and at peace. They'd made the right decision to move here.

Grants Pass hosted an annual festival event called Boatnik that started Friday and would last throughout the weekend. There were boat races on the Rogue River that ran through the north side of town, a carnival, and a car show at Riverside Park.

Each year the daily attendance at Boatnik had increased and now ranged from twelve to fifteen thousand. The festival brought in over $100,000 each day; the city's motels were full, restaurants were always busy, and business at retail stores was thriving. People came from all over the state; the city was crowded and bustling with activity.

The motel where the Taylor and Gonzalez families were staying was two blocks from the river, and parking was at a premium along the two main streets. By nine o'clock Friday morning Jumpy and Sandy were waiting outside when their realtor pulled in, fighting through the town's traffic. BJ waved to them as they drove out.

"Wish us luck," Jumpy called back.

———

When Jumpy and Sandy arrived back at the motel, BJ and Carol were in the pool playing dodge ball with Dane and Carson. The boys were clearly winning.

Jumpy waved to them. "We'll be out in a minute. Got some news!" He and Sandy changed into swimsuits, each grabbed a beer, and joined the Taylor family at the pool.

"Well, what happened?" Carol asked, leaving the boys alone in the pool. "Any luck?"

"I don't think I'll be able to sleep tonight—" Sandy began but Jumpy interrupted her.

"I thought we were in for another long, hopeless day. Our realtor had five houses on the schedule. One house was in the city, but it was *too* much in the city. And then another in the county, too far out and isolated."

Sandy laughed. "Then another one in the county was nice, but quite old and needed a lot of work. Even needed a new well."

BJ was looking impatient. "What about the house near our property?"

Jumpy and Sandy shared a smile. "We've made an offer," they said in unison.

"Tell us about it," Carol said. "I don't remember it, although BJ said we passed it on the way to our place."

"Well, it has white vinyl fencing along the edge of the property on Lower River Road," Sandy began. "The entrance is in the middle. The house is set back about a hundred yards."

Carol nodded. "I think I remember it now."

"There's a small apple orchard to the right of the driveway, between the fence and the house," Jumpy added

"Oh, Carol, the house is everything we wanted—three bedrooms, two full baths, a den, a separate laundry room, and a dining room. There's even a sewing room and a mud room at the rear entrance. It's immaculate, freshly painted too, and the kitchen's been remodeled."

Jumpy continued the description. "And it has a two-car garage and an animal barn that I can convert to a workshop."

"When will you know whether you got it?" BJ turned to Carol. "The house is about a quarter of a mile from our property."

"When we said we wanted to make an offer, our realtor sat down at the kitchen table—where our kitchen table will be—and set up her computer and wrote up the purchase offer contract! The owners have twenty-four hours to accept or to counter." Jumpy grinned. "But Sandy's right. Waiting for an answer will be hell, although the realtor thinks we have a good chance."

"Good things are going to happen for all of us. I have a feeling," BJ said and slapped Jumpy on the back.

"Is everyone up for pizza tonight?" There were no negative votes. "So pizza it is." Carol raised her beer bottle in a toast. BJ went back to the motel manager for recommendations; he hadn't steered them wrong yet. "What's the best pizza restaurant in town?"

"The best place, as far as I'm concerned," the manager said, "is The Wild River Pizza Company on E Street, just past Mill Street."

BJ entered the address in the GPS; they piled into one car and headed out.

Although it was Friday evening, the restaurant wasn't busy yet. Most of the crowd must have been at Riverside Park, and they settled at a table for six. Soon the boys spotted two girls playing video games and decided to meet them. The waitress took their order and brought them a pitcher of beer.

Jumpy poured for everyone, then raised his glass in a toast: "May all our lives be filled with love and happiness." As they clinked glasses, he reached for his cell phone. "Darn!" He glanced down at the number. "Excuse me. I have to take this." He covered his other ear to block the background noise.

"Yes, that'll be okay. I'll take care of it right away. Thank you for all your help." He replaced the cell in his pocket. Looking at Sandy, he smiled. "We got it! I'll need to deposit the earnest money in escrow tomorrow morning." They were shouting and hugging each other.

"Now, we really have something to celebrate," Carol said.

"A round of drinks for the house." Jumpy called and held up his half-empty glass. "We just bought our first home, here in Grants Pass!" The crowd in the restaurant applauded. Several people came over to introduce themselves and welcome them to the community.

———

They decided they would all go to Boatnik at Riverside Park, after Jumpy concluded his real estate business. He was at the escrow office promptly at nine o'clock with the money order he'd purchased at a local bank.

"In thirty days or less, we'll be living in our new home," he told Sandy. "Hey, why are you crying?"

Sandy sniffled and wiped at her eyes. "These are happy tears, dear!"

"After breakfast, let's walk down to the park and festival. All right?"

10

OREGON

The boys had already gone on ahead to the carnival area to see whether they could meet some local young ladies. Carol and Sandy went to the park to check out the vendors for any household items they might need for their new homes.

BJ and Jumpy were crossing the Sixth Street Bridge when the man in front of them picked up a little girl and stood her on the two-foot-wide cement railing. He grabbed her hand, and they continued walking together.

"That's dangerous!" BJ exclaimed. "She can't be more than four years old."

"Downright dumb too," Jumpy added his agreement.

The sidewalk pedestrian traffic was heavy, and the two lanes of cars crossing the bridge were bumper to bumper; it seemed that everyone was headed for the park. One of the cars blasted its horn as it passed and that must have startled the little girl. She jerked her hand away, stumbled, and fell back, twenty feet down into the mild current of the river below.

BJ didn't hesitate. With Jumpy following he dashed between the cars to the other side of the bridge. He slipped off his shoes and handed Jumpy his wallet. "You be my spotter, pal." He waited on the cement railing until the child appeared under the bridge. Catching a glimpse of her, he jumped. He had no idea how deep it was and hoped there wasn't anything just under the surface.

When he surfaced, Jumpy was shouting to him. "Five feet in front and just to your right!"

BJ swam with the current a few strokes, then plunged beneath the surface, straining to see in the murky river water. Ahead he could make out what looked like light-colored cloth. Deciding that must be the little girl, he grabbed for her. Almost out of air, he struggled to reach the surface, trying to hold the child's limp body above the water. The crowd on the bridge erupted into shouts and applause. Within moments, a sheriff's river patrol boat had come alongside and helped him and the child into the boat.

The deputy was on their radio at once. "Need an ambulance to meet us at the boat launch." Within minutes, the little girl was on her way to the hospital. "You sure are one lucky SOB," the deputy was saying to BJ. "You must have jumped right between those boulders. You could have killed yourself."

Within minutes, a reporter was there from *The Daily Courier*, the Grants Pass local newspaper. BJ was shivering from the wet and cold, and after a brief interview, a sheriff's unit escorted him to their motel for a change of clothes and then brought him back to join his family.

"Jumpy!" BJ called when he found him again. "Thanks, man. I couldn't have done it without you." He grasped Jumpy's hand, then threw his arms around the other man's shoulders; their strong bond of friendship was firmly sealed. They finally caught up with Carol and Sandy.

"Did you hear the roar of the crowd and the sirens?" Carol asked. "I wondered what all the fuss was about."

BJ and Jumpy shared a meaningful glance, then shrugged and laughed.

They spent the rest of the day checking out the classic cars on display. There was one that caught BJ's eye, a fully restored 1956 Chevy hardtop. It had a 396 engine, a lot of chrome, a white leather interior, and gleaming red and white paint. He stopped to look because there was a *For Sale* sign on the windshield. He copied down the information and crammed the paper into his pocket.

"Oh no, you don't! We have too many irons in the fire now for you to go running around in an old car." Carol laughed and tugged at his arm to keep him walking.

It had turned out to be a great day for all of them.

———

The next morning, BJ went to the motel's office to pick up a copy of *The Daily Courier*.

"I'll be damned!" There was a picture of him on the front page and a headline that read: *Retired Police Officer Saves Local Girl From Drowning.* Standing there in his pajamas he read slowly through the story: they were calling him a hero. He returned to their room. "Holy crap!" he called to Carol. "Honey, look at this."

"So you didn't know what all the fuss was about yesterday," Carol said after she'd finished reading the story. "You could have been killed! Why didn't you tell me?"

"I don't know." BJ poured his first cup of coffee. "I sure didn't think it would make the papers."

He had just sat down to read the rest of the news when the phone rang.

Carol answered. "Good morning. Yes, this is Carol Taylor." She listened for a moment and then covered the mouthpiece. "It's Diane Wilson from Mayor Blake's office," she whispered and handed him the phone. "She wants to speak to you."

"Hello. This is BJ Taylor."

BJ took the phone from Carol and listened for a moment. He cleared his throat awkwardly. "Well, er.... Thank you, but it's really not necessary." Again he held onto the receiver and listened. "All right, I'll see you tomorrow morning."

Carol tilted her head, curious. "What was that about, dear?" she asked when he'd hung up.

"The mayor of Grants Pass wants to give me an award on behalf of the city for heroism." He was feeling more than uncomfortable. "They've insisted. The mayor intends to give me the keys to the city. And we're to be there at his office in city hall, tomorrow, Monday morning at ten."

"And you were going to get away from it all—no more being the people's hero—'you're just here to protect and serve.' Right?" She winked at him.

"Hell, I don't have any decent clothes to wear." He frowned, thinking. "Everything's still packed and on the moving van."

Carol was finishing her makeup, her lips pursed to apply the pink lipstick BJ preferred. "We'll buy some today at one of the men's stores—whatever's open."

There was a knock at the door, and BJ went to open it. Jumpy was there, excited and grinning broadly. "Have you seen the morning paper?" He indicated BJ's picture.

BJ nodded. "Yeah, I got one earlier." Then he told Jumpy about the call from the mayor's office.

"Man, you're a celebrity." Jumpy laughed. "Is it okay if I touch you?"

"You're involved in this too. I told the reporter you were my spotter."

"Bullshit! I don't want anything to do with it." Jumpy backed out the door.

"Come on, man. Don't leave me hanging out there."

"What do you want me to do?"

"Just come down to city hall with me, Jumpy. I'll explain how we were partners." BJ was almost begging.

"Right now, I have to make a call to Santa Ana. We have all our household goods in two sealed pods stored in a warehouse," Jumpy said. "We didn't want to have them shipped until we knew where our new home was."

So he and Jumpy were in the same predicament, with everything either of them owned packed in a moving van or in storage. BJ's cell buzzed and he answered it. The number was Carl's, from the van lines. "I thought you guys weren't going to be here until this afternoon."

"Yeah, I know, but things changed. We're about thirty minutes away."

"Okay." BJ gave the driver the address of the storage units. "I'll be there in thirty." He phoned the boys' room. "Hey, guys. I need you ready in fifteen minutes so we can all be there to meet the moving van."

Fortunately the units were side by side in the main row, and the driver decided to back in. BJ opened the units while Carl's two helpers guided him into a spot that would be practical for unloading. For the next hour, the van workers carefully placed all their furniture and personal belongings in the units. BJ handed the crew a generous a tip for the extra trouble, and he waved them on their way. He located the shovels, rakes and other tools he would need for working on the land and wearily loaded them in the pickup.

Back at the motel, Carol handed the boys some cash. "You guys get your own breakfast because your dad and I are going shopping. We're meeting the mayor of Grants Pass tomorrow."

11

Colombia

Miguel leaned across the fine Italian desk, his every word intense. "Jake, you know how my business has grown. I control the city and nearly everyone in it. Now is the time to expand."

Sitting before him in silence, Jake Zapata nodded. "*Sí*, Señor Vargas."

"My goal is to take over the whole damn country: drugs, vice, and gambling," Miguel continued. "Hector may be the kingpin now, but I'm going to relieve that asshole of that status—and in the very near future."

Like a good, loyal soldier, Jake was waiting for his marching orders.

In order to put his plan into effect, Miguel needed someone he could trust on the inside at the Hector Compos cartel. That would not be easy. "Hector knows you work for me. He must be completely convinced that I kicked you out of my organization and that you want to work for him." Miguel paused. "He'll try to trick you into admitting you've been sent to spy on him... he may even try kill you."

"I can do it, boss," Jake said; his voice was calm and strong.

"Just wait. Hear me out—you may want to reconsider. I'll understand completely."

Again, Jake listened to Miguel in respectful silence.

"Only you and I and Rafael will know of this plan. I want complete control of all the drugs in the country. And I want Señor Campos and his crowd dead and buried. All of them." Miguel paused a moment, allowing the thought to linger, imagining the power and wealth that would soon be his.

Miguel had purchased a full, square block in the industrial area of Bogotá. It would be his future residence and business compound. The block consisted of warehouses, a construction yard, and several other businesses. He instructed the construction company that they could have anything of value found in the buildings. That would be their payment for demolishing the structures and hauling away the debris. Within a month, the block looked as if nothing had ever been there. It was completely leveled, ready for the new Vargas estate.

The following month, Miguel boarded a plane to Brazil to meet with the world-famous architect Ramón G. Santiago. It was a smooth, enjoyable trip. He was alone in first class and appreciated the extra attention. This was his first time visiting Sao Paulo, Brazil, but before leaving he had done his homework on the Internet. He had reservations at the InterContinental Sao Paulo. The luxury hotel would suit his needs well. It was located a few blocks from the city's business district, conveniently near entertainment, fine dining, and night clubs. This was a business trip, but the evenings were his to enjoy.

Miguel phoned Señor Santiago. Sometimes, but not often, Miguel was uncertain whether he was polite enough. Rules of etiquette in Brazil were vastly different from the ways he had learned coming up in the underworld of Colombia. "Would you like to meet at my hotel?" he'd asked the architect. "The lounge at the InterContinental Sao Paulo is private and quite comfortable." Their meeting was set.

Señor Santiago arrived precisely on time. He was considerably shorter than Miguel, and probably weighed two hundred pounds. He was wearing a stark white suit, black dress shirt, and white silk tie. His neatly trimmed goatee and moustache were white and matched his suit.

Miguel extended his hand. *Buenas dias,* Señor Santiago. May I order you something from the bar?"

"Thank you, I would be honored," Santiago said.

They both sat, easing into the comfortable armchairs arranged around the dark wood tables. Miguel gestured to the waitress. He made certain that his guest ordered first, and then he ordered something for himself, light and no alcohol. He needed all his wits and attention focused on the project at hand.

"Señor, I have a very elaborate and extensive plan that may take considerable time to develop."

The architect nodded. "That is what you have indicated in our telephone conversations."

The waitress returned with their drinks and placed them on the table. "Is there anything else I may help you with at this time?" She was speaking to both men, but she was looking directly at Miguel.

"No, thank you," Miguel replied. "Not at the moment."

Santiago said, "Would it be agreeable if we used first names?"

"Of course!" Miguel smiled and raised his glass for a toast. "In fact, I would prefer it." Santiago responded and they touched glasses. The two men continued to discuss business for over two hours.

"We should meet at my office tomorrow morning at ten. Would that be acceptable?" Santiago asked. He handed Miguel his card as he left.

It had been a long day. Miguel wanted to be well rested for his meeting tomorrow. His suite was lavish, and he decided to make use of its whirlpool bath immediately.

The next morning, after Miguel had finished showering, he reviewed the layout for his proposed new compound. He'd spent hours planning it, dreaming it, and imagining its special features. He was certain that Santiago would have helpful suggestions to improve it. He ordered breakfast from room service, poring over his charts and drawings while he ate.

Engrossed in his work, Miguel didn't hear the buzz of his cell phone at first. The third buzz brought him back to the present. There were very few people who had his number; the display indicated it was Rafael.

"Hope I'm not disturbing you, boss. We've got a problem here," Rafael was saying. "Before I take any action, I wanted to check with you."

"What's the problem?"

"Five guys from out of town brought in a string of twenty ladies. It looks like one guy is the boss and the others are his enforcers. They told our girls to get the hell out of the area, or they would cut up their faces if our girls dared return."

"Where?" Miguel asked, instantly concerned.

"Around the airport," Rafael said. "They're operating out of an old motel."

"Okay. Here's what you're to do. Take as many of our men as you need. While their girls are out working the streets, these guys will probably be together at the motel. Use silencers to eliminate them. Then get rid of the bodies. I don't care how. Make sure it's someplace where they'll never be found." Miguel drew in a deep breath, and paused for a moment. "As for the ladies, gather them up and tell them they'll be working for us.

I don't think they'll ask about the other guys, but if they do, just tell them they had to go back home 'unexpectedly.'" Miguel was silent for a moment.

"Will do, boss," Rafael said. "Anything else?"

"Yes. I want you to look the girls over and see if they're up to the quality of the ladies we use. Those you decide to keep... I want you to take them shopping for good working clothes. Then, take them out for dinner and drinks. The next day, take them to the clinic... you know which one, right? Have them checked for drug usage and diseases. Let them know that if they do a good job for us and bring in lots of cash, they'll always be treated fairly."

"Got it," Rafael said.

"Now, if any of them don't make the cut, find them a job and put them to work some place within the organization." Miguel prided himself on the way he took care of those who worked for him. Rafael assured him it would be done just as he ordered. Miguel hung up the phone and turned his thoughts back to the meeting with Santiago.

An hour later, Miguel handed the driver of the limo Santiago's business card.

"Ah, you're going to see the famous architect." The driver entered the address into his GPS and handed the card back to Miguel. "You know, he gets visitors from all over the world. Last week, some men from Italy. The month before, a man from Florida, in the United States."

"Yes." Miguel said. "He is very well known." He didn't want to talk about his plans. Besides, although they could understand his Colombian Spanish, he had difficulty understanding their language, which he'd discovered was Portuguese. Fortunately, Señor Santiago spoke many languages fluently.

"We should arrive in ten minutes, if there's no problem with traffic," the driver said. They stopped before a soaring twelve-story building where Santiago's logo, carved in a large slab of granite, dominated the entrance.

One of the architect's employees was there to greet Miguel, and he ushered him to the elevator. He pushed the button for the twelfth floor. Santiago was waiting for him when the elevator eased to a stop and the doors slid open. They shook hands and went into Santiago's personal office that was decorated with the architect's collection of artwork and statues. There was a large conference table at one end of the room where massive windows looked out on a panoramic view of the city below.

Santiago pushed a key on his desk phone and murmured something Miguel didn't understand.

"I have asked several of my staff to join us for this planning session," Santiago began. "They are experts in their respective fields of construction, electronics, security, and explosives. Their knowledge will be of great importance, I assure you. Each man is sworn to secrecy about the information and design of any contract."

Santiago stopped speaking when the door opened and a lovely young lady entered carrying a tray with a coffee pot, cups and saucers, and a plate of delicious looking pastries. "Thank you," he said, and she turned and left. Their meeting resumed.

Miguel described his project as he had envisioned it. He laid out the plans he had brought with him, in addition to the city street diagram of Bogotá's utilities.

"What I want is a single story, twelve thousand square foot main house with six bedroom suites, each with its own private bathroom. It must have a gourmet kitchen too." He pointed to something on his tentative diagram. "A library and study right here. Of course, I'll need a formal dining room for entertaining clients."

"What did you want in this section?" Santiago peered down at the cramped writing.

Miguel smiled. "I want a billiards room, right there... and a TV entertainment room, over there."

"Swimming pool?" Santiago pointed to a blue rectangle.

"Yes, in ground. Can the spa be connected, like so?" Miguel waved a pen over the drawings. "I'll need a garage with room for five vehicles. And a wash rack... right here."

Santiago leaned over the drawings and studied what Miguel had brought. "Yes, that should work, depending on the subsoil."

One of his experts looked closely at something else on Miguel's plans. "Is this where you planned the secret passageway?"

"Yes. Connected to an underground shelter capable of withstanding a bomb blast and holding up to thirty people. At the other end of that room, can you build another a reinforced tunnel that leads up to a garage and storage room on the surface—that's away from the main house?" Miguel said.

Velez, Santiago's security expert, pointed to the perimeter. "You want this reinforced concrete, correct? Señor Miguel, I'd suggest at least four feet thick and ten feet in height. Around the entire block?"

Miguel nodded, pleased with how their discussion was progressing. "Only one gate and armed exit ever visible, that anyone on the outside knows about." He paused and looked to Velez, to make sure the security expert was following and approved his plan. "There will be razor wire on the top and outer edge of the wall. I want surveillance cameras and motion detectors, mounted at thirty-foot intervals. Can you install motion-controlled exterior lighting that will illuminate every square inch of the property if necessary?"

Santiago's experts were busy making notes.

"Behind the main house will be the swimming pool for my guests—I'd like a vanishing-edge pool. The patio should accommodate up to two hundred people and room enough for tables and umbrellas for shade." Miguel glanced up at the serious faces around him, uncertain who would supervise the more decorative aspects. "These are two built-in, commercial-size grills at each end of the patio. I want the house and patio surrounded by lush gardens and flowers. Then—here and here," he pointed, "there should be pathways leading to a waterfall cascading into its own pool and over here a koi pond with lily pads."

Santiago's construction engineer spoke next. "I think you'll be pleased with our landscape architect. What are these buildings?"

Miguel's drawing showed six small, single-story homes in a row. "They're houses for my men. However, I'll need two other buildings. This one is twenty feet square. The other will be fifty by sixty feet, but underground. It should have only one exit and entrance. The larger building must be built with shower rooms and a changing area. This building would need a high functioning air supply and air filtration system...." Miguel didn't share the purpose of the buildings, but it was important for this team to know about the need for electrical, water, and plumbing connections.

Miguel's last request involved several small, block buildings that were to be placed at strategic locations. "I want the illusion of a peaceful sanctuary." He certainly did not want his compound to look like a drug warehouse. Entering the gate and proceeding to the main house, trees and other landscaping would obstruct the view of the rest of the property.

Santiago's experts began asking several more questions about the overall project. Miguel gave as much information as he could, but reminded them again of the need for secrecy. Santiago was the only one who knew Miguel's last name and where the construction would take place.

Miguel was staying for one more day, then he would fly home. Santiago would personally stay in contact by email or cell phone. Miguel paid the architect in cash; both men seemed pleased with the arrangement. Now the work could begin.

During the following two months, there were numerous calls and emails between the two men; finally, the plans were complete and construction could start. Miguel arranged to bring in the different trades and subcontractors from outside of Colombia. He did not want any of the information seen by the locals or anyone local to ever work on the project.

The water, power, and gas lines inside the property were closed temporarily. Then the massive perimeter wall was built, hiding any further work from view. Heavy equipment started digging trenches for utility lines and the underground buildings once the wall was completed.

The details were coming together, and Miguel was thrilled. There was still much more to be done. He hired an interior decorator from Mexico to give his home warmth and charm.

While construction and landscaping continued, he was buying up the businesses and vacant buildings across the streets surrounding his block. Now no one could spy on him easily. His plan was to convert the smaller buildings into homes and let his people and their families their families live there.

Six months later, his dreams had come to fruition. It had been an expensive undertaking. Miguel was proud of the beautiful main house and the lavish gardens. He was anxious to show off his home to everyone... well, to almost everyone.

No drugs were ever used in his home or on his property. No drug use was allowed in his presence—and that included his guests. He began making plans for the social season.

12

OREGON

On Monday morning, BJ and Carol arrived at the city hall of Grants Pass and were escorted to the mayor's office.

A tall man with salt-and-pepper hair greeted them. He held out his hand. "Good morning, Mr. Taylor. I'm Mayor Warren Blake."

"Good morning, sir." BJ shook the mayor's hand. He noticed the mayor's firm grip and, as he often did, judged the other man's sincerity by the firmness of his handshake. "Pleased to meet you. I'd like to introduce a special friend of mine, Fred Gonzalez. We call him Jumpy. He also was helpful in saving the little girl. He was my spotter when I jumped into the river."

"Thank you for your help too." The mayor smiled and grasped Jumpy's hand. "That's an interesting name, Mr. Gonzalez."

A serious Jumpy shook the mayor's hand.

BJ glanced around the room. There were several other people there, including the sheriff, the police chief, and more newspaper reporters.

The mayor stepped behind his desk. "Mr. Taylor, on behalf of the community of Grants Pass we wish to show our appreciation with this plaque." BJ was standing beside him, feeling self-conscious in the stiff new clothes he and Carol had bought, and accepted the plaque while the reporters clicked cameras and lights flashed in his face. "We welcome you and your friend Mr. Gonzalez to our fair town."

Even less useful was the symbolic key to the city. BJ accepted the gift and smiled for the reporters. The small group applauded; Carol seemed to be applauding the loudest.

After the brief ceremony, the sheriff approached BJ and Jumpy. "Frank Patterson," he introduced himself. "I'm the county sheriff. Would you boys care to join me for a cup of coffee?"

BJ glanced in Carol's direction. She nodded. "See you later," she mouthed.

The three men left city hall and walked down the street to the closest coffee house and settled in at a table toward the back.

"What's on your mind, Sheriff?" BJ asked.

"Please, gentlemen. Call me Frank like everyone else does." He motioned to a waitress.

"Hi, Sheriff," she said. "You guys here for lunch?"

"No, just coffee all around," the sheriff told her. "I'd

like to know more about you two boys. What agencies you were with and what kind of work."

Jumpy laughed.

"No offense, Frank, but we're retired. We've put in our time." BJ took a sip of his coffee and smiled. "They make good coffee here."

"I'm not trying to get personal, but I may have a place for you in my reserve unit."

BJ grinned and Jumpy shook his head.

"I'll be glad to tell you about my background," BJ said cautiously. "Everything. Foot patrol, beat car, detective division, vice, narcotics, and homicide... for thirty-two years in Riverside, California."

"I've worked the beats, narcotics, gangs, missing persons, and was a high school resource officer for Santa Ana," Jumpy said, although he sounded reluctant. "Now tell us something about you, Sheriff."

"I served with the Los Angeles County Sheriff's Department for thirty years before we moved to Grants Pass. I was elected sheriff two years ago. It was a close race." He hesitated for a moment. "The local man had let the department slide into near collapse."

BJ was curious. "Was it hard being the new kid on the block?"

"Maybe. A little bit at first. But I brought fresh ideas and manpower to the department. My deputies seem to trust me—they're a solid bunch. But I also created a twenty-man reserve unit to assist the regulars for covering the whole county."

"Sounds like you're doing a fine job for the area," Jumpy said.

Patterson shook his head. "When I took over as sheriff, my budget was cut. I had to close down the Homicide Section—entirely. The three men who worked Homicide went back on patrol. I badly need a couple of guys with experience to open it up again and work some cold cases." The sheriff looked from BJ to Jumpy and back to BJ.

BJ stared down into his coffee cup and stirred the remnants, thinking. He raised his hand and their waitress appeared instantly with a steaming pot and refilled their cups. He was retired, he had a house to build, and he'd promised to spend more time with his family.

Patterson thanked the waitress. "You would have full arrest powers. Your weapons would be provided by the department, but you would work in civilian clothes. Our reserves are only required to work thirty hours a month, at their convenience." Again the sheriff hesitated before continuing. "Currently, we have two unsolved, missing-person cases and one homicide. All of them are getting stale, but they're still on the books. The downside is it that it's strictly volunteer work."

BJ and Jumpy exchanged a glance. "Thanks for the offer, Sheriff. I'll need to think about it and talk it over with my wife," BJ said. "I'm sure Jumpy wants to discuss anything with Sandy too. However, do you mind if we get rid of these ties? I'm not used to wearing one." He was tugging at the annoying knot.

"By all means, eighty-six the ties. I'll be on my way, gentlemen, but please consider my offer." Patterson pushed back his chair and shook hands in farewell.

The sheriff was pausing to chat with just about everyone in the café.

BJ waited until he had left. "I need to buy a chain saw today. Ride along with me and we'll talk." Outside, Jumpy climbed into the truck, and they headed for the nearby Ace Hardware store.

"What do you think?" Jumpy said at last, breaking the silence.

"Truly, I think it'd be a kick in the ass. It's only thirty hours a month, and we can pick our time. If it gets to be more than that, we can always quit. They can't cut our salary!" BJ chuckled as they turned into the parking lot.

"I'm up for it, I suppose, if Sandy doesn't object," Jumpy said.

"I'm sure, when we explain to them that were not in harm's way, and it's only a few hours a month, they'll both be okay with it," BJ commented thoughtfully. Still, he didn't want to commit to anything without asking Carol.

Inside the store, BJ explained to the clerk that he needed a chain saw. The clerk recommended a mid-sized Husqvarna. It was a well-respected brand, and this model also included a pair of heavy-duty, plastic work glasses. BJ paid for the saw and asked for a quick course on its safe operation.

They headed back to the motel, but when BJ drove

around to their rooms, a red and white 1956 Chevy hardtop was parked in his usual space. He parked beside it, intrigued. He and Jumpy strolled around the classic car, admiring it.

Carol stepped from their room. "Honey, someone named Mr. Olson left the car here, for you. He said there's a note in the glove box."

BJ walked around to the passenger side, opened the door, and reached into the glove box. He pulled out the envelope on which his initials were scrawled across the front and read the note:

Dear Mr. Taylor,

I have three more beautiful, classic cars, and I would give up any one of them for my precious granddaughter. She is the little girl you saved. Thank you for giving her back to us.

Sincerely,

Red Olson.

PS. The title has been signed over to you, and you can find it behind the driver's visor.

BJ rushed back to Carol and kissed her. He flung his arms around her waist, picked her up, and whirled her about. "I can't believe it! That's the car I fell in love with!" He kissed her again.

"What's going on here?" Jumpy asked.

"Carol, grab some beers please." BJ was grinning, still in shock. "Jumpy, you're not going to believe this."

BJ slid into the driver's seat. "Come on everybody get in the car!"

The boys had heard the commotion and come out to see what was happening. Jumpy and Sandy were sitting in the backseat; BJ and Carol were in the front. Dane and Carson were on the outside peering in. Everyone was talking at the same time.

"Hey, Dad, you're going to let us take this to college, aren't you?" Dane said.

"No frigging way!" BJ laughed and playfully swatted at him.

"Here boys, take the empty beer bottles and put them in the room, because we're going to cruise the town!"

Early the next morning, Carol called Sandy. "Would you like to come shopping with me and then we'll go to lunch?" she asked. "BJ and the boys are moving some of our boxes out to the house at Rogue Lea Estates, and then they'll be working on the land." She listened for a moment and started to hang up.

"Sandy? Are you still there? BJ wants to know whether Jumpy would like to go with him and the boys."

Carol waited for another long moment. "Jumpy's in the shower," she told BJ. "She's going to ask him." She laughed. "Okay, I'll tell him." She turned to BJ. "Jumpy says he'll be here as soon as he dries off.

BJ placed the boxes and tools in the truck beside the new chain saw. "We'll need to buy gas and oil for the saw and some work gloves. Boys, you're going to drive the Chevy to Rogue Lea. I'll follow you. Be extra careful with that baby, and park it in the carport. We'll unload the boxes before heading out to the property."

Carol gathered up the rest of their belongings, packed their suitcases, and loaded them in the car. She did the same in the boys' room, and checked out of the motel.

"It's going to feel different without you guys here," Sandy said. They spent the next several hours getting to know the city. They stopped for lunch at a quiet little restaurant.

"I've been thinking," Carol said and paused for a moment. "The boys are leaving for college next week, and we have three bedrooms at our house in Rogue Lea. Why don't you guys stay with us until you close escrow?" Carol rested her hand on Sandy's.

"I'm not sure," Sandy said. "That's so sweet of you."

"It would save you a lot of money. You know you're welcome."

"I'll ask Jumpy." Sandy smiled. "Thanks for the offer."

"If you don't have anything on your schedule this afternoon, why don't you come with me? I need to buy groceries and unpack the boxes that BJ's left at the house."

"Schedule?" Sandy laughed. "I don't have a schedule, not anymore!"

"Great. Let's get together for dinner tonight. We can discuss it then."

BJ, Jumpy, and the boys worked on the property for the rest of the day. BJ would fell a tree, limb it, and cut it into logs. The boys carried the logs to the edge of the property and stacked them in orderly rows. Jumpy raked the slash into a pile they would burn at a later time. By the end of the day, they could already see the improvement in the land. Dirty and sweaty, they drove Jumpy back to the motel.

"We're having dinner with BJ and Carol in a couple of hours." Sandy was brushing at Jumpy's shirt. "You're a mess!"

Jumpy waved to BJ as he pulled out of the drive. "See ya' later," he called to him.

Carol had unpacked enough to cook spaghetti and the meat sauce her family loved, prepare a salad, and toast some garlic bread. The men had showered and changed clothes. They were ready for their first home-cooked meal in what seemed an eternity, but had been less than two weeks.

"Hon," Carol was saying as she stirred the sauce. "I was talking with Sandy today. I suggested they could live here for a couple of weeks until they close on the house. It'd help them, don't you think?"

BJ was helping set the table. "I think it's a great idea."

"The boys are off to college in four days."

BJ passed her, headed back into the kitchen, and playfully pinched her butt. "You're always looking for someone to help. A nurse never stops—right?"

Carol laughed at his teasing. "But they're our friends."

"Yes, they sure are, and we're lucky to have them."

At dinner, the two couples discussed their plans further.

"I told Jumpy about your offer," Sandy said. "Are you certain you still want to do this? It would save us a lot."

BJ spoke first. "Of course. We wouldn't have offered if it weren't doable."

They finished dinner and cleared away the dishes, but remained gathered around the table.

Jumpy asked again, "And you're sure we won't be crowding your space?" He put his arm around Sandy.

"Not at all," BJ said.

"You know you're welcome to stay," Carol added.

After dessert, they spent the rest of the evening playing cards.

For the next two days, BJ, Dane, and Carson worked on the land clearing trees.

BJ and Carol had an appointment with Mitchell's Construction, the contractor that Sheriff Patterson had recommended. There were hundreds of floor plans to choose from. If a client had his own design, he would use them.

He and Carol wanted to get started as soon as they possible. Carol had told him, "I want Thanksgiving Dinner in our new home." It would also be great if the exterior were complete before the rainy season hit.

They found a plan they liked, a house of 2,200 square feet, and signed the contract.

13

Oregon

By the next week, BJ and Jumpy had made an appointment to meet with Sheriff Patterson. They'd both agreed to accept his offer and join the department as reserve deputies. On the drive out to his offices, they had chatted, sharing some of the most embarrassing moments of their careers... and the worst.

"I understand if it's too personal, buddy," BJ began, "but once you mentioned bad dreams. Still having them?"

Jumpy had stared ahead at the road for several minutes but finally shook his head. "It's better now. But that was when I decided it'd be wise to retire. If we're going to be partners, I guess you should know."

BJ felt slightly uncomfortable. "Only if you want to."

"I shot and killed a man in a hostage standoff. There was this father, you see. He was high on meth and had been beating his wife. He was threatening to kill her and his daughter who was two years old...."

"Gosh, man," BJ said softly. "These are the stories I don't miss one bit."

"Well, the father had barricaded them in a one-story apartment. It was dark, but the porch light was on when I approached the front door—service revolver readied, of course. Suddenly, the door swung in and the man was standing there. He was holding a pistol in his right hand and his daughter in the other. The man yelled, 'You fucking pig!' and raised his gun to shoot me."

BJ sighed. "Oh, shit." How well he knew what was going to happen next.

Jumpy swallowed and cleared his throat. "I had a split second to make the decision, to shoot or not. I hit him in the right collarbone and reached to grab the little girl before the guy crashed to the ground. The bullet ricocheted off the bone and traveled down into his lungs." He paused and shrugged. "He drowned in his own blood. The department determined it was a good shoot…. Still, it took *me* a long time to come to grips with it."

"Believe me… I understand, pal."

They rode along in silence after that, each man with his own thoughts, and within ten minutes BJ had parked at the county complex.

"Gentlemen, welcome to the Josephine County Sheriff's Office." The sheriff ushered them into his office and pressed a button on his desk phone. "We'll have you sworn in and get your gear in a few minutes." He slid two sets of keys across the desk toward them. These are to the 4WD SUV assigned to the previous detectives in Homicide."

Jumpy laughed. "Nothing like filling another guy's shoes!"

BJ picked up one set of keys. "You must have been in a hurry—and you were counting on us taking the job too." He grinned, turned to Jumpy, and winked. "My partner and I have decided we'd like to negotiate for a higher salary. Right, Jumpy?"

"I wish I could," Patterson said. "You have no idea how much your help is needed. Pull up those chairs, boys. Here are the three cold cases I told you about." He handed them three stacks of manila file folders.

BJ whistled softly. "You weren't kidding, were you, Frank?" He was no longer in a joking mood.

"You guys can decide on how you want to work them. If you'll excuse me, I have a meeting with the mayor. Captain Smith will handle your swearing in."

A deputy had showed them to a small cubicle they could use for their office, a place where they could review each case in private, and then left them alone.

"I think this gig is going to be a blast," Jumpy said.

"Your sense of humor is strangely developed," BJ teased in return. "Here's a three-year old murder case. Damn!"

"On the bright side, the two missing person cases are only a year old."

"Let's work on the case of the missing young girl first." BJ handed Jumpy several files.

"All three cases are from an area near the small city of Cave Junction. Did you notice that?" BJ asked his partner.

"Yes, it's within the county."

BJ picked up an information sheet in the file and read out loud. "Population less than two thousand. You're kidding! They call that a city here? Hmm.... It was a timber town until recently and before that silver mining."

Jumpy glanced up from his reading. "I have a vague memory of the place. In the '60s and '70s it was popular with hippies coming in from California." He chuckled for a moment. "I think many of them still live in the area in their tie-dyed, psychedelic clothes and rusted-out VW vans. They wanted to practice free love, grow pot, and smoke pot. They still do."

Cave Junction was on the western edge of the Cascade Mountains, thirty miles southwest of Grants Pass on US 199, the highway that ran to the Pacific Ocean. The area around Cave Junction was now mainly mini-ranches, horse farms, or plots of acreage for those who simply wanted to get away from everyone else. Law enforcement for the community was split between the Josephine County Sheriff and the Oregon State Police. On a typical day, one officer or one deputy would be working the area, while Grants Pass would be the closest agency for any backup. It was not unusual to hear gunshots in the rural area, property owners guarding their small fields of pot. There seemed to be a general attitude of "shoot first, ask questions later," and local law enforcement could do nothing about it. Rarely, it might be someone shooting deer, because many of the locals believed deer season never closed. US Forest Rangers would often request backup when they arrested poachers.

Their most recent case was a twelve-year-old girl who went missing about one year ago. The information in the file wasn't very helpful: there was lots of paper, but much repeated information. There was a three-by-five-inch photograph and a few short notes from interviews conducted by Deputy Stewart Miller, who had been assigned to the case. There was a copy of the always sad and hopeless reward poster. Last was a hand-written report by the deputy outlining the steps he had taken in his investigation.

"First, we should talk with Deputy Miller." BJ looked to Jumpy for agreement.

"He might have something else to add since then," Jumpy said. "You never know." They went in search of Captain Smith.

"How can we reach Stewart Miller?" BJ asked. "He was the deputy who was handling the Becky Hanson case."

"Shit, that'd be a good one!" the captain replied. "'Cuz he ain't around here anymore."

"Do you at least have an address for him?" Jumpy asked.

Captain Smith laughed. "I guess that would be someplace in heaven or hell. He was in a boating accident about six months ago while vacationing in Washington State. He died from his injuries."

They returned to their office. BJ picked up the files. "And we thought this was going to be a walk in the park.... Let's take the files with us and do some homework." BJ tossed Jumpy the keys to their unit. "You drive the unit, and I'll take my truck."

Carol and Sandy were making lunch when they arrived at the house in Rogue Lea.

"When the hell are we going to get time to go fishing?" BJ glanced longingly at the rods and reels in the backseat of the truck.

"We need to plan a day and stick to it," Jumpy said.

"We should be looking for a boat and trailer too. The current in the river makes it almost impossible for shore fishing." BJ sniffed appreciatively as they walked into the house. "Something smells mighty good."

Sandy was setting the table. "Hope you guys are hungry."

"We are!" BJ and Jumpy spoke in unison.

"Where are the boys?" BJ asked.

"They took our car and went into town. Not your new baby, BJ. I believe they had a date for lunch with a two girls they met last week." Carol smiled as if she had disclosed a secret, but she knew even more.

After lunch, BJ and Jumpy settled into the family room and opened the files once more.

"We should interview the girl's parents again," BJ said. "Then perhaps we can visit the school and talk with the teachers and the bus driver."

"Yeah." Jumpy nodded. "And let's check on any video cameras around that area where she was last seen, including at the bus." He was making notes.

"Good idea," BJ said. In the file were the parents' address and their phone number. There was also a detailed description of the clothes the girl was wearing the day she disappeared.

"Do we want to call her folks first?"

BJ stared at the file for a moment. "No, I'd rather show up unannounced. It's about a forty-minute drive from here. Let's take off now, stop at the school first, and then head to the girl's home."

"Sounds like a plan," Jumpy said.

BJ transferred the GPS from his truck to the sheriff's unit and entered the school's address.

Highway 199 twisted and turned, an up and down route that provided a scenic drive. The highway offered stunning views of mountains and valleys and occasionally passed through stands of dense forest. The last few miles downhill opened into a broad valley.

The school was located on the east side of town and included elementary and middle grades. They drove into the school yard and parked in a spot marked for visitors.

Jumpy glanced around, taking in the school yard. "Darn! No cameras here."

They walked up the front steps and entered through the double doors. Directly ahead was a sign: *Principal's Office.* An arrow pointed to the left.

The door to the office was open; inside a woman behind a desk was working at a computer. She glanced up as they entered. "May I help you gentlemen?"

BJ and Jumpy produced their badges for her inspection. "We're with the Josephine County Sheriff's Office, ma'am," BJ said. "Are you the principal?"

"No, I'm her secretary." The woman smiled. "The school's principal is Mrs. O'Connell. She's in the next office. I'll let her know that you're here."

A few seconds later, a short, heavy-set woman wearing glasses came from one of the offices.

"I'm Helen O'Connell." Her voice was high and squeaky. "How may I be of assistance?"

"May we speak with you in private?" BJ asked.

"Yes, of course. Please come into my office."

"We're investigating the disappearance of Becky Hanson last year." BJ reached for the small notebook he always carried in a shirt pocket. A thirty-year-old habit didn't die at retirement.

"I told Deputy Miller everything I knew about her right after it happened." Mrs. O'Connell's expression changed from helpful concern to sadness.

Jumpy was also taking notes. "Are there any security cameras on the school grounds?"

The principal shook her head. "Our school budget didn't leave any monies for them. We never had a need for them before."

"Could we have a copy of Becky's last report card?" BJ asked. "What kind of student was she?"

"Certainly." She picked up the phone and spoke to her secretary. "Mandy? Will you make a copy of Becky Hanson's report card for these gentlemen? Thank you." She turned back to them. "She was a good student, above average and conscientious, and excellent attendance. There was never any report of trouble, either on campus or on the bus."

"Could you show us where she was last seen?" Jumpy asked.

Mrs. O'Connell nodded and they left together, walking down the steps to the broad drive in front of the school. "The buses line up right here." She gestured along the driveway. "Each bus has an individual number marked on its side, so students will know which bus to get on. It avoids confusion."

BJ nodded. Not much had changed in the bus drill for elementary schools, he guessed. "Thanks for your time, ma'am. Please call the Sheriff's Office if you hear anything new at all. We'd appreciate it." He handed her one of Frank Patterson's cards, with his own name and personal cell number scrawled on the back. He and Jumpy were so new they didn't even have business cards. That would be his first request from the department, tomorrow morning.

"Next stop, the parents' house."

They climbed back in the unit and drove west three miles outside town to an address on Holland Loop. By the entrance a wooden bear stood on his hind legs and held a sign that read: *Sawdust Creations.* They continued down the drive, passing other wooden sculptures that had been created by a chainsaw master. Two dogs rushed out from nowhere and barked wildly as they followed the unit.

A woman came to the front door. "Who is it?" she shouted over the barking dogs. "State your business! Hush!" The dogs stopped barking as if the woman had thrown a switch.

"Are you Greta Hanson?" BJ called to her. He would not leave the unit until the dogs were under better control.

"Yes." Her tone of voice had changed instantly.

"We're here on a follow-up about your daughter's disappearance."

She shouted at the dogs; they obediently left the side of the car, tails between their legs, and wandered off behind the house. A man appeared from the same side of the home; he was covered in wood shavings from head to toe.

"They're here about Becky." Tears were rolling down her cheeks; the man put his arms around her.

"There, there, Greta," he murmured. "I'm sorry, dear. I'm Becky's dad. Do you have any new information about our daughter?" His lips were pale and trembling.

"No, actually we don't. We've just been handed this case, and we wanted to revisit all of the people whose names are listed. We're hoping we might be able to uncover a new lead." BJ looked from the bereft mother to the father and wondered how he could even get one of them to continue the conversation. They stood before him, their tears streaming.

"Do you have any questions for us?" Jumpy had walked up to the man and extended his hand. "Fred Gonzalez... and my partner, BJ Taylor."

"Sorry." The man wiped his eyes with a gritty handkerchief. "Ray Hanson." The men shook hands. My wife, Greta."

"Pleased to meet you, ma'am," BJ said. "I wish it were under other circumstances."

"I appreciate you folks starting the investigation again," Mr. Hanson said. "Would you boys like to come in for a cup of coffee?"

Jumpy and BJ exchanged a glance. They would be able to talk with the Hansons after all. They sat at the kitchen table while Mrs. Hanson poured coffee.

BJ cleared his throat. "I need to ask some questions that you might think inappropriate. Is that all right? We need to have the answers."

"We understand," the Hansons spoke simultaneously.

"Are you Becky's natural parents?"

They nodded emphatically. "Yes."

"Is there any reason whatsoever you can think of why Becky might have wanted to run away—like any family disagreements, punishment, a boyfriend, or drugs?"

"Oh, no, nothing like that," Mrs. Hanson finally spoke. "Our Becky was a happy, young girl with a bright life ahead of her. She was involved in several activities at school and had so many friends. None of them were troublemakers either." Her tears were welling again.

"I'm so sorry, Mrs. Hanson, but I had to ask." BJ was looking around their house. From where he was sitting, the home seemed well furnished and neat and clean.

"May we see Becky's room?" Jumpy glanced at BJ who nodded in approval.

"All I've done is make her bed since she left for school that morning last year." Mrs. Hanson pushed back her chair and led them to her room.

"Does she have a computer or cell phone?" BJ was studying the rest of the room. It appeared to be a typical teenager's room: posters of her favorite singers and celebrities, school awards, and plush toys scattered at the head of her bed. There was a hair brush on her dresser. "Would you mind if we take the hair brush with us?" he asked. He turned to Jumpy. "Bring some evidence bags from the unit. We'll return everything later."

"Of course, you can take the brush. We bought her a cell phone a few weeks before she disappeared," Mr. Hanson said. "She had the phone with her that day."

"Is there any other way we may be of help to you?" Mrs. Hanson asked.

"Could you give us the name and address of your family doctor?" BJ asked. "And the cell phone number too." He wondered why those leads hadn't been followed earlier.

Mr. Hanson looked puzzled. "Our doctor is Dr. Miles Haggle. His office is on Sixth Street in Grants Pass."

Jumpy returned with evidence bags and a camera. After gathering the hairbrush and taking several pictures of the girl's room, they thanked the Hansons and started the long drive back home, a scenic drive east away from the setting sun.

"I really feel for the parents," BJ said. "I can't imagine how it would feel to lose one of my sons." He glanced across at Jumpy. "Sorry, pal, I know you do. But this... I've got a bad feeling."

"Yeah," Jumpy agreed. "Most disappearances aren't solved nicely."

14

COLOMBIA

July was a beautiful time of the year in Bogotá. The rain and fog had finally cleared away for the month, and the clear, dry, and sunny weather was ideal for the party Miguel had planned. The guest list would include Miguel's business associates. He preferred to refer to them that way, no matter how the "business" might have begun. Among the guests would be the who's who, VIPs, and the celebrities who made their home in Bogotá.

It was surprising how many were addicted to cocaine. Most of them didn't wish to buy from the gangs. That would take them into unsafe parts of the city, and there was the risk the quality would be degraded. Rafael always handled transactions with the VIPs. Sometimes he would receive oral sex or a quickie as part of his service. Occasionally a husband or boyfriend would complain about this part of the arrangement.

"If you don't like it," Rafael would tell them, "you can always buy from the nearest gang. The quality might not be the same. The gangs cut the snow with something else. You can never be sure of the quality. And you're never certain you can trust them...." He would shrug meaningfully. Miguel's staff promised secrecy, a rare commodity in the world of drugs. Rafael's reminders seemed to take care of the whiners, and business would continue as usual.

Miguel's extensive house staff was preparing the grand, spacious home for the throng of guests that would soon arrive. Groundskeepers were busily trimming hedges, mowing lawns, and neatening flower beds throughout the complex.

The men who worked for Miguel were required to be neatly groomed: a fresh haircut, their nails clean and manicured, and any facial hair closely trimmed. Miguel had arranged for a tailor to fit his staff with black suits. Most of them had never owned a suit in their lives, and some had physiques that made the tailor's job a challenge. The women who worked for him must be attractive and well-mannered. They, too, were provided with appropriate clothes for the evening.

Through his secretary, Miguel had contracted with a much sought-after catering service. The caterers put together an elegant meal, a cosmopolitan and international feast featuring delicacies from around the world. They would also provide the wait staff and bartenders, but Miguel had first thoroughly checked each employee's background. Miguel's guards would always be there too, providing security at the perimeter.

Miguel had hired a popular dance band to perform for the evening, and a popular singing star was flying in from Mexico. He wanted everything to be perfect. Two hundred invitations had been mailed, and all except three were promptly accepted. The three families were out of the country on extended vacations, otherwise someone from Miguel's organization would have demanded an explanation. An invitation from the boss was not actually an invitation, it was a command.

The leading criminal attorney Juan Moreno had an appointment with Miguel and had requested an extra invitation. "We have a guest visiting from America. Her name is Allison Denney. Would you mind if she comes with us?"

"Of course." He pressed a button on the desk, and his secretary entered the room. "Another invitation for Juan, please. The name will be Allison Denney." The young lady nodded and left. "It's done, my friend. Now, to business." He and Juan spent the next half hour discussing several minor legal matters. Moreno's law firm had represented Miguel on more than one occasion with satisfying outcomes. Over time, they had grown close, and Miguel would often confide in him. Their business concluded, the men shook hands in farewell.

"I'm looking forward to your party next week," Moreno said in parting.

Miguel sighed and eased back into the chair behind his desk. There was one call he needed to make, one he would have liked to avoid. He dialed the number. The dial tone rang on until, after many mysterious clicks, someone answered.

"This is Miguel Vargas. I wish to speak with Hector Campos, please." A few minutes passed before Hector's gruff voice came on the line, mumbling that it was nice to hear from him and asking what he might need.

"I've hired some bakers. So I'll need about 140 kilos of flour and 225 kilos of seeds," Miguel replied in the code that referred to cocaine and marijuana. Yes, my new chef is baking some fine pastries. I've moved into my new home at Numero 6, El Pablo Placita—in the Industrial area. The gate code for your people is the same as at the old hacienda," Miguel lied. He listened for a few minutes to Hector Campos's crude mumbling. "I'll need to know when you'll be making delivery."

Campos grudgingly promised the delivery for the day after tomorrow, at ten in the morning. There would be a black SUV and another vehicle that looked like an ice cream delivery truck with the sign *Frozen Treats for Everyone* on the side.

"That will be satisfactory," Miguel said and hung up. There was no need for any further pleasantries. Neither man liked or trusted the other.

On the promised day, Jake ordered the gate opened for the two vehicles; they'd had arrived exactly on time. Miguel's men were waiting and hidden in two pickups, ready to transfer the goods, but not far enough into the property that Hector's people could see them. After the transfer had taken place, Miguel's representative paid Hector's men; the ice cream truck and SUV drove away, and the heavy gates slid shut.

Miguel's men drove the pickup trucks to the main underground building, offloaded the cargo, and carried the bundles downstairs to the storage area. In the underground room fiberglass tables were arranged with weighing scales, baggies, and rubber bands. One man, without a shirt, was wearing shorts and flip flops; he was in charge of what transpired in this building.

Twenty women sat around the tables; they wore thongs and flip-flops. Six cameras were placed around the entire room, covering it from every angle. The women's job was to break down the bundles and separate the drugs into smaller quantities. Working in the nude prevented anyone from stealing or using any of Miguel's drugs. After they finished their work they would shower and change back into their own clothes before leaving. The women were paid well; they knew if they ever disclosed any information about their work, they would lose their jobs and probably their lives.

The cameras throughout the complex were connected to computers in one blockhouse. The videos and cameras were monitored twenty-four hours a day. Two industrial-sized generators were located in another block building; they were designed to supply energy to the complex if power was ever lost or deliberately sabotaged. At night, a minimum of six men, carrying AK-47s and armed with Smith & Wesson 40 mm handguns patrolled the inner perimeter of the complex. They were accompanied by trained attack dogs. In the center of the property stood a twenty-five foot tower built to resemble a Spanish church bell tower. Two men worked the tower at night using infrared, night-vision glasses and high-powered scopes. From their vantage point they could view the entire property.

Miguel returned to the main house, again focused on the upcoming celebratory evening. It would be nicer still, not having to deal with Hector any longer. Soon, he would take over everything.

15

COLOMBIA

The night of the party, Miguel spoke to the handlers of the K-9 units. "Be alert for anyone nosing around in areas that are off limits. The guests should be confined to the house and courtyard."

Some of his men would serve as parking attendants, keeping the driveway clear for the arrival of next guests, while Miguel waited at the front door to greet his guests. "Welcome to my home." He would shake hands with the gentlemen and place a light kiss on a lady's cheek.

Someone from his elegantly dressed staff would usher the couple to the courtyard. A single gentleman would be escorted by one of the lovely young women who worked for Miguel; the single ladies would be accompanied by a handsome young assistant. The tables were set for eight, each elegant setting of crystal stemware, china, and silver was displayed on a white linen tablecloth, and freshly cut flowers graced the center.

A bandstand was located at the outer edge of the courtyard. Lights shone on ice carvings of swans, and they appeared to shimmer. Soft music was playing in the background, just enough to set the mood but not interfere with conversation. Miguel was pleased. Everything was going as he'd planned, and even the weather was cooperating.

"You should be proud of your new complex," one of his secretaries said to him. He was proud.

Three of Miguel's classic cars were displayed to one side of the driveway. His personal armored limousine was parked beside them. Many of the guests had been driven to the party by chauffeurs. When a guest stepped from his vehicle, one of Miguel's men would drive the car to the parking area while another would escort the chauffeurs to the garage. There the caterers had set up tables and chairs and provided food and drinks, but there would be no alcoholic beverages served for the drivers. They were provided decks of cards and poker chips to pass the time.

Juan Moreno, his wife Carmela, and their guest Allison Denney were among the last to arrive. Juan introduced Miguel to Allison. "Miguel, I should like to present our guest from the United States, Miss Allison Denney. Miss Denney, my good friend Miguel Vargas."

He took her hand in his, struck by her beauty. She wore a long, white dress that enhanced her curves; her shoulders were bare. A gold chain draped from around her neck down into her cleavage. He guessed she was around five foot six; she was slender, but not skinny, and glowed with physical fitness. Her long, blonde hair she wore parted in the middle, its glossy length swinging past her shoulders. Her bright blue eyes sparkled with intelligence.

"Señor Vargas, thank you for extending the invitation," she said.

"You are most welcome, Miss Denney. I'm pleased you were able to attend," Miguel said. "I'd be honored if the three of you would join me at my table for the evening." One of the wait staff escorted them to his table.

Juan leaned closed to his wife. "I think our Miguel likes Allison very much." His wife smiled and nodded. He turned back to their house guest. "Allison, Miguel is a very rich and powerful man." He winked across the table at their host.

"Señor Vargas?" Allison tilted her head in his direction and smiled. "You've never married?"

Miguel shook his head. "No, Señorita."

"Please," she said. "We don't need to be formal, do we? You may call me Allison."

Miguel nodded. "Of course. It's Miguel—for you and Juan and Carmela only." He had invited two other couples to sit at his table, the Mayor of Bogotá and his wife and the Chief of Police and his long-time mistress.

Miguel checked with Jake to make certain the seating

arrangements were as he'd requested. He didn't want anything to spoil this evening, what he had counted on for such a long time. In the courtyard he found the guests were engaged in conversation, laughter floating above the happy group. Liquor was flowing. Only a few had taken their designated seats.

Miguel crossed the courtyard to the bandstand, and the music stopped instantly. He grasped the microphone. "May I have your attention please." The crowd in the courtyard grew quiet. "Ladies and gentlemen, tonight is a very special occasion for me. My new home is now complete, and I look forward to sharing it with you. If you will please find your seats, dinner will be served. Afterwards there will be entertainment and dancing in the courtyard. For those who would like to see my new home, my assistants will arrange a tour."

The caterers began serving, and the band was playing again, something soft and low. Miguel thought he recognized some old folk songs from his childhood. He sat down and nodded politely to the mayor and police chief and the ladies with them. He was never quite sure whether the ladies were wives or not. Respectfully he addressed them all as "Señora." He noticed that Juan had switched the place cards so he would be seated beside Allison.

He turned to her. "Please tell me more about yourself."

"I'm from America and a linguist by trade," she began in fluent Spanish, surprising Miguel. "You know, I'm a friend of Juan and Carmela."

"How long will you be staying in Bogotá?" Miguel asked.

"I don't have any definite plans at the moment. It's a wonderful city, and Colombia is a beautiful country."

Juan was talking with the mayor about the election that would take place in a few months. "How's the campaign progressing?" The mayor was a friend of Miguel's, and Miguel had been a large contributor to his campaign.

The police chief asked Miguel, "Is there anything you need regarding security in this neighborhood?" He gestured, indicating the rest of the area outside Miguel's new compound.

"*Gracias, mi amigo.* Nothing now." He preferred it when no one else knew about his business, especially the police.

The police chief was beginning a story. "We found the body of a man, burned to death. He was stuck in a barrel, in a dump near here several years ago. It's an odd case that's never been solved," he said. "We might look into it again soon."

"Probably a drug deal gone bad," Juan said

Miguel deliberately ignored the conversation. "Is everyone enjoying the party?" They must have gotten his message; the others at the table began discussing something else. He turned to Allison. "Your Spanish is incredibly good and without a trace of an accent."

"Thank you, Señor Vargas. It is nice of you to notice."

"Please call me Miguel as others do. This is the second time I've asked." He looked directly into her eyes. "Allison the linguist.... And what is a linguist, may I ask?" He was secretly embarrassed that he didn't know.

"I suppose it would best be described as someone who speaks many languages and makes a living at it," she said.

"And do you speak many languages?" Miguel asked, more intrigued by this woman.

"Yes. English, Spanish, Russian, French, Italian, and Chinese."

"I would love to learn English from you." Miguel meant what he'd said. He'd love to learn anything from her.

"It'd be my pleasure to teach you." Allison smiled and their eyes met again.

The meal was served, the exquisite feast that Miguel had so carefully planned. Soon the dishes were cleared, replaced by a selection of desserts.

Overhead, the dance floor in the courtyard was strung with balloons and streamers. The evening's entertainment began with one of Mexico's favorite female recording stars, Señorita Sylvia Perez, followed by the world-renowned magician Señor Tony Marcus. The band was playing again, and soon dancing couples crowded the floor.

"Miss Denney—Allison?" Miguel bowed before her. "May I have the pleasure of this dance?"

She smiled up at him, a glowing lovely smile. "Of course. I'd be delighted." She stepped into his arms, and they glided onto the dance floor.

16

COLOMBIA

"This is control," a voice had boomed and crackled from Jake's radio. "We have a silent alarm tripped near the front gate."

Jake had ordered the men to use the high-intensity lights to sweep the area, and he raced toward the direction of the gate. When he arrived, several of his men were standing over a figure on the ground, already cuffed and gagged. They had dragged him into one of the blockhouses and were questioning him.

He was one of the chauffeurs, and he had slipped away from the others.

"What in the hell are you doing? You're roaming around where you don't belong!" The man said nothing, and Jake slapped him hard across the mouth. The guy would need more persuasion. "Get some rope," Jake called. The men tied the chauffeur securely to a chair.

"If you don't answer my questions, I'll make you wish you had—and I'll keep on until you do," Jake snapped. "What's your name?"

Again the man was silent.

He walked behind the man, grabbed his right thumb, and wrapped a piece of wire around it. Then he inserted a small wooden stick under the wire and began to twist it, tightening the wire with every turn.

The thumb was turning blue, tears were running down the man's face, but still he didn't answer. Sweat was rolling down the chauffeur's face. His eyes were shut, and his jaw was clenched.

"I'll keep tightening it until your damn thumb drops off," Jake said calmly. "Then I'll do the other one." The wire cut through the skin; blood squirted over the room. Jake reached down, smeared his hand in the man's blood, and wiped it on the guy's face. "You're going to end up with no thumbs... Maybe you'll even bleed to death."

"All right! Please stop! I'll tell you what you want to know," the chauffeur begged.

Jake eased off on the wire slightly but kept it in place. "What's your name?"

Tears were rolling down the man's face. "Ricardo...."

"Who're you working for?"

"I'm a driver for the Sanchez family."

"That's bullshit, you asshole! Don't jerk me around— or I swear I'll take both your fucking thumbs off."

"No, please don't hurt me anymore! I'll tell you everything." The man was pleading. "Hector Campos had me contact the regular driver for the Sanchez family. I was to tell him that his family would all be killed, if he did not let me take his place driving tonight."

Jake stepped back, curious. The other guards had come closer to listen.

"I told the Sanchez family that their driver called me to replace him—because he was sick. They're totally unaware of what has happened."

Jake glared at the man, leaning in close to the blood-smeared face. "Why does Señor Campos want you to spy on Señor Vargas?"

"Hector gave me an infrared camera and wanted me to take pictures of his entire complex."

Jake nodded and one of the men found the camera and pulled it from the chauffeur's jacket. "What do you want us to do with him?"

"Keep him here until I talk to Miguel. He'll make this decision." Jake wouldn't disturb Miguel during his party. Take off your uniform," he ordered. Ricardo stripped to his undershorts. "Here. Get it cleaned and pressed up at the house. *Pronto!*"

They waited together in the blockhouse. Jake was studying the man, sizing him up. *"Hola!* Send me Saldaña. He's about the same size. We'll let him drive the Sanchez family home. I'll send you, Pablo, to pick him up. *Sí?"*

Miguel and Allison had danced together for the past three dances. He was thoroughly enjoying her company. "Would you mind if I called you again, Allison? Perhaps we could spend more time together while you're here in our fair city."

"I'd be flattered, Miguel." She reached into her handbag, took out a business card, and wrote her cell number the back.

He took it from her, holding her hand a moment before he let go.

"I'll be expecting your call." Her voice was warm, soft, and inviting." Please don't wait too long."

Miguel felt a sudden rush come over him; it was a pleasant tingle of arousal, something he had not felt in a long while. There was plenty of sex in his life, but this was different.

His guests were starting to leave, and Miguel again waited at the front door, bidding them farewell and thanking them for coming. Chauffeurs were bringing the cars around to the front drive. One by one the gleaming expensive cars drove off into the night.

When the last guest had left Jake approached Miguel about the incident with Campos's employee Ricardo.

Miguel was furious. "Only a fucking weasel like Hector would try such a stunt! I want to know more about this guy." He turned sharply, headed for the blockhouse where his men were holding Ricardo, striding so fast Jake couldn't keep up.

Miguel reached the door, slowing before he entered. He wanted to seem calm and make Ricardo less fearful that something else might happen to him. Hector's "chauffeur" was sitting in the same chair, cradling his right thumb. By the expression on his face, he was still in a lot of pain.

"Ricardo, I'm Miguel Vargas. I have some questions." He kept his voice steady. "Do you feel well enough to speak with me?"

Ricardo nodded and glanced up.

"What's your job in Hector's organization?"

"I'm one of his drivers," Ricardo said softly.

"Do you like working there? Are you treated okay?"

"He pays good money... but I stay out of his way as much as possible."

"What were his instructions for you tonight?" Miguel asked.

"Señor Campos wants to know how your complex is laid out, and how many men are working here." Ricardo rubbed his thumb and moaned.

Miguel paced the room, chin cupped in his hand. He stopped and considered Ricardo thoughtfully for a moment. "After you were to take the Sanchez family home, what would happen next?"

"Tomorrow, I was to send the pictures to Señor Campos's computer." The man shrugged. "Then I had hoped to visit my family here in Bogotá."

Miguel turned abruptly and waved, dismissing the others from the room. He was about to set a plan in motion and didn't want anyone else to know about it. "Ricardo, has Señor Campos ever threatened your family?"

"He threatens everyone who works for him."

"Do you believe he'd cause them harm or even kill them?" Miguel asked.

"Oh, yes, he has… too many families already."

Miguel was ready. "Ricardo, come with me to the house. Someone will take care of your wound."

"I'm very sorry, Señor Vargas, for any wrong that I have caused you."

They walked together from the blockhouse to the mansion. Miguel instructed the staff to treat Ricardo's thumb. He glared at Rafael. "I don't want that guy's thumb getting infected. Wasn't Raoul an army medic? Get him to treat the wound."

Miguel waited while his young staff member cleansed the wound with an antiseptic, applied an antibiotic ointment, and bandaged the thumb, wrapping the gauze securely up to the man's wrist. "Boss?" Raoul asked. "He should probably get a tetanus shot too."

Miguel nodded. "You take care of it. You have it in your kit?"

The young man nodded.

"Rafael? Go find this guy some clothes." He was tired of the sight of this guy standing around in his shorts.

Miguel waited until they were alone again. "Now, Ricardo, I want you to listen to what I have to say. Let me finish before you decide to accept or not. I want you to work for me, but you'll be spying on Hector. I'll provide you with another camera and an untraceable cell phone. Your mission will be to give me all the information you can on the exact location of Hector's coca fields, his packaging places, and the guards. I need to know his routes of distribution and the names of people who visit him from out of the country. I'll need to know his daily routine. Get me any information that might be helpful."

Ricardo's eyes widened in disbelief. "But, Señor Vargas, my family.... What about them?"

Miguel interrupted him. "Don't worry, I'm coming to that. How many are in your family?"

"My parents and two sisters. I also have a brother who lives in Mexico."

"Is your brother involved in *any* kind of crime or narcotics?" Miguel needed to know.

Confusion was spreading across Ricardo's face. "No, Señor Vargas, he owns an auto repair business."

"How long has it been since you or your family have visited your brother?"

Ricardo thought for a moment. "It's been over twenty years."

That would be perfect for Miguel's project. "Here's the rest of the plan. I'll pay you three times what Hector pays you. We'll move your family inside my complex where Hector can't harm them. When you finish getting the information I need. I'll fly you and your family to

Mexico, where you can live with your brother. I'll give you enough to provide a comfortable living, for all of you, for the rest of your lives. You'll need to make your decision quickly—Hector will be expecting those pictures by morning."

Ricardo faced Miguel. "You are not like Señor Campos." He hesitated for a moment. "I have wanted to leave for such a long time, but I was trapped. I feared for my family. Now, I can start again and be safe, in a new country." He drew himself up straighter. "Sí, Señor Vargas, I will work for you. You will be most happy with the information I give you."

Miguel didn't like sentimentality, but he needed a job done and would keep his word, as much as he needed to. "By the way, how many pictures did you take tonight?"

"Only two," Ricardo admitted.

Miguel laughed. "We'll need to get a few more so Hector is satisfied that you did your job."

They sent the photographs to Hector the following morning along with a short text message. *I will be visiting my family for two days,* Ricardo wrote, *and then I will return to the compound.*

Miguel dispatched three men with Ricardo to help his family move into Miguel's complex. Theirs was a small house with meager furnishings. They loaded their belongings into a truck and left, without indicating where they had gone.

Jake was at the gate when the truck arrived. He waved them in and hopped on the running board as they drove past. "Go to number three house," he instructed the driver.

The house was much nicer than the one they'd left. His parents and his sister had their own bedrooms; the house had two bathrooms and running water. The house was furnished with everything his family would need. Miguel's staff would provide their food.

Miguel watched from his home, satisfied. Now he had total control over Ricardo and his family. If the guy fucked up in any way, he'd kill all of them. Ricardo must know that too.

Miguel was at his desk studying Allison Denney's business card, turning it over in his hand and rereading her cell number. "Ah, yes...." He smiled, thinking how very much he wanted to get to know her and what a pleasure it would be to make love to her. She had flirted with him the night of the party. Should he wait longer, another day or two, before he called? He didn't want to seem over anxious; sometimes that gave a woman the upper hand.

Oh, what the hell, he thought and punched in the number. He let it ring and ring and ring. Finally a recording clicked on. It was Allison's voice, asking him to leave his name and number and she would return his call "as soon as possible." Damn, how he hated talking to a machine.

Allison had just returned from a game of tennis. A light was blinking on her cell. She pushed the playback button and listened. There was no message; the caller was unlisted. She had hoped that it might have been Miguel. She'd never been attracted to a "bad boy" before, and she was certain he was one. She placed her tennis clothes in the hamper and stood in front of the bathroom's full-length mirror. She had a good body and didn't mind admiring it. She appreciated when other people admired it too, like Miguel had.

"I have plans for that Latin devil," she said to her reflection. She turned from side to side, checking her tan lines.

The steam from the shower was fogging up the glass. The heat felt grand against her skin and tired muscles. After she finished shampooing, Allison reached for the soap and slowly applied it to her arms and shoulders. She sighed. It felt like silk gliding over her body. She moved her hands to her breasts, the nipples aroused and tingling. She imagined Miguel taking each in his mouth, kissing them, arousing her more. How she would love that.... She leaned back against the tiled walls, letting the warm water cascade over her. Just thinking about him.... She let her hand slide between her legs, caressing herself slowly, back and forth.

Visions of Miguel flashed through her mind. *Oh, my God, it feels so good...but I wish it was him, deep inside me. Oh, God...!* She was breathing faster and her legs shaking when she climaxed. The explosion was deep inside, repeated contractions and pulsations. But she'd really wanted Miguel—not this way. She felt weak, barely able to stand. For a moment she sat on the tiled floor of the shower, knees drawn up to her chest, and longing for *him*.

17

Oregon

The day after the men joined the Josephine County Sheriff's Office, Jumpy and Sandy met with the loan officer of First Oregon Bank, arranging the mortgage for their new home.

BJ decided to call on Dr. Haggle for any medical information he might have on Becky Hanson. The doctor's office was located on Sixth Street in a large older home that had been converted to accommodate a medical practice. The parking area was where there had once been a backyard.

Inside, a small, thin woman sat at the reception desk; she was talking on the phone scheduling an appointment. She was wearing a white uniform with a name badge that read: *Sugar Brown*. BJ tried not to chuckle, thinking how her name would sound if reversed.

"May I help you?" she asked without glancing up, still entering information into her computer.

"I'm BJ Taylor from the Josephine County Sheriff's Office. I understand that Dr. Haggle is the family doctor for Becky Hanson." He held out his badge for her inspection.

Sugar finally looked up, clearly startled. "What are you are looking for?"

"We would like to view Becky's medical records." BJ said.

"Please take a seat, Mr. Taylor. I'll let Dr. Haggle know you're here. He's with a patient now, but I'm sure it won't be long."

BJ sat down in one of the uncomfortable chairs facing the reception desk; he was sure the seating was designed to bring the doctor more business: patients with back problems. He thumbed through a stack of magazines. All seemed to be of interest to women—not even a *Time* magazine and definitely no *Field and Stream*. Most of the doctor's patients were probably female, judging by the patients in the waiting room.

Sugar opened the door. "Mr. Taylor, Dr. Haggle will see you now."

Dr. Haggle was standing behind an impressive desk when BJ walked into his office. "Roger Haggle." He extended his hand in greeting, and they shook hands. "Please, sit down." The doctor motioned to a chair facing his desk. "Mr. Taylor, you understand that I can't let you see Becky's file without a court order. Perhaps I can answer a few questions." Haggle folded his hands and leaned on the desk.

BJ smiled. "Thanks. That's a good place to start. Prior to Becky's disappearance did she have any signs of trauma or sexual activity?" He was prepared to take notes.

"I reviewed the file before you came in. I can tell you that Becky is a normal teenager. She was a virgin, as of the last time I saw her, which was a little over a year ago. Her mother had brought her in because she had a severe cold that was lingering on. There were no signs of trauma during the times I examined her," Haggle said.

BJ waited.

"I'm afraid that's all I can share at this time...."

"Without a court order, right?" BJ said, finishing the sentence for him. "Thank you for your time, doctor."

The doctor had been another dead end. Why hadn't the other detective obtained a court order? Frustrated, he drove back to the Sheriff's Office.

"We'd like a list of the local radio codes," he asked the young officer who had helped them before. "Thanks." He looked over the list. Somehow every county was different, yet strangely the same. No wonder civilians could listen in on their calls. "Oh, one more request, if you don't mind. Could Jumpy and I have some business cards? Nothing fancy. Just something that states who we are and our phone numbers so folks will know how to reach us."

He'd discovered two more interesting notes in the Hanson file. Deputy Miller had notified the National

Crime Information Center, officially telling them about a missing child. So NCIC had already been informed. The other was that he had contacted the two landfills in the area. At the same time he had set up a phone hotline for any tips or leads. Absolutely nothing had come in for him to follow up. Anything else the deceased deputy had had on his mind, but did not act upon, had died with him. BJ decided to contact the school again and request a list of all the students who took the same bus as Becky. He wanted to interview them again before any more time had passed. Within hours, the school had sent him an email with thirty names and phone numbers. He'd review them at home on his own computer.

"How did it go at the loan office?" BJ asked Jumpy when he and Sandy arrived home.

"The loan's approved and wired to the escrow office. Now, we wait for the title company to do a title search, and we'll be able to close in about three days." Jumpy was sounding proud and relieved. He laughed. "Do you think you'll be able to put up with us that much longer?"

"We're enjoying your company," BJ said. "Do you have anything planned for tomorrow?" He was studying the list of names from the school bus.

"Free as a bird."

"Let's make a few phone calls and set up interviews." BJ showed Jumpy the list and told him about his visit to Dr. Haggle's office. "I'll call the sheriff and give him an update."

"How about we call the girl's mom? Maybe she'll remember who Becky's best friends are," Jumpy suggested.

"Super idea. I'll call her right now," BJ said. The phone rang and Greta Hanson answered on the third ring.

"Hi, Mrs. Hanson," he said, "this is BJ Taylor from the Sheriff's Office. I was wondering if you could tell me who's Becky's best friends are? Also, did any of them take the same bus that Becky was on?" BJ listened, nodding and making notes while the girl's mother talked. "Thanks, Mrs. Hanson. Yes, we'll keep you posted if we learn anything." He hung up.

"Well?" Jumpy asked.

"There's a Cody McNeil, who was Becky's close friend. They were on the same bus, and they sat together in the same seat. Yes," he murmured, "here she is on the list." He dialed the number and waited; a recording clicked on. "Sorry wrong number," he said politely and hung up. "We can try later."

They decided to divide the list and used their personal cell phones. They were able to set up nine appointments for interviews on Saturday and six on Sunday, taking advantage of the time the kids would be out of school.

"I don't want to let this interfere with my family time and put my retirement on hold." BJ was looking longingly at his fishing gear.

"Yeah, you're right," Jumpy agreed. "It just grabs at you and you feel for the parents."

"Let's at least take our gals out for dinner tonight and talk it over with them," BJ suggested.

"I saw a place on F Street that looks interesting," Jumpy said.

"What's their specialty?"

"Beer, I guess."

"Why do you say that?"

"Well, the name of the place is The Brewery." Jumpy grinned. "I'm just pulling your chain, pal. It's a steakhouse."

"Sounds like a plan."

They arrived at the restaurant just after five, but there was already a waiting line. They were told there would be a twenty-minute wait for a table, unless they wanted to dine in the bar area.

"We wouldn't mind that at all," BJ said. The waiter showed them to a table against the wall and past the bar. BJ and Jumpy chose the seats that would allow them to keep their backs to the wall.

"Just an old habit." BJ winked at Carol as he helped slide in her chair.

"After so many years, it's just automatic," Jumpy said. Sandy and Carol nodded. They were accustomed to it too. He picked up the menu and glanced through the pages.

The room was large, accommodating twelve tables and a shuffleboard against the opposite wall. The long, ornate bar was built of antique cherry wood. There were white linen tablecloths on all the tables and a vase of fresh-cut flowers in the center of each one.

"Can you see anything in this dim lighting?" BJ asked Carol.

She laughed. "Is it time for you to get cheater-peepers too?"

"It is rather dim in here," Sandy agreed.

There were five other couples seated at the tables and only a few patrons at the bar. Several people were talking much louder than BJ thought necessary. The cocktail waitress came to their table to take their drink orders.

One of the louder patrons at the bar squinted in BJ's direction. "I know you. You're that asshole-hero that jumped into the river and got the kid before she croaked. Aren't you?" He was a large man, and he was pointing directly at BJ. "You think you're hot shit, right?"

BJ ignored him. The man left his barstool and headed unsteadily toward their table.

Carol put her hand BJ's arm, but he was already standing. "Honey," she said softly, "he's had a bit too much to drink. Let it go... please."

BJ was out of his chair, putting himself between their table and the drunk. Jumpy had quietly slipped off to one side.

"Let me buy you a drink." The man waved the glass in his hand, sloshing some of his drink on the floor.

"No thanks, we've just ordered," BJ said. He was standing with one foot slightly forward, automatically assuming a defensive stance.

"Oh? So you're too fucking good to drink with me, huh?" The stranger was advancing toward their table.

"Please. Stop where you are, sir." BJ's voice was low and steady. "Turn around and go back to your seat."

"Fuck you and your bitch!" He charged at BJ.

"That's my wife! Now you apologize!" BJ blocked the man's approach to their table. He moved quickly to the left, grabbed the man's right hand, twisting it behind him, then pushed his face against the table. The man's drink sloshed across the tablecloth in front of Carol and Sandy, and the vase of flowers toppled over and spilled into Sandy's lap.

The man's friend was off his stool. He was holding a beer bottle and charging at BJ's back. Jumpy grabbed him around the mid-section to restrain him, while the bartender had already called the police. The other patrons at the bar applauded.

The restaurant manager raced into the bar. "What's happening, Stan?"

Just then, four city policemen arrived. BJ and Jumpy explained what had happened, and the belligerent drunks were cuffed and taken away.

One policeman was asking Carol and Sandy for more details. "Are you sure you're all right, ladies?" A busboy was changing the tablecloth and resetting the table.

"I'm in shock. I hardly knew what was going on before it was over," Sandy told the officers.

Carol nodded. "Me too."

BJ apologized to the rest of the patrons for disturbing their dinner. Several drinks arrived at their table, courtesy of the other guests in the room.

"I'll be pleased to offer your meals complimentary," the manager said. "It's the least we can do to apologize for the disturbance and inconvenience."

"Well, Jumpy, you said it looked like an interesting place." BJ grinned and they all laughed.

At last BJ and Jumpy had a chance to talk.

"I understand completely," Sandy said after Jumpy had described their frustration with the one case they had started working.

"When a child disappears...." Carol let the words trail away. "Somehow, those are always the worst cases, aren't they, dear?"

"Whatever you can do for those parents and their grief is important," Sandy agreed. "You've got to do what you can."

18

COLOMBIA

Miguel called Allison again later in the afternoon.
"Hello, Señor Vargas." Her voice was low and
sultry. "I've been waiting for you to call. I was thinking
I'd need to hire someone to show me the highlights of
Bogotá."

"Who is this? Did I dial the wrong number?" Miguel
laughed. It felt good to be able to joke with someone.
"Are you free for dinner this evening?"

"That is a definite yes," Allison said without hesitation. "How should I dress?"

"Casual is right for where we're going. I'll pick you
up at seven." Miguel wanted to leave all further conversation for later in the evening.

"I'll be ready," she said.

Miguel spent the rest of the day taking care of business. He would be providing the necessary money
drops to the elite and entering the information in a

special ledger that contained the dirty little secrets of the city's rich and powerful. Mostly they were beholden to him; he could destroy them in a heartbeat and they knew it. All it would take was for a certain piece of verifiable information or photograph to reach the right places....

It had happened not long ago. He had quickly released a piece of information to the media. He sat back and watched the person squirm with embarrassment and then collapse in ruin. It was in his clients' best interest not to anger him or cross him in any way. Miguel Vargas could be loving and loyal, but he was also cunning and dangerous.

Miguel's driver followed the winding entrance to the Sanchez Estate and drove directly to where Allison had been staying. She was smiling and waiting for him by the guest house. He had told her "casual": she was wearing white pants and a loose, pale blue blouse. He thought she looked beautiful.

Miguel spoke first. "It impresses me when a lady is ready on time."

"That works both ways," Allison said.

The restaurant he had chosen was in the heart of Bogotá; it was renowned for extra fine South American cuisine. Miguel had reserved a table beside the large stone fireplace. The head waiter escorted them to their table and placed a leather-bound menu before them. Miguel helped Allison with her chair and sat down across from her.

He didn't glance at the wine list. "The lady and I will have a bottle of Dom Perignon."

Unknown to Allison, three of Miguel's bodyguards were seated at the neighboring tables, and another was lounging casually near the front door. They were armed with Israeli Uzi submachine guns. Some establishments provided their own security, but Miguel preferred to trust his personal guards.

Their waiter returned. "Señor Vargas, are you and your lady ready to order?"

Miguel was familiar with the menu. There was one item, a truly South American dish, he was certain she would enjoy. "Yes, Diego." The waiter liked it when Miguel used his first name. "We're having one order of Bandeja Paisa. Bring two plates."

Bandeja Paisa was a monster of a meal containing shredded meat, crispy fried *chicharon*, avocado, sausage, eggs, the light corn cakes called *arepita*, beans, and white rice, and the portions were always huge.

They ate slowly, savoring each bite.

"This is delicious!" Allison exclaimed. "The blend of flavors is delightful."

Miguel nodded. "I think this platter could feed three people." He could hardly take his eyes off Allison, admiring her. Her complexion was smooth and flawless; her skin glowed.

She glanced up and caught him staring at her. "Is there something wrong?" She tilted her head and regarded him, questioning.

"No, no! Not at all. You're incredibly beautiful," he said. "In Colombia, we admire beauty. Our Colombian beauty queens enjoy a very elite status among us. You could easily be in that ranking."

Allison smiled. "A few years back I placed as second runner-up in the Miss America Pageant."

Miguel slapped his palm against the table. "I knew it!"

"Thank you for the compliment," Allison said. She set her fork aside. "I can't possibly eat another bite. It was excellent. But I would like another glass of champagne." She raised her glass for Miguel to pour.

"I'm pleased that you enjoyed the dinner.... I hope you didn't mind that I ordered for you." Miguel lightly touched the napkin to his lips and poured the last of the Dom Perignon. He leaned back into the chair. "You mentioned you'd be happy to teach me English."

"Yes, I remember that quite well," Allison answered.

Miguel reached across the table and took her hand in both of his. "I would be so happy if you would do just that. In fact, I have a proposition that would be very lucrative for you."

Allison was reaching for her evening bag. "What do you have in mind?"

"I'd like to have you teach a group of my men and me English. I will set up a classroom on the patio or in the library, and you can give us lessons. I want them do be able to communicate well in English. I too wish to speak English—without any trace of an accent. I promise we will work very hard to learn."

"Miguel, you realize that will take time. My visa might expire before we're finished."

"I'll pay whatever you ask. And I'll take care of the visa." Miguel had never said "please" to anyone—not since the day his father was killed—but he was almost ready to now.

"It sounds very important to you, Miguel. How can I refuse?" She placed her other hand on his.

"Thank you for your kindness. Would it be convenient to start next week?"

"I believe so," she said.

He and Allison thanked the head waiter. He walked away, signaling for his driver to follow.

"Miguel? You don't pay?" Allison asked and glanced back at their table.

"No. We have an arrangement," he said, but did not explain further. They strolled through the restaurant, allowing time for his men to check the perimeter outside and to prepare the car. Once inside the limo, Miguel raised the privacy shield between them and his driver.

He didn't intend to try to make love in a car, not when the comfort of home was a few minutes away, but he kissed her softly on the neck and caressed her cheek. She turned toward him and they kissed again. His heart beat faster, and they clung to each other in a warm embrace.

"Shall we go to my place?" he whispered. She nodded. They both knew she would be spending the night.

Allison settled on the living room couch while Miguel uncorked a bottle of vintage port from his extensive cellar. He poured two glasses and sat down beside her. A fire blazed in the fireplace, giving off enough light and warmth to enhance the already romantic mood. A white bear skin rug near the hearth added to the atmosphere.

"It's been a wonderful evening, Miguel." Allison moved closer.

Her delicate perfume was intoxicating, like everything else about her. Miguel set his glass aside. "Would you like to take a moonlight swim in the pool?" He looked deep into her eyes.

"I don't have swimwear with me." Her tone was coy and teasing.

"In the guest bedroom, you'll find a white terrycloth robe. That's all you'll need," Miguel whispered. "I'll meet you in the pool." They stood and shared a long and passionate kiss.

The underwater lights in the pool glowed upward, turning the water a pale luminous turquoise. Miguel was already in the pool when Allison stepped to the edge, slowly untied the robe, and let it drop to the ground. She stood for a moment, the pool lights reflecting up and dancing off her body.

What a gorgeous woman, Miguel thought.

She stepped into the shallow end, taking the steps one at a time, and walked toward him until the water was to her shoulders. He moved toward her until they touched. She pressed her breasts against him. Arms around each other, they turned slowly, kissing, their hands busy exploring each other.

They stayed in the pool less than twenty minutes. Miguel suggested they go back inside by the fireplace. They emerged from the pool, and he wrapped the robe around her.

"I have never made love on a bearskin rug before," Allison said as she sank to her knees on the soft fur.

"Neither have I," Miguel said and joined her on the rug. He had brought the wine glasses with him.

"Are you warm enough?" he asked

"Just right." She snuggled closer to him.

Did she want him as much he wanted her? Miguel caressed her arm slowly, gently, and she looked up at him. "Miguel, I hope this isn't only a one-night stand for us. I think we have something special."

"I agree," he said, kissing her gently on the neck.

"You excite me. Not just sexually. I tingle the moment you walk into the room. Maybe it's the bad boy in you." She grabbed his hair and pulled him to her, pushing her month hard against his.

Miguel laid her down on the rug and untied her robe, completely exposing her. He began kissing her neck again and working his way to her breast, pulling her nipples into his mouth and flicking his tongue around its hardness.

"Oh, baby, that feels *sooo* good." Allison arched upward to meet his lips. He continued from one breast to the other and then to her navel while she moaned, low and soft. She had a thin patch of neatly trimmed, blonde pubic hair. Below it she was glistening with arousal, and he tasted her for the first time—sensually pulling on her labia and paying attention to her sensitive clitoris, teasing the slick pearl with his tongue.

She was resting her hands on his head, returning a slight pressure, and she was murmuring, "Yes, yes...."

"Stay with me. I'm about to explode." Miguel nodded and continued giving her pleasure. "This is the first of many to come," she moaned.

Encouraged, he was trying to hold back.

Allison clenched her teeth, buried her fingernails in his hair and she gasped loudly, startling him. "Oh, that was wonderful, sweetheart," she sighed, trying to catch her breath. "You really know how to please a woman. Now I'll return the favor." She reached down and rubbed his already erect penis. She took him in her mouth, using her tongue to stimulate him and tease him.

He moaned and begged of her. *"Oh, Dios!"*

She lifted her head for a moment and looked up into his eyes. "I want you to remember this night forever." She took him into her mouth again. It didn't take long for him to come. Allison crawled back up on top of him until they were facing. "Did you enjoy that as much as I did?"

"Oh, yes," Miguel said.

"Were not finished yet, are we?"

"Not by a long shot, sweetheart. We're just getting started." Miguel pulled her face close to his, pressing her mouth open for their tongues to seek each other. He was soon ready again.

"I want you inside me." She reached down, guiding him deep inside her and sighed with pleasure.

Miguel's heart was pounding and, as he had with Miss Cherry, he feared it might burst. Beads of perspiration ran down his face, as he forced himself deeper, in and back. He was vaguely aware that she was climaxing, small pulsations that nearly drove him mad, and finally they erupted together in one explosive climax. They collapsed into each others' arms, lying there in silence.

"Stay. I'll be right back." She kissed him on the forehead and returned with a cool washcloth, slowly caressing him with light gentle strokes.

He had known the pleasure of many women, but none had come close to the intense feeling of pure passion he'd experienced with Allison. Their relationship promised to be strong and exciting.

Since she would be teaching English at Miguel's house five days a week, Allison moved most of her belongings into one of his guestroom suites.

She had never been around a man like Miguel before. He was both scary and exciting. Sex with him was the best she'd ever known; she wanted to enjoy it as often as possible. It would be hard not to fall in love with him; at this point, she wasn't trying to resist. The days seemed to fly by, and Miguel was beginning to confide in her more, talking about his business and discussing his plans for the future. She had heard rumors that he controlled the drug trade in Bogotá. It was hard not to hear about it.

19

Oregon

On Saturday morning, BJ and Jumpy left headed for Cave Junction and the first of nine interviews. It was another stunning and scenic drive, tempting BJ with views of the river. Someday, he would have a chance to fish it—he hoped.

All the kids they had talked to wanted to help, but none had any new information that was helpful.

"Let's try the McNeil girl again." BJ pulled out his cell phone and scrolled through the list for her number. "Good afternoon, ma'am. This is Deputy Taylor from the Josephine County Sheriff's Office. We're in your area conducting interviews today concerning Becky Hanson's disappearance. Would it be possible to speak with your daughter Cody?" He listened for a moment." He turned to Jumpy. "Damn kids are busy these days. She's at band practice at school. Her mom says she won't be home for another hour."

Again he listened to more explanations pouring over the phone. "Would it be all right with you if we dropped by the school and talked with her there?" After assuring her they would be in a marked sheriff's car and that his partner would be with him, he received the mother's permission. She would call ahead and let the girl know they were coming.

"Thank you very much," BJ said, and then hung up.

"Sounds like a good, cautious mother to me." Jumpy nodded his approval. "If the band's going to be practicing for another while, let's grab a quick burger and then head over to the school."

"I'm up for that, and I'm buying," BJ said.

They were both in civilian clothes. They walked up to the front doors of the school only to find them locked. Peering through the windows, they signaled to a boy inside and displayed their badges. He pressed down on the release bar, and the door swung outward.

"Can you show us where the band room is?" Jumpy asked the boy. "We'd appreciate it."

The boy walked with them down one corridor after another. "It's at the end of that hallway," he said and pointed to another set of double doors.

The class was packing up their instruments when BJ and Jumpy walked in. Cody raised her hand and waved.

"I'm Harold Poke, the school's band teacher," a tall gray-haired man introduced himself. "How may I help you?"

"They're from the Sheriff's Office," Cody said. "And they want to talk to me." The rest of the students froze and stared at them, while the teacher asked to see their ID.

"Could you please stay, Mr. Poke? We want to ask Cody some questions," BJ said and squeezed himself into the small desk next to Cody.

"Class, the rest of you can go now," Mr. Poke said. He went to the other end of the room and began straightening stacks of sheet music.

"Cody, we know you and Becky are best friends. We're still trying hard to find her." BJ held his notebook and pen readied to take down anything the child might say. "Think back to the last day you saw Becky. Were you getting on the bus together?"

"No, sir," the girl answered without hesitation. "I was at the front of the line and didn't see Becky until I took my seat in the second row against the window." She sat primly erect at the desk, her hands folded in her lap.

"Were you sitting on the side of the bus facing the school?" BJ continued.

"Yes, sir," she said.

"What happened next?"

"I don't remember for sure. Oh, yeah. I took a picture with my cell phone of the rest of the kids getting on."

"Do you still have the picture?" BJ asked.

"I don't know. I take a lot of pictures with my phone, but I don't know how to erase them." She smiled and looked embarrassed. BJ himself didn't know how to erase the photos on his new phone either; Carol always handled it for him. "So I guess it's still there." She began rummaging in her backpack for the phone.

"Would you mind if we take a look at it?"

"Sure, it's okay."

BJ quickly scanned through the volume of photos until he found the one of kids getting on the bus. They huddled together, staring down at the phone.

"That's Becky in the back of the line." Cody pointed to a girl on one knee; her right hand was deep in her backpack that lay on the ground.

"Who is the guy behind her?" BJ asked.

"Oh, that's Mr. Iverson. He's the school janitor."

BJ looked at Jumpy. "I don't remember any mention of him in any reports." Jumpy shrugged and shook his head.

"Do you mind if we send this photo to the department?" He handed the phone to Jumpy, who emailed it within seconds.

The girl shook her head. "That's okay with me."

"What happened next?" BJ said as he was writing Iverson's name in his notebook.

"I was talking with the girls in the seat behind me and forgot about Becky not being there." Cody began to cry softly. "Am I in trouble for not paying attention?" she said. Worry had transformed her sweet young face.

"Not at all, Cody. You've been very helpful." BJ put his arm around her shoulders. *Poor kid,* he thought. She might have been the last one to see Becky alive. The thought nagged at him.

"Do you need a ride home?" Jumpy asked.

"I live next door to Cody," Mr. Poke said. "I always take her home after band practice."

BJ and Jumpy looked at Cody directly. "Are you sure this is all right with your mom?"

"Yes. This way she doesn't have to drive out here twice on Saturday. Thanks, Mr. BJ and Mr. Jumpy."

Sunday afternoon they were back in Cave Junction for interviews with six more kids who rode the same bus as Becky Hanson had. The first five didn't add anything new to their case. The last was a boy named Todd Gilbert. BJ repeated the same question and nothing seemed forthcoming.

Jumpy leaned near to him. "You know, when I was a kid I remember some odd things at school. Most of it was nothing. But, it might be able to help us a lot. Have you noticed anything strange or even different at school during the past year?"

"No." He looked thoughtful for a moment. "Oh, yeah. My friend and I discovered that Old Poopy-Pants wears diapers." He laughed at what he'd just said.

BJ broke in. "What do you mean?"

"We were playing ball behind the school. One kid hit a foul ball that landed in one of the trash bins. My buddy and I went over to get it. We climbed in. I was tossing out the black plastic bags, trying to find the ball, and one of them broke open. It was some stinky old diapers with shit and blood on them." Todd pinched his nose with his fingers.

"Yes," BJ said. "Go on."

"We knew the bags belonged to Mr. Iverson. After that we started calling him Old Poopy-Pants." Todd laughed nervously, but then looked embarrassed. "We didn't call him that to his face. After we found the ball, we put the bags back in the bin and went on with the game."

"Thank you for your help, Todd." Jumpy said. "That was really one foul ball, wasn't it?"

The boy grinned and nodded.

They left and headed back to their unit.

"Are you thinking the same thing I am?" BJ was feeling the first hint of excitement, the beginnings of something about to happen in a case. "If those diapers belong to Becky, that means she's still alive, and he's got her hidden somewhere." Along with the excitement came worry.

"Let's double-back to the school and see if there're any bags in the bins," Jumpy said.

"If there are, we can call the refuse company and find out when they make their pickup at the school. Then we can follow the truck to the landfill and take any other evidence we may find—without getting a warrant."

Sunday, late afternoon, there was only one vehicle in the parking lot at the school, an old and dirty Dodge pickup.

"I don't have any idea where the janitor lives. He wouldn't live there, would he? I'm guessing that's his pickup." BJ decided to park outside the school grounds.

"We need to check those trash bins without anyone noticing," Jumpy said.

"Suppose we go home and drive back after dinner when it's dark." BJ turned around and headed east to Grants Pass.

Excitement and nervousness hung over them at the dinner table. "We're going back to the school after dinner," Jumpy told Sandy.

"Are you sure you should?" Sandy sounded concerned.

Carol sighed. "I rarely ask anymore."

BJ and Jumpy had changed into dark clothing were planning their trip back to Cave Junction. "We'll arrive just as it turns dark," Jumpy said.

"Please be careful, my big guy." Carol hugged BJ as he left. "Remember? You're supposed to be retired."

BJ turned off their lights a block away and coasted up to the school. The old Dodge pickup was still parked in the same place. BJ wondered when it had last been driven. The trash bins were located beside a rear door at the back of the school.

"Jumpy, take a position on the other side of the door in case anyone comes out. I'll check the bins." As they crossed the parking area, headed for the two bins, BJ slipped on a pair of latex gloves.

The heavy plastic lids didn't have any locks. The amount of trash and garbage heaped inside wouldn't allow the lid to close properly. BJ lifted the lid and shone his small flashlight on the first black plastic bag. He held the flashlight between his teeth so he could use both hands to untie the bag. He found nothing but school trash; he tried another bag. The odor was distinctive and overwhelming. Had he hit pay dirt? He retied the sack and lifted it out.

They hurried back to the unit. How he wished it had a trunk. They wrapped the bag in two more plastic sheets, but they'd still need to drive with the windows open. BJ turned the ignition, eased into gear, and drove away slowly before turning on the lights.

They were feeling hopeful. They exchanged a fist pump and a high five, certain that whatever they'd found would help their case. "I'll need to call Sheriff Patterson and give him a progress report." BJ slapped his palm against the steering wheel.

"We're due to close on the house tomorrow," Jumpy said. "We need to do the walk-through at ten in the morning. Then, after that, the new furniture is being delivered."

"When I finish with the sheriff, I'm meeting our contractor out at our property," BJ said.

"We'll touch base later in the afternoon."

The next morning, BJ arrived at the office before eight. Captain Smith was at his desk reviewing some documents when BJ knocked at his door. "Come on in, BJ," the captain said and closed the file.

"Captain, do you and Sheriff Patterson have a few minutes? I have some new information on the Becky Hanson case that may be important."

Five minutes later the three of them were in a conference room, the doors closed.

"What have you learned?" Sheriff Patterson asked. Over the next several minutes BJ outlined the information he and Jumpy had gathered on the Hanson case.

"I'd like to call the trash company and have a special empty truck sent to the school to pick up the two containers," BJ said.

"Why a special truck?" the captain asked

"That way there won't be other trash in the truck to contaminate any possible evidence." BJ said. "When the trash truck is far enough from the school we can check for any other bags containing diapers in them and mark them as evidence."

"What's your next move?" the sheriff continued.

"Where's the closest DNA lab?" BJ asked.

"Portland," Captain Smith said.

"We have the girl's hairbrush. I'd like to see if there is a DNA match between her hair and the diapers."

"It'll take awhile before we get those results. In the meantime, we'll run a background check on Iverson." The sheriff pushed back his chair. "Great job, BJ. You and Jumpy are a credit to the department."

BJ returned to his cubicle and dialed the school's number. "Is Mrs. O'Connell in?" he asked. There was a moment of silence before she picked up. He identified himself. "We met the other day about Becky Hanson."

Helen O'Connell had a good memory, and she sounded pleasant and cooperative.

"Mrs. O'Connell, would you be so kind as to give me any information you have on Mr. Iverson, the school janitor?" He paused while she asked him what he would need. We'll need his full name, address, birth date, social security number, and how long he's been employed with the school." He waited, listening to the clicking of her computer keyboard in the background.

After a moment she came back on the line. He wrote down the information and read back his notes. Mrs. O'Connell assured him he'd written everything correctly. "Thank you, Mrs. O'Connell. You've been most helpful."

BJ brought up NCIC on the department's computer and referred back to his notes about the janitor. First, he entered the name Earl Iverson and the rest of the data except for his address. There was nothing under that name, but the birth date and social came up with an Earl Morrison. Morrison had escaped from a mental hospital in California over a year before he was hired as a janitor at Cave Junction Elementary. There was no confirmed address. Were there any quarters at the school, somewhere the janitor could have been living?

BJ went back to the Captain's office. "Could I get a search warrant for the school?"

"It's not needed in Oregon. The school and grounds are state property," the captain said. "However, we'll need to wait for the DNA results before we approach the school." The captain was thoughtfully scanning the wall of legal books, searching for a particular volume. "BJ, did you actually see the janitor put those bags in the bins?"

"No, I didn't. Could we try to retrieve any finger-prints now?"

"Where's the bag?"

"In the back of my unit," BJ answered.

"Bring it in and I'll get our print expert. We can meet in Interview Room 1," the captain said.

BJ put the bag on the floor.

"Phew! This is a stinking job!" The deputy carefully dusted the outside of the bag and tried to hold his breath. The odor was fouling the air in the room. "Damn! There're all kinds of prints—good ones too," said he said.

"Do you think you could check one of the diapers, also?" BJ was pleading.

"Okay, man, but this is going to cost you." The deputy reached for one of the plastic coated diapers, holding his breath again.

"Yeah, got one off the plastic liner," he said.

Things were starting to come together. The tech packaged everything and sent it to Portland's DNA lab. He'd filled out a rush request and sent it by overnight courier.

The deputy ran the prints locally, but nothing came up. Next he ran them on the national data basis known as AFIS. Within minutes, he had a hit. The same guy, Earl Morrison, showed up.

"We've got the SOB," the deputy said.

BJ placed the print data in Becky Hanson's file, then it would be a waiting game. He was off to meet with his contractor.

20

OREGON

The workmen were removing the forms surrounding the concrete slab that had been poured two days ago.

BJ walked over to inspect the foundation. "You guys are moving right along."

"As long as the weather holds, we'll be okay," John said. John Briggs was a well-respected contractor in the area, and had built dozens of beautiful custom homes throughout the county.

"We'll be snapping out the lines showing your room layout in a few minutes." He was studying the blueprints. "Any changes?"

"No, we're still pleased with the plans," BJ replied.

"It will take us nearly two weeks to complete the framing, and then the trusses will go up," John said.

"I'm looking forward to seeing that." BJ shook John's hand as he prepared to leave.

"I'll give you a call. We hire a crane to offload the trusses and hoist them up into position." John was pointing to a cross-section view of the blueprints.

BJ waved goodbye and drove down to Jumpy's new house. A moving van was in the driveway, and men were carrying furniture inside.

"Sandy, is Jumpy here?"

Sandy directed a mover where to place the piece of furniture he was carrying. "He's at the storage unit picking up our other belongings."

"Think he'll need any help?" BJ stepped out of the way of another mover.

Sandy wiped her forehead. "I don't think so. There's nothing heavy and he's almost finished.

"I'll hang here and wait until he gets back, if you don't mind. I need to bring him up to date on the Hanson case."

"Would you like something to drink while you're waiting?"

"No thanks, not right now," BJ said.

A few minutes later, Jumpy arrived with a trailer in tow, piled high with what they had brought with them from Santa Ana. Together, BJ and Jumpy carried the boxes into the house.

"I need to stop by your place and pick up whatever we still have there," Jumpy said.

"If you're done with the trailer, let's drive it back. You can meet me at Rogue Lea, then we'll load my truck with the rest of your things and come back here."

Jumpy poured two cups of coffee, and they found a quiet corner away from the movers.

"Here's what's been happening with the Hanson case." BJ described the morning's discoveries at the Sheriff's Office. "We're waiting until we hear from Portland." He crossed his fingers, and Jumpy nodded.

The next few days were a flurry of activity; both families were busy with personal matters. Early one following morning, BJ was reading the paper when his cell rang, breaking the silence.

"BJ, you need to get Jumpy," Captain Smith said. "Get your asses down here as soon as possible—we got news." The captain rang off.

The conference room was bustling with activity when BJ and Jumpy stepped in. Sheriff Patterson reviewed what BJ and Jumpy had put together on the Hanson case.

"The DNA results have confirmed a match for Becky Hanson," he said. "At the time the bag was placed in the trash bin, Becky was still alive. We know this because of the soiled diapers." He shook BJ's hand and then turned to Jumpy. The room erupted with cheers. "We need to proceed with caution and lay out our plan to find her, while making sure the janitor is isolated and can't do her any harm... any more harm, that is."

Over the next two hours, BJ, Jumpy, a small group of sheriff's deputies, and a representative from the District Attorney's Office laid out a plan. The fewer people involved, the better. They certainly did not want the press latching onto the story.

Three sheriff units, with four deputies each, headed toward Cave Junction on Highway 199. It was a clear, sunny day in the mid-70s. BJ's unit had taken the lead, and Jumpy was following in his own vehicle. The plan was to drive to the fire station and have the deputies change into firemen's gear.

Jumpy and Sheriff Patterson, who would remain in civilian clothes, would arrive at the school ahead of the others. At a prearranged time, they would pull the fire alarm. The firemen would drive the sheriff's units behind the school, and the deputies would arrive in the school's main parking lot driving fire trucks. They would enter the school as part of the fire drill.

Jumpy and Sheriff Patterson's assignment was to locate the janitor, Earl Morrison. If he was in the crowd outside, they would arrest him. Once BJ was notified of the arrest, he and the other deputies would shed their firemen's gear and begin the search for Becky Hanson.

Their plan worked. Jumpy located Mrs. O'Connell, the school principal, and she identified Mr. Iverson. He was a short, stocky, and balding man in his mid-fifties who was a bit overweight. He was standing to one side with a group of teachers. Sheriff Patterson circled around back while Jumpy approached the janitor from the front.

Sheriff Patterson arrived first, and placed his hand firmly around the janitor's upper arm. Holding him tightly, he leaned over and whispered in his ear. "Sir, my name is Frank Patterson. I'm the Sheriff of Josephine County. I'm placing you under arrest for the abduction of Becky Hanson."

Jumpy had joined the sheriff and grasped Mr. Morrison's other arm; they escorted him to one of the sheriff's units. Even in the fresh air Morrison's body odor was pungent and overwhelming. Before placing him in the backseat, they gave him a pat down and cuffed him.

Jumpy was immediately on the radio to BJ. "He's in custody. I'm coming in to help with the search." He raced to the school's back entrance.

Sheriff Patterson asked Mrs. O'Connell to delay the children from re-entering the school building for a few minutes. BJ and Jumpy found the door marked *Janitor*. It was locked. They radioed Sheriff Patterson, who asked Mrs. O'Connell where they could find the keys.

Within seconds BJ's radio came to life. He listened as Patterson's words crackled through the air.

"Go to the principal's office. In the middle top drawer you'll find the master key to all the school's locks. It has a red-rubber cover on it," the sheriff said.

"Copy," BJ answered. Jumpy and two other deputies were waiting by the door. BJ's hands were shaking as he inserted the key into the lock. "The janitor's quarters are in the basement." They pushed open the heavy, metal door.

"We can't just rush down there; we don't know if he has set any booby traps. Be careful. Take your time." They closed the door behind them, and BJ radioed the sheriff to not let the teachers and the children back in the school yet.

"Sheriff? If we find her, she may need medical attention. Have the firemen send an ambulance to the back of the school, without red lights and sirens.

"Already done," the sheriff replied.

Outside the firemen were gathering their gear and heading back to the station with their trucks.

BJ and the other deputies were slowly descending the dimly lit stairs, flashlights beaming off the walls. "Look for any tripwires... anything that looks suspicious."

After the bottom step, the passage continued down a hallway that led to a large, high-ceilinged room with cinderblock walls. To the right was a vast boiler used to heat the entire school. Someone switched on an overhead light.

In the corner of the room was a twin bed, a makeshift closet with a chest of drawers, a small bare table, one chair, and dirty dishes piled everywhere. There was a small refrigerator and a hot plate that looked like it hadn't been cleaned any time recently. Throw rugs on the floor were old and threadbare. The trash can was overflowing, and the stench of body odor permeated the room.

Morrison's dirty clothes lay at the foot of the bed. It

was evident he didn't practice good hygiene. There was no evidence of Becky Hanson.

"Keep looking, I know she's here someplace!" BJ began calling her name. "Becky, if you can hear us, yell out or knock on the wall!"

The men listened intently. There was no sound.

"Look for a sealed compartment or trapdoor," he told them."

One of the deputies called out, "BJ, over here!"

BJ couldn't tell where the voice was coming from.

"Over here! Behind the boiler," the deputy repeated. They crowded into the small space. The light was poor, and again they used their flashlights. There was a metal door with a large padlock.

"Shit!" BJ muttered.

"Shall I shoot it off?" Jumpy reached for his side arm

"Hold it. If she's in there, it could scare the crap out of her. Spread out and look for any keys." He tapped on the door and called her name again.

"He must have them on him, the bastard!" Jumpy said.

"Radio the sheriff that we need any keys that Morrison might have on him," BJ ordered.

In an instant, Sheriff Patterson was back on the radio. "He has a whole damn ring of keys," the sheriff said. "I'm taking them off his belt. Christ, he stinks. I need a Hazmat suit just standing next to him!" There was a moment's silence. "Send one of the deputies up to help watch him, and I'll bring down the keys. I want to be in on this first hand."

In less than two minutes, BJ had the keys in his hands.

"I needed to get away from the smell," Patterson whispered to BJ, and they both laughed for a moment.

One by one, BJ tried the keys. Finally one slid in and he turned it. The lock sprang open. Jumpy was behind him, feeling for a light switch. He flipped the switch, and light flooded the room. The five men cautiously stepped inside.

In the far corner was a young girl huddled on a mattress. One hand was chained to the wall; her other hand covered her eyes. The only items on the mattress were a wadded-up blanket and a dirty pillow. The men hung back, out of shock and respect, while BJ walked very slowly toward the girl.

He knelt down beside the bed. "Is your name Becky Hanson?" he asked softly.

Through her sobs, she nodded.

"We're from the Sheriff's Office, honey. We're going to take you to the hospital, where your mom and dad are going to meet us."

God, how he hated these cases. She was not in good condition at all. Her body was filthy dirty, and her hair had not been cared for since she was kidnapped. Her hair, which might have been a pretty blond at one time, was so knotted that it looked like she had dreadlocks. Her nails were long, dirty, and broken, and she was pitifully underweight. She was wearing filthy sweat pants and a faded, dirty tee shirt. Her feet were bare and had open sores. From what he could see there were bug bites all over her body too.

She had curled up, her head tucked down to her knees, and she was crying. Finally, she looked up at him. "Why did it take you so long to find me?" Then she began crying again.

"Honey, I'm sorry. I don't really know. I've just moved to Oregon myself." BJ tried all the keys again and finally unlocked her wrist from the chain.

The sheriff had already called for the paramedics to send down a gurney.

BJ dialed the Hanson residence on his cell phone and Greta Hanson answered. "This is BJ Taylor. We've found your Becky. She's alive, but in poor condition. Can you and Mr. Hanson meet us at Grants Pass Community Hospital in about forty-five minutes?" He listened to her for a moment. "Of course, you can speak to her." He handed the child his phone. "Here, Becky. It's your mom."

Becky took the phone. All he could understand was "Mom" and then the girl cried some more.

He took back the phone. "Yes, Mrs. Hanson, this is for real."

It gave him a tremendous sense of pride and delight to make that call and to hear the excitement from her parents on the other end.

Upstairs, the paramedics were starting an IV in Becky's arm and had wrapped her in blankets. She had been kept in the dark so long she was having trouble adjusting to the light. "Keep your eyes closed until we get you into the ambulance," Jumpy said as he helped tuck her in.

"Becky, your mom and dad are going to meet us at the hospital," BJ told her as the paramedics carried the gurney up the flight of stairs. Jumpy was leading and opened the door into the school's hallway. He held it open for the paramedics and saw two guys rushing toward them—one was carrying a TV camera and the other was holding out a microphone.

"Shit, it's the press," he said. "How the fuck did they find out?" He raced ahead and blocked their path. "This is a police matter. You're interfering." He prevented them from advancing any further. The gurney wheels plopped down on the tile floors, the sounds echoing about the school hallway. The paramedics rolled Becky to the school's back exit where the ambulance was waiting.

"Where are you taking her?" shouted the reporter with the mike.

"To the fire station," BJ called back. He hoped he could throw them off track. The men retreated and scattered in opposite directions. BJ called for a deputy to place crime scene tape across the janitor's door. "Stay here until the CSI team arrives."

21

COLOMBIA

Miguel's men were unloading a truck filled with new school desks and a large chalkboard on wheels. He directed them to arrange the classroom on the patio, where it could easily be moved into the library in case of rainy weather. A note pad, pens and pencils, and a copy of the text book, *Spanish Converted to English*, were placed on each desk.

Tomorrow would be the start of their English lessons. The men were scheduled to be in class from eight in the morning until four in the afternoon every day, five days a week.

"Miguel," Allison was explaining, "the only way to learn a language completely is called 'immersion.' It's important that the class is conducted in English and that—after the first week—the men speak nothing but English. That way they begin to think in the language too. That's often the most difficult part with adult learners. Even if your men are dedicated, it will take at least three months."

Miguel had nodded in agreement. "That's makes perfect sense. I'd never really thought about it."

"That's natural. People who grow up learning one language, whatever their native language is, never give the matter another thought. Don't you worry, dear one, I'll give you extra attention after class." She winked at him playfully.

"I was counting on it," Miguel said.

"I mean I'll work on your diction." They both had laughed.

Ricardo had contacted Miguel. They arranged a time and place to meet and review the information he had acquired, including photographs of the airfield by the river and where the drugs were stored before shipment. There was a short list of visitors who had business with Hector in the last few weeks. One that seemed of particular interest was General Omar Augustus of the Colombian Army.

"I've seen that guy before," Miguel said. "He's the asshole who's supposed to be fighting the drug trade in Colombia. He's in bed with Hector! He's the one who's tipping him off when there is an upcoming raid from the army." Miguel laughed at the irony.

Miguel called Jake to meet with him. "It won't be necessary for you to join up with Hector after all. My plans have changed." He noticed the change in Jake's demeanor. It was as though a ton of weight had been lifted from his shoulders. "I appreciate your willingness, Jake. It's good to know I can always depend on your support."

All the men Miguel had chosen to attend the English classes were young and had completed high school. A few of them had had minor scrapes with the law in the past but never anything serious. All were unmarried. He wanted them to live in America, and he didn't want them getting homesick for a wife and kids. His plan was to take over the Colombia drug trade and expand into America. They would be setting up grow houses and function as runners and dealers, while cutting out the American middlemen. Miguel's profits would soar.

"*Buenas días, estudiantes,*" Allison addressed the class in perfect Spanish. "However, my students, within one week you will speak only English in class. Furthermore, after class you will practice what you have learned with each other." She handed out several assignments. "We will go over these the following day." Her teaching methods were easy to follow, and she was patient with them; she was most patient of all with her special student Miguel.

One Friday evening, Miguel and Allison were on the patio, finishing dinner, when one of his staff stepped from the house; the man was waiting, trying to attract Miguel's attention.

Miguel sighed, set down his fork, dabbed his lips with a napkin, and motioned to the man. Allison had rarely seen this man before, but he clearly knew Miguel. He came close and whispered in Miguel's ear, too softly for her to hear; he turned and left them alone.

Miguel appeared saddened by the news he had just received. They ate in silence for the next several minutes.

"I'll be leaving tonight and won't return until Sunday evening. There's something I must attend to."

"Is there something wrong?" Allison asked. She placed her hand on his, trying to reassure him.

"I just received word that my mother has passed away."

"Oh." Allison remained silent for a moment. "Would you like me to go with you?"

"No... thank you for offering. Excuse me. There are things I must see to before I leave." He pushed back his chair from the table and stood, abandoning the rest of his meal.

Miguel phoned Rafael and Jake. "Meet me in the office, within the hour. It's urgent." He told Rafael to bring some peasant clothing that would fit him and a disguise, including facial hair and makeup. "Jake, bring your personal pickup. Make sure it's fully gassed and ready for a trip."

The men arrived within minutes of each other. Miguel told them he was going to visit his old village to attend his mother's funeral and did not want to be recognized. Jake's old King Cab truck was in excellent mechanical condition, although it looked like an old farm vehicle.

Miguel was removing extra cash from the safe. "We may be gone overnight."

"Have the kitchen staff prepare some food," he directed.

The three men were on their way within the hour. Leaving the city and traveling at night, they were soon on a rural dirt road that was winding through grasslands, jungle, and forests. There wasn't much traffic late at night, and they had come well armed. There was always a chance they would encounter army patrols or guerrilla bands that kidnapped people and held them for ransom. Miguel was well known by both groups, but at night someone might shoot first without identifying his target.

The road passed through the edge of the village where Miguel had killed Pedro; painful visions of that day flashed through his mind. A few minutes later, they entered an even smaller village, made up mostly of farmhouses and small huts.

Miguel signaled to Jake to slow down. "This is the one we're looking for."

They pulled in behind the church, ate their sandwiches, and drank beer.

"Nothing to do now until daylight," he said. "You two get in the truck bed. I'll use the front seat. We'll try to get some sleep." He unrolled one of the sleeping bags. Jake and Rafael each grabbed a handgun and a sleeping bag and settled down in the back.

The next morning, Miguel awoke to the sound of someone tapping on the window. It was Jake. He sat up rubbing his eyes, not fully awake, briefly wondering where the hell he was.

"Where's Rafael?" Miguel muttered, still getting his bearings.

"He went over to those trees to take a piss." Jake was holding his crotch. It was not yet quite light. Miguel needed to relieve himself but decided to use an empty beer can rather than risk being seen before putting on his disguise.

Rafael returned and unbundled a package containing the familiar white cotton pants, shirt, sandals, and serape of a peasant. Miguel changed quickly, and Rafael applied makeup to his face, hands, and feet that made him appear weathered and much older. Next he added a bushy mustache with some kind of adhesive; the finishing touch was a tattered sombrero.

"The funeral is at nine," Miguel said. "I'll find somewhere to hide until then. Pick me up at noon, right here. He stood there looking like someone else, not the Miguel they'd always known. Jake and Rafael drove away from the village to wait.

After they drove off, Miguel walked down the road to where his old home had been, only to find it empty and in shambles. He hid inside, waiting for the hours to pass.

Nine o'clock finally came, and the small church filled as the villagers filed in, and the Mass started on time. It was so long ago that he'd lived there that he didn't recognize anyone. Miguel stood inside the entrance, his head bowed low. He watched the peasants walk past the casket. Each made the Sign of the Cross and spoke softly to the family seated in the front row before filing into the rustic old pews. He listened to the priest continue the words of the Mass he had once known well. As the funeral mass ended he moved to the far side behind a pillar and remained there until the end.

For a brief moment Miguel had been alone in the church, and he had walked up to the casket to stare down at his mother. He touched her hand, whispered a prayer, and his eyes filled with tears. She had always been sweet and gentle, and she had loved him.

The men from the village carried the casket to the cemetery, and the villagers walked behind the men. Miguel kept at a distance, following them as they wound their way through the old rock houses to the cemetery. There he stood behind a tree, but close enough to hear the priest pray. Miguel's thoughts turned back to when he was a boy and the happier, simpler times with his family. Strange how life could change a boy's plans. Never in his wildest dreams did he ever think he would become a killer and a drug lord.

A young woman approached the casket and placed a single rose on top. Her two children did the same, and they huddled together, sobbing. A man walked up from behind and put his arms around them. The priest said, "Elena, your mother is now with God, where she will suffer no more."

That's my little sister and the others must be her family. The rest of the people left the grave site. Miguel longed to talk to her alone, but how could he? At last the man took the children by the hand, walking back to the village. Elena fell on her knees to pray.

"I have lost my father and my brother and now my mother... all my family is gone," she said. She turned and looked up at the stranger who had touched her shoulder. She didn't recognize him.

"Elena, it's Miguel, your brother." He tried to smile, but his sadness must show through, even through his disguise.

"I need to talk with you, Miguel," she said softly. "You look so different... and so much older." She stood, uncertainly reaching for his hand.

"It's the disguise. I can't be seen here in our village, because the police are still looking for whoever killed Pedro." He leaned down and kissed his little sister on the forehead.

"Where have you been all these years? We thought you were dead."

"It's better that you don't know." Together they walked slowly from the cemetery and sat down under a nearby tree. "Was that your husband and children I saw with you earlier?"

"Yes, my husband is your old childhood friend, Javier Lopez. Maria and little Miguel are our children."

How he envied the love in her voice. "Are you happy and do you have enough... enough money?"

"Javier is a good man and works very hard in the fields. We love each other and our children are well." She placed her hands over her heart.

Miguel reached into his pocket, pulled out a folded cloth, and handed it to her. Inside the cloth was 2,000,000 Colombian pesos.

"Please take this. Use it to help your family—any way you want. You must tell no one, not even Javier, where it came from. I will make sure you receive more, from time to time... when I'm able." He enfolded her in his arms. "I must go now."

"When will I see you again?"

"I'm not sure if it can ever happen again... but I will always keep track of you and your family, and you will always be in my heart." Miguel kissed her on the forehead once more, turned, and walked away down the path.

Rafael and Jake were waiting in the truck. Even through his disguise they must have read the sadness in his eyes.

Jake opened the door for him. "Are we ready to go home?"

"Yes, my business here is over. Probably forever. Let's go." He threw off the sombrero and ripped off the fake mustache. He wondered whether Rafael had applied the hairy thing with duct tape.

They drove in silence for over an hour, winding their way through the countryside, until they arrived at a small bridge where two vehicles blocked their way. Rafael stopped fifty yards from the bridge, and threw the truck into reverse. The guerrillas ahead of them were heavily armed and aiming at them. Rafael checked the rear view mirror: the armed men were closing in from behind. They were clearly out-numbered and out-gunned.

"Stop! Get out of the truck!" the leader shouted. They were firing bullets into the air as a warning.

Miguel, Rafael, and Jake slowly climbed down from the truck, hands in the air, but each was still carrying a gun, tucked through their belts, well concealed by their shirts.

"Get on your knees," the leader said. "Hand over all your money."

Rafael reached into a pocket; he held out several crumpled peso notes.

Miguel sighed. Thank God, he had just given Elena the 2,000,000 pesos.

A young man walked up to Jake, tipping his head to one side. "I know you. I worked for you and Señor Vargas." He was smiling but carrying an AK-47, readied and at port arms.

Jake smiled in return. "Hey, Paco. I remember you too." Jake turned to Miguel. "Señor, he worked the gate at our old compound."

Paco lowered his voice. "Help me get away from these guys, please."

Miguel was still holding his hands in the air, but he nodded.

"They are dangerous men. Be very careful," Paco whispered. He turned and called to the men at the bridge. "I know these guys. They're from Bogotá and they're friends of Hector Campos."

"Bullshit! Tell them to empty their pockets or they die," the lead man shouted back.

Paco pointed the AK-47 at Jake and continued talking, softly but urgently. "I'm on your side. Are you armed?"

"Yes," Jake said.

"Please, do as I say. You must start walking toward the bridge, with your arms up. When we get close, I will shoot the leader—he's the one with the military cap. You guys must shoot the other three. Then run to the bodies and grab their weapons. Hide behind the trucks and fight off the other four that are behind your truck."

"Sounds like a plan," Miguel whispered. "Maybe our only plan. When we get ten feet from them, Rafael, you step to the left. Jake, step to the right. I'll crouch down so Paco will have a clear shot. Do this when I say 'go!'."

Slowly, they began walking toward the bridge. The guerrillas appeared to relax, allowing their rifles to point more toward the ground. The man in charge grinned and started to laugh, throwing his hands up in the air. He clearly thought they'd won this confrontation easily. Paco held his rifle readied, waiting for Miguel's signal.

When they were close enough, Miguel shouted, "Go!" He crouched down and pulled his gun from his belt. Paco took his shot: four hits to the leader's chest that sent him flying backward. Jake and Rafael had stepped aside, as if they had rehearsed their moves many times, and began shooting at the others. Bullets scattered wildly.

The guerrillas who had trapped them reached Jake's truck and began firing. Paco was hit in the back. A burst of gunfire jerked his head back, and he fell forward, blood streaming from his mouth, dying before he hit the ground. Miguel, Rafael, and Jake picked up the AK-47s and took up a position behind the guerrillas' vehicles and returned fire. The last of the guerrillas were trying to hide behind Jake's truck, when bullets struck its gas tank. The truck exploded in flames, sending chunks of truck and body parts high into the air. When the smoke cleared at last, the guerrillas lay dead.

"Jake, I'm sorry about your truck. We'll get you a new one," Miguel said, studying the bloodied landscape. "When—if—anyone finds this scene, they'll figure two bands of guerrillas had it out. Now let's grab one of their trucks and get the hell out of here."

Picking the better of the two, they piled in, with Jake behind the wheel.

"Check to see how much gas we have. There's about fifty miles of rough roads. It'll be dark in two hours so make sure the damn headlights are working," Miguel said.

Jake switched on the lights and got out of the truck to inspect them. "Yeah, they're fine, and the tires look all right too." Two shots rang out and hit the side of the truck. Jake scrambled back into the driver's seat. They peeled out in a cloud of dirt and blood.

"We must have missed one. He was probably hiding in the trees." Rafael turned and peered out the passenger side window.

"I feel sorry for the kid." Miguel rested his head against the seatback. "He saved our butts. Jake, do you know anything about his family?" He closed his eyes and fell asleep, thinking about Allison. They drove the rest of the way home in silence.

The English classes continued for the next twelve weeks without any interruptions. All attendees had mastered basic English.

Of course, Miguel had received extra tutoring every evening; now they even made love in English. Miguel could read, write, and speak English, almost as if he had been born in the United States. The few, small traces of Spanish he carried would soon be gone. He told Allison he could even dream in English.

He often looked in the mirror and admired the handsome man who looked back at him. He was proud of what he had gained through the years, even though a great deal of it was by violence, lying, cheating, and murder. Hector Campos remained very much on his mind. The time had come to make several monumental decisions and a few very calculated moves. His plans needed to be exact, with no room for error. He would take over Hector's cartel, this time without a bloodbath.

22

Oregon

The paramedics were loading Becky onto the ambulance. They had hung a second IV and were closely monitoring her vital signs.

"Stay off the radio until we're closer to the hospital," BJ told the driver. "The fucking reporters are monitoring your calls to get more information." *God, they were like vultures… worse than vultures, actually. A vulture at least provided a useful service.* How in the world did they learn about their plan in the first place? He and the other deputies piled into the cruisers parked around the school.

The more he thought about it, the more it seemed like the only person who would benefit from the story leaking out would be Sheriff Patterson. BJ recalled the sheriff had said: "I want to be part of this." That was immediately before he brought the keys downstairs to the janitor's room. The sheriff must have wanted to have his picture taken and give the reporters an interview about how he had singlehandedly solved the Becky Hanson kidnapping. They had foiled his plan when Jumpy sent the reporters off in the opposite direction.

BJ called the Grants Pass police dispatcher. "This is Deputy BJ Taylor with the Josephine County Sheriff's Office. We're en route to Grants Pass Community Hospital with a kidnap victim. Please call them—on a land line, not the radio. Tell the ER to stand by for a medical emergency." He paused while the dispatcher confirmed a piece of information. "Most important, send a couple of units to keep the press away. No one is to give *any* interviews or statements of any kind regarding the person in the ambulance." The wailing of the siren trailed behind them while BJ continued to think. If he could cause a diversion, maybe the press would follow and there wouldn't be a major scene at the hospital.

One of the other detectives knew the newspaper hotline; he punched in the number and handed BJ his cell. "You need to get over to the county jail. They're bringing in a guy who might be implicated in a major kidnapping case." He switched off before the reporter could ask any questions.

The paramedics taking care of Becky had called the hospital to report her vital signs to the ER staff. BJ learned later that she had held the blanket over her eyes throughout the ride. They switched off their sirens several blocks away from the hospital and coasted into the ER entrance.

Two city units were parked by the hospital's ambulance entrance; four officers stood next to them. Their instructions were to keep everyone away, including the press. One officer was to remain posted at Becky's hospital room door until she was released.

The medical staff was waiting immediately inside the doors to the ER. Apparently BJ's diversion had worked: there were no reporters. Mr. and Mrs. Hanson drove up within minutes and didn't even bother parking. They left their car in the ER driveway behind the ambulance.

The Hansons rushed toward their daughter, but the staff blocked their way as the paramedics wheeled Becky into the hospital. One nurse stayed with them. "Please, we want to stabilize her first. If you're seen with her out in the triage area, the reporters might see it too. As soon as we have her in a separate room, of course you can go in."

Now that he knew the girl was in good hands, BJ wanted to check out what was happening at the Sheriff's Office.

They took Jumpy's truck and headed for the jail that was located in the basement of the sheriff's building. There were so many questions he wanted to ask Morrison, but didn't know whether he would be allowed in on the questioning. His head was spinning: Why did he kidnap her? Did he molest her? What had he planned for her future? Was he going to leave her there to die? The paramedics said she probably couldn't have lasted much longer. Had he planned it all in advance?

The jail was less than three miles from the hospital, but at this time of year there were tourists in town, and the roads were heavy with traffic. They snaked their way through the city. BJ spotted the sheriff and the other units pulling into the back entrance of the jail.

"Catch up to them," BJ said and Jumpy pulled in behind the last unit. There were TV cameras and reporters everywhere, all struggling to catch a glimpse of Morrison. They wanted a statement from Sheriff Patterson.

"Is it Becky Hanson?" someone shouted.

"Is the girl alive?"

Another reporter had climbed onto a chair. "Where is she at this time?"

"Did he kill her?"

"How was she killed?" a different reporter persisted.

"Has he confessed?"

The sheriff raised his hands. "Quiet please. We've got the SOB." The mob surged toward him while the deputies hustled the blanket-draped Morrison inside. The local TV stations were airing everything as it unfolded. Soon the sheriff's station was crowded with hundreds of people standing about outside, all hoping for more information. It wouldn't be long before someone from the school in Cave Junction gave out

Iverson's name and perhaps his photograph, even though the school officials had been asked not to. They didn't know Morrison was his real name, they knew him only as Mr. Iverson.

Carol called Sandy. "Have you been watching Channel 11?"

"No, why?"

"Our guys have caught the man who abducted that little girl." Carol was almost crying with relief. Then she and Sandy were crying and laughing at the same time.

"I guess we'll have to wait until they get home to hear the whole story," Sandy said.

"They're too busy right now to answer their cells," Carol said. "I've tried once."

"Call me tomorrow when you get more news." Sandy hung up.

The deputies escorted Morrison down the hallway and into an interview room. It was sparsely furnished with two chairs, a small table, and a large expanse of two-way mirror that was also shatterproof. Cameras were mounted on three walls close to the ceiling, and a recorder was ready and on the table. A deputy cuffed Morrison to a chair bolted to the floor and then left the room. The sheriff and several deputies were looking through the one-way glass, observing Morrison's nervous demeanor.

"We'll wait awhile before we go in." Sheriff Patterson had conferred with the state District Attorney. "Has anyone read him his rights yet?"

"Yeah, I did," one of the deputies said, "before I put him in the unit and brought him here. It's recorded."

Patterson decided that BJ and Russell Lowe, the department's top interviewer, would handle the questioning. Morrison was wringing his hands and sweat was dripping from his chin through the heavy stubble of his beard.

BJ studied him through the glass. The guy must know he was in deep shit and wasn't sure what to do next.

BJ and Russ stepped into the room, introduced themselves, and shook his hand. Belatedly BJ wished he'd brought some hand sanitizer.

"Would you like some water or coffee?" Russ asked

"Just water and a cigarette." Morrison muttered.

Russ stepped up to the glass, tapped on it a twice, and then returned to his chair. In a few moments, someone knocked on the door, and the requested items were delivered to Morrison.

BJ watched, satisfied. Soon Morrison's fresh DNA would be on the bottled water and the cigarette butt.

For the next four hours, BJ and Russ questioned Morrison while he drank more water and finally requested coffee. During that time, he had asked to use the bathroom several times, but the interviewers pressed on with their questions and ignored his requests. Morrison's body odor was so strong that Russ left the room for a few minutes.

"How much water has he had?" For the past hour Captain Smith had been watching though the one-way mirror and listening to the interview. "Is he dehydrated or nervous—or what?"

"I've heard diabetics might have unusual thirst, I think," Russ shrugged. "Not sure though."

"You guys are doing a great job. Strictly by the book." He patted Russ on the shoulder.

"Is there anything you need?"

"Yes, as a matter of fact." Russ grimaced. "We could use a can of air freshener. Would it be okay to take him to the shower room, let him clean up, and have him put on an orange jump suit?"

"Hmm.... let me think on it for a moment. I'll check whether any of the techs might need any other samples."

"We'll need something to eat for the three of us too," Russ said. "It might be a long night. We want to keep the asshole talking."

The Captain thought for a moment and allowed his request. "Take this kit with you." The tech gave them specific instructions on what to collect and from where.

Russ went back into the room and whispered to BJ about the plan; he nodded and unlocked Morrison's cuffs.

"We're going to let you go to the bathroom and shower. We'll give you some clean clothes too. We've sent out for some food, so let's get started." BJ pulled Morrison to his feet. He and Russ accompanied him into the bathroom and then to the shower.

When they were finished, a bright orange jump suit and a pair of one-size-fits-all slippers were waiting for Morrison. They secured him, now with a set of ankle chains, and returned to the interrogation room. A nearly empty can of air freshener was on the table: someone had sprayed the room, but it still had an odd odor.

It had been a long day, and BJ had thought about calling Carol, but then decided against it. Jumpy would probably tell her what had happened. Then he and Russ were cuffing Morrison when the food arrived.

Burgers, fries, and soft drinks—the all American meal was at hand.

———

Another set of investigators from the Sheriff's Office were en route to the hospital, one of whom was the child psychologist who worked for Josephine County. It would be possible to talk with Becky Hanson only after receiving permission from her primary doctor and her parents. Ruth Donahue, the child psychologist, asked who was in charge of Becky's care.

"It's Dr. Newport," one of the staff informed her and pointed. "You can find him in his office—down there."

Dr. Newport had just finished with the girl's exam and was transcribing his notes when plain clothes deputies Jackie Osborn and Blaze Parker appeared at the door of the cramped cubicle he called an office.

Jackie held out her badge. "Dr. Newport? Could we have a few minutes with the Hanson girl?"

"You can have thirty minutes, no longer. She's still in a very fragile state. However, Mr. and Mrs. Hanson must okay it first. There's a release form they'll need to sign—pick it up from the clerk at the desk. They have the final say." Dr. Newport returned to studying a set of x-rays.

Ruth Donahue had followed the deputies into the cubicle; the psychologist had sat down and was asking a few questions. Dr. Newport promised he would give her more time later.

The deputies headed for Becky's room, displayed their badges for the city cop at the door, knocked lightly, and walked in. The reunion must have been a happy one, they reported later. "You could tell they'd been crying," Jackie told BJ. "Her parents' eyes were red, and Becky's eyes were red. I guess they were happy tears because they kept on flowing."

"I asked them if it'd be okay to have a short talk with Becky, and they both agreed. I asked Deputy Parker to take them to the cafeteria for coffee." Jackie sighed as she told BJ and the sheriff about the interview. "Becky was holding on to her mother's hand so tightly that it was turning white. She didn't want to be alone with any strangers."

"Do you blame her?" BJ asked.

"What did you do?" the sheriff asked.

"I said, 'It's all right, sweetie, your mom can stay.' I took out my notepad, and Parker and Mr. Hanson went to the cafeteria. Thirty minutes wasn't nearly enough."

BJ shook his head. "I'm sure you did a fine job with the poor girl."

Jackie shrugged. "I thanked Becky for her help. She and her mom agreed to chat with us again, when she felt a little stronger." She hesitated for a moment. "As I was leaving, Becky looked into her mother's eyes and whispered, 'Mom, that man did awful things to me.' Then she started to shake uncontrollably. I notified the nurses' station on my way out."

"What about Parker? Did he get anything from the dad?" BJ asked.

"That's odd. Not a word. Parker reported the only thing the father had to say was how wonderful it was to know she was alive and that she'd be home in a few days."

BJ shrugged. "Different people react differently to a crisis. Maybe delayed shock... who knows?"

"When will she go home?" the sheriff asked.

"It could be longer than 'a few days'," Jackie said. "I wasn't able to get a lot, just the edge of the story. I didn't want to press her too early."

"When you get together with Ruth Donahue you'll probably be able to piece more of it together."

"God, I just hate it when it's kids," BJ said.

They all understood what he meant.

23

Oregon

BJ and Russ continued the interview with Morrison after they finished their meal; they didn't want to push him too much, fearing he might lawyer-up. After several more hours, they placed him in a cell, far away from the other prisoners and posted a guard for suicide watch. Questioning would begin again in the morning.

The CSI team arrived with a van billowing with paper bags, loaded with the forensic evidence they had gathered from the school janitor's quarters and a mountain of photographs.

Morrison maintained that Becky had flirted with him and teased him until he could not take it any longer. The day he abducted her, he had stood in the doorway and called her back into the school before she got on the bus. He told her that her mother was on the phone and wanted to speak with her. The hallways were empty, and as they passed the door to the janitor's room, he pulled her inside and down the steps. He took her backpack, because he figured that was where she kept her cell phone. He put her in a separate room and locked the door.

"I took good care of her the whole time she was there," he said.

BJ and Russ had shared a glance.

"Tell us how you took good care of her," Russ said without a trace of irony in his voice.

"At night, when the school was empty, I'd take her to the cafeteria and get bits of food. I made sure I didn't take too much, so no one would notice any was missing." He looked pleased with his cleverness. "I checked the Lost and Found for clothing she could wear after hers were soiled."

BJ shook his head in disbelief.

Morrison continued without prompting. "Once a month, I'd take her to the boys' shower room and wash her body with the dirty towels the boys left in the hamper after gym class. I was being nice to her."

Russ resumed his questioning, while BJ studied the man. Never once did he mention he had molested or tortured her, but it was evident by her condition.

The next morning, the questioning continued. The District Attorney, David Nightingale, and his assistant, Laurie Gilsen, were peering through the one-way glass. "I'll need a copy of the entire interview and a full list of all the evidence obtained as soon as possible," Nightingale said.

He had come prepared with the proper court orders and sent his assistant to the hospital to obtain copies of all medical records, tests, and any photographs taken on admission. She was to talk to everyone who attended Becky, for any additional information.

"I'll begin putting together the charges and preparing for the preliminary hearing," Nightingale said.

"You've got jack shit on me." Morrison's smile was an ugly smirk. He was probably sure he had fooled them. He sat defiantly, arms folded across his chest, leaning back in the chair.

"Is that what you think, Earl?" BJ leaned closer. "Well, let's do a quick review here. First, we know your real name isn't Iverson. It's Morrison. Second, you're wanted in California for escaping from a mental hospital. Third, we have your DNA from the crime scene. It was on—and in—the victim, as well as on the mattress and bed covers." He wished he could say what he was thinking: *We not only have you, but we've got you hogtied like a calf at a Texas rodeo.* Police were expected to treat their suspects nicely, tenderly, with more rights than their victims ever had.

"I want a lawyer!" he shouted and slumped back in his seat, glaring up at them defiantly.

"Oh, you'll get one," BJ said as he and Russ left the room. The man was sick. He wished he could do everything in his power to see that the only daylight this man would ever see was through the bars on a window in a prison cell.

It was close to noon the following day when BJ arrived home. Carol greeted him with a warm kiss and a long hug.

"Are you hungry?" she asked.

"No, not really, he replied. "I just need to take a break from all this crap and get my mind on other things. Any calls from the contractor?" he inquired.

"No, none at all," Carol said. "Maybe you should go out there and see how things are progressing."

"Yeah, I think I will." BJ settled down in his favorite chair and closed his eyes. "I'm just going to rest for a moment." Within seconds, he was asleep. He rarely took a nap in the middle of the day. The tension was finally subsiding and letting him relax; he would allow in only good dreams.

He opened his eyes. Carol was starting a pot of chili in the kitchen and it smelled wonderful. He had a good life. And two great sons and a beautiful, loving wife to share it with.

"Honey, I think we should go cruising in the '56 Chevy tonight," BJ suggested. "It's Friday, and Jimmie's Drive-in will be packed with classic cars. We can grab something to eat and cruise Sixth and Seventh with the group."

"That would be fun." Carol looked up from stirring the sizzling meat. "This is better if it simmers overnight anyway. I can freeze it tomorrow. I'd like to get to know some of the other wives."

"I'm going out to the land and check with John." BJ picked up his keys and headed for the door. "Hopefully, there's been some progress." As he was pulling into their driveway at the property, John was getting into his truck. John stopped and waited for him.

He walked around the perimeter, admiring the completed framework. "Wow, you guys really have been busy."

"We're trying to get it dried-in as soon as we can," John said.

Curious, BJ asked, "What does the term 'dried-in' mean?"

"We need to get the roof shingles laid and the exterior walls sheeted, and then the windows set so we can work on the inside if it starts to rain," John explained. "Then we'll put the meter box in place so there won't be electrical cords getting wet."

"How's the time looking?" BJ asked.

"You guys should be able to move in within four months, providing nothing unforeseen comes up." John walked back to his truck and waved as he drove out of the yard.

The timing should work well, but the construction would be cutting things a bit close. Four months would be mid-fall. Maybe he and Jumpy could still get in some fishing or hiking.

24

COLOMBIA

Allison was having lunch with Miguel early one afternoon when she turned to him. "It doesn't bother me about the business you're in. I just want to be part of your life."

"Is that so?" He faced her directly. "What kind of business is that?"

"Well, let's see." She smiled and placed her hand on his. "You travel in the highest circles of society and employ a large number of people. And yet, you don't seem to have any sort of job. Also everyone is fiercely loyal to you."

He squeezed her hand. "So you think you'd like to help me with my plans for the future?"

"Yes, I know I can help you." She leaned close to kiss him on the cheek. "Please let me try."

Their conversation continued for another few minutes. "Let's go into my study. I want to be sure no one's listening." He reached into the desk and pulled out a large map of the United States.

"Where do you think fields of growing pot plants would be less likely to be noticed—or discovered?"

Allison paused a moment, studying the map, and then placed a fingertip on a small town in Oregon. It was called Cave Junction. "I took a trip there one time to see the Oregon Caves. I couldn't believe how dense the forest was. It was beautiful."

"Cave Junction," he repeated the name thoughtfully. He had never heard of the place and only remotely knew about the state of Oregon. "I want to set up at least fifteen houses near that town for growing marijuana indoors."

"How does that involve me?"

"You are an American citizen, sweetheart. No one would blink an eye if you were buying a house. You will purchase them for me, but under different names," he explained. "I will get you multiple identifications. The houses need to be well secluded from other properties. All of them should be over two thousand square feet on at least twenty acres of property. The men that you helped with English will be living there, two of them to each house."

"So...." She smiled. "I was grooming your gardeners?"

"It might take as long as three months for you to purchase all the houses."

She grimaced. "I remember the last time I bought a

house. I thought I'd grow old before the sale was finalized."

Miguel shook his head. "No, these purchases will be all cash. It might take another month to bring in the necessary materials to make the plants grow. There are special lights, special soil...." He sighed. "I would like to supervise it personally, but I still have another business matter to handle here."

"You mean the other cartel?" she said softly.

Ricardo had been supplying a steady stream of information for the past several weeks. Miguel was certain now that he was fully informed about Hector's operations. He had promised Ricardo he would fly him and his family to Mexico. He'd also told him he would provide the family enough money to live comfortably for the rest of their lives.

That posed a problem—actually two problems. It would cost him money he didn't want to spend, and Ricardo would be alive to double-cross him and possibly even blackmail him. The more Miguel considered it, he decided he should simply kill them all. That way he could save money and get rid of his "problem."

Ricardo was scheduled to be in Bogotá next week to meet Rafael at an outdoor marketplace. He was to mingle with the crowd under some pretext and then change clothes. Rafael would drive him to the compound and collect his family for a "family reunion and picnic."

They drove thirty miles into the countryside, to a secluded field they had used frequently for disposing bodies. Rafael eliminated the family first. Before he died, Ricardo begged, "Why is Miguel doing this? I did my job for him."

Rafael shot him between the eyes and drove away.

Miguel made contact with a skilled counterfeiter in Bogotá who dealt in forged American passports, driver licenses, and social security cards. He gave the man a long list of names, birth dates, pictures of each of his men, and a bogus address near Cave Junction, Oregon. Miguel included his information as well. The skilled forger was to be paid exceptionally well for completing this large order. Two weeks later, Rafael arrived at the man's home. He carried a duplicate list of names; Miguel had requested that he check all the papers for accuracy. When he was sure everything was correct, he placed a suitcase full of cash before the man.

"I'm sure you would like to count it, Señor."

"Of course," the gentleman said. He removed his spectacles from a case, slipped them on, and leaned over to count the stacks of $100 United States currency.

Rafael reached into his pocket, pulled out a syringe, and jabbed the contents into the man's neck. The deadly concoction killed him within seconds. Rafael searched the room for any evidence that would connect Miguel to ever having been there. When he had found none, he picked up the suitcase of money and walked back to his car. He placed the money in his trunk and grabbed a 20-liter can of gasoline. He doused the interior of the home and tossed in a match. Buy the time he had reached his car, the entire house was engulfed in flames.

Miguel did not want any outsider knowing anything about his plans, especially the information the slick counterfeiter would have had.

"Are you sure you want to get involved?" Miguel asked Allison. "If you say yes, there's no going back." *And,* he thought, *she will be mine until I decide otherwise.*

"Yes," she said without any hesitation.

"I like this way of life. Now I know you really trust me."

"You can't tell your friend Juan Moreno why you have decided to go back to the United States," he warned her. "When the time comes, just say your goodbyes and leave."

Allison paused a moment before answering. "Juan and Carmela have been my close friends for years—almost twenty years, since I was a little girl."

"That's how it must be."

"All right. Yes."

"One more thing, my dear," Miguel said. "I need you to show me that you can be trusted by completing a deed of my choice."

"And… if I…?"

"Here, in Colombia," Miguel said calmly, "there can be all sorts of accidents, so many things that are never explained." He shrugged, appearing totally bewildered by these possibilities. "Drownings, shootings, disappearances.... So many things that aren't explained." he repeated and met her gaze: she understood him perfectly.

"You name it," she had said confidently on that fateful day. "The man who loves me would never harm me." She felt certain of that.

Miguel had bowed his head for a moment, as if deep in thought. "There is a young man who wants to join my organization as a bodyguard. He told me he would be willing to take a bullet for me to prove his loyalty. I'm going to give you both a chance to prove you can be trusted."

Allison was feeling faint, but tried not to let it show. *My God, how in the world can I go through with this?* she thought. It was difficult sleeping that night; she would be put to the test the next day.

Miguel had showered, dressed, and left the bedroom before she awoke. The smell of frying bacon was coming from the kitchen. She hurried and dressed and joined him in the private covered courtyard where he was reading the morning paper.

"Good morning, sweetheart." He didn't glance up from the paper when she sat down beside him. "Slept well, I hope."

"Not well at all." She rubbed her eyes. "I had terrible dreams that kept me awake most of the night."

"Some breakfast?" Miguel was smiling, but his smile was somehow different.

"Food is the last thing on my mind right now," she said very softly.

They sat together in silence while Miguel finished eating.

"Well, let's get to it, shall we?" Miguel pushed his chair back from the table. "Please stand up, my dear."

A young man had walked out to the middle of the courtyard. He was dressed in jeans and a tee-shirt. He stood with his eyes pressed shut, his arms at his side, and he was trembling.

Miguel handed her an automatic handgun. "It has only one bullet in it. You're to shoot him in the stomach from five feet away—so you won't miss."

Her hands were trembling as she raised the gun to fire. Aiming at his mid-section, she took what felt like an eternity to pull the trigger. The sound was deafening. The young man took a step backward, but he was still standing. At first the man thought she had missed too. Perhaps he thought it didn't really hurt that much getting shot. She dropped the gun, sobbing.

"It was only a blank." Miguel smiled. "You've both passed the test. I had to be sure." He put his arms around her.

"You bastard!" She looked up into his face through tear-filled eyes.

"You're right, baby. But now I can tell you the rest of the plan." He waved the young man away, and they walked back into the house. It took him nearly an hour to calm her and reassure her. Then he made love to her—passionate, fierce and desperate love—because now she really belonged to him.

"You are not only beautiful, but you are smart. There will be much work for you after purchasing the houses." He handed her a long note pad so she could take notes: she was his partner and his secretary now.

"First, you'll go to Medford, Oregon. Lease a small warehouse in an industrial area. Make certain the front windows are tinted with dark film so no one can see inside. There must be a roll-up door in the back, large enough for a truck to enter. Do not have any utilities connected."

"How will the door work—without electricity?" Allison asked a reasonable question.

He ignored her. "Hire someone to paint a sign on the front window that reads: *Used Electrical Supplies*. We'll be in contact with burner phones. When you've completed that part, I'll provide you with a list of supplies. You'll purchase them and have them delivered to the warehouse. Always pay in cash." He paused, hesitating for a moment, in deep thought.

Allison waved her pen over the tablet. "Won't that seem suspicious—no electric or water?"

"My men are strong, they can lift the door."

Allison raised an eyebrow. "Manpower is always slower than electricity…. If someone is in a hurry?"

"You're right. I'll have them tap into the city system, on someone else's meter." He cleared his throat and stared out the window for a moment. "When our men are settled in Cave Junction, I'll send my contacts in California up to Oregon. They will show them how to construct the equipment and set up the electrical and water to grow marijuana indoors." Again he waited, making certain Allison had written everything down precisely as he had dictated.

"I don't want *any* outsiders knowing the locations of our other properties. They will complete the set-up in one house only. Our guys will repeat the process in the rest of our grow houses. They know how to harvest, separate, and bundle. They will be schooled in the transfer of money from sales."

"How will we handle the money? Bank accounts might be traced."

Again Miguel ignored her. "Each house will produce at least $400,000 a year. That's $6,000,000 for all fifteen houses. In the warmer months, we'll grow pot in the denser forest areas. By the time I arrive in Oregon, we'll also be dealing in cocaine. In our network, we'll need bundlers, transporters, couriers, and sellers. The demand for the product is there, and we will have cut out the middleman."

Taking notes, Allison recognized how thoroughly he had thought through this plan. She would be playing a big part. There was always a chance she would be caught and would face prison. To take such a risk, the payoff would certainly need to be a substantial one.

"You are asking me to become a criminal." She held her head high, the writing tablet set aside for a moment. "What price are you willing to pay for that?"

"I would like you to become my wife," Miguel said. "You will share in everything I have and will have."

Allison was silent, processing what she had just heard. "That sounds like you're taking it for granted that I will say yes." Again she waited a beat. "If that is your way of proposing, maybe I'd like some time to think it over."

"You do love me, don't you?" Miguel asked gently.

"Yes. In a twisted way, I do."

Miguel kissed her hand and held it for a long time.

"When will our wedding take place... and where?"

"After everything is settled in Oregon. When I have control of the cartel—perhaps in ten months. You will come back here, with your family, and we will have a grand wedding and a reception and a honeymoon like no other." He pulled her close to him, reaching for her blouse and unbuttoning it slowly, one button at a time. He touched her shoulder and gently pulled down one bra strap... then the other.... His caressed her breasts and bent to take each nipple into his mouth.

25

OREGON

The DA had filed charges, and the trial of Earl Morrison was set to start in thirty days.

Morrison had gotten his lawyer as he requested, a hot-shot defense attorney from Portland, who wanted to make a name for himself. Attorney Byron Samuel Singleton had a long enough name, although most people at the courthouse referred to him BS Singleton. The shortened name seemed to fit him well.

Singleton's first move was to schedule a news conference with the media on the courthouse steps. The major networks were present and news vans were lined up, wires going everywhere, and a podium with a dozen microphones had been set up at the top of steps.

"I'm here today to tell you that my client was intimidated, coerced, and entrapped by law enforcement. I have proof that he was never read his rights. That alone is reason enough for him to be released. I will use every means at my disposal to prove his innocence." Singleton shouted and waved his arms.

"What will you use as his defense?" one reporter called to him.

"You'll have to wait for the trial," he answered and walked hurriedly to his car. Reporters were following him, pushing microphones in his face and shouting all sorts of questions. None received any answers.

"Typical BS Singleton," one reporter muttered.

Articles in the morning paper questioned the Sheriff Office's rush to judgment in Morrison's arrest and cast doubt as to whether or not he was truly guilty.

"What utter bullshit!" BJ exploded after reading the paper. He felt almost ill. He felt certain that with all their carefully collected evidence—the DNA, Becky's testimony, and so much else—that the asshole Morrison was on his way to prison. He sighed in resignation. "Stranger things have happened."

BJ let Jumpy's phone ring four times and was about to hang up when a sleepy voice finally answered. "Don't tell me you're not up."

Jumpy mumbled something into the phone.

"Let's go fishing on the river tomorrow morning and catch some Steelheads."

"Sounds like a plan to me," Jumpy mumbled sleepily.

"I'll pick you up at six. Pack yourself a lunch." BJ smiled at the thought of finally getting the chance to go fishing.

At five the next morning BJ was asking the owner of the bait shop what the Steelheads were biting on and about the best way to rig his pole.

"You need to use six-pound test line, with a silver spoon and a number six hook with a juicy night crawler attached." The shop owner talked while packaging BJ's purchases. The morning sun had not peeked over the horizon when he pulled into Jumpy's driveway. Jumpy tossed his gear into the bed of the pickup and climbed in.

"We have a fifteen-minute drive to this spot some- one told me about. It's a small peninsula where you can walk out to the end, throw your line to the other side, let it drift down in the current, and hook up and reel in your catch," BJ said. He glanced over at Jumpy, who had already fallen back to sleep.

BJ pulled off the paved road and onto a bumpy dirt road. They traveled for almost a mile until he came to an abandoned house.

"That's strange," he said to his sleeping companion. His fishing source hadn't mentioned there would be a chain stretched across the road and a wire fence on both sides. He couldn't drive any further. He pulled to one side and parked on the edge of the rough road.

"Wake up, Sleeping Beauty." He shook Jumpy by the shoulder.

They packed up the gear and began walking on a lightly worn trail to a downward slope. The growth on both sides was well above their knees, and thorny blackberry bushes tugged at their pant legs as they passed. In the distance was a stand of madrone trees.

"That's it—right ahead!" BJ shouted and picked up the pace. As they passed the trees, he could see the peninsula. It was partly rock and partly sand with scattered tuffs of grass, but it was solid enough to walk on.

"Let's rig up the poles before going out to the end. We can take a net and the bait with us." BJ suggested. It was seven o'clock, a perfect time for morning fishing.

They cast out toward the other shore and let the current take their lines downstream. In less than ten seconds, Jumpy had a strike. He set the hook and began reeling in the fish. By the time Jumpy landed his fish, BJ had a strike. Their luck continued until they'd both caught their limit.

They were acting like a couple of crazy kids. They'd laugh and give each other high fives every few minutes.

"We should get the fish back to the cooler and on ice," Jumpy said.

They gathered up their gear and the stringer of gleaming Steelhead trout and began the trek back to the truck. Jumpy stumbled against a clump of blackberry bushes and yelled out when the thorns caught at his leg. The bushes were moving, and a black bear stepped out into the path. They looked at each other for a fraction of second, and the bear reared up on his hind legs. He sniffed at the air, catching the scent of fresh fish. The bear dropped to all fours and started toward them.

BJ remembered from somewhere, probably from when Dane and Carson were in the Boy Scouts, that if confronted, to never turn his back to a bear. "Drop the fish!"

Jumpy dropped their string of fish.

"Now, for God's sake, walk backwards, away from the bear. Very slowly."

The bear sauntered into the path and hungrily devoured the fish—BJ's and Jumpy's magnificent catch.

When they thought they were far enough away, BJ and Jumpy turned and ran for their truck. Safely inside, they gazed down the trail. The bear was nowhere in sight—and their fish weren't either. BJ chuckled, pounding his fist against the steering wheel.

Sweat was still trickling down Jumpy's face and neck and into his collar. "What in the hell is so funny?"

"If we tell this story to Sandy and Carol or to anyone else, they'll never believe us."

When they got to Jumpy's house, Sandy was outside pruning flowers in the garden. "How was the fishing?"

"They weren't even biting," they said in unison. Then they started laughing again.

"I don't think that bear lives in those berry bushes, like it's his permanent address," BJ said thoughtfully. "We're going back again. Next time, we're bringing home some fish."

"Damn straight," Jumpy said.

At their property, BJ inspected the progress on their new home. John's crew was busy putting on the siding.

"We'll be starting drywall next week," one of the workers said. "Anything you want to ask John about?"

"No, just stopped by to see how it's going.

"Tell him hi for me," BJ said, pulling away. He was really quite happy with the progress. Carol was on the phone when he stepped through the doorway.

"Did you guys have a good time fishing?"

"You would not believe it if I told you." He grinned and shrugged. "You just wouldn't believe it."

26

COLOMBIA

Slowly and deliberately, Miguel was teaching Allison everything about his business and how to set up the new locations in Oregon.

Allison insisted that all their conversation be in English, which gave him added knowledge of the language. Day after day, they spent hours planning the move to the United States: nothing was to be left to chance. He had arranged for the start-up money to be available when she arrived in Medford, Oregon. Allison had packed, said her goodbyes, and boarded a plane to the United States.

Now was the right time for Miguel to start his take-over of the drug cartel. Hector had one secret known to only a few in his organization. Ricardo had supplied the information during one of their private briefings. Hector would travel to Bogotá every three months for a brief visit with his illegitimate daughter and her mother. He would be in disguise and surrounded by bodyguards. He lived in constant fear of the DEA, and that someone was always looking for a way to kill him.

The girl and her mother lived on the sixth floor of a luxurious condo in an affluent area. The woman posed as the widow of a wealthy businessman. Hector would only stay for a few hours and then drive back to his compound in the jungle.

Miguel directed Rafael to stake out the building for several weeks and record all the activity on film. It wasn't long before a pattern emerged that revealed the comings and goings of Hector's other family. Records showed that the title to the condo development company was held in the name of a hotel chain located in Miami, Florida. Even more interesting was that the current manager of the complex was a frequent user of cocaine on Rafael's list.

Miguel was familiar with a poison called Peruvian Mist. It was odorless, tasteless, and colorless, derived from the sweat glands of a poisonous frog in the jungles of Peru. Anyone inhaling the slightest amount would painlessly die within eight hours; the poison could never be detected. He made inquires about how to obtain the poison. Then, he wire-transferred the money to the manufacturer and included specific instructions on how to encapsulate the contents.

Soon five small plastic vials arrived by overnight messenger. The package also contained a burner phone set to electronically discharge the vials into the air by the operator of the phone. Rafael called the condo manager and arranged a meeting at a nearby restaurant.

Rafael looked up from his table. "Good morning."

"Good morning to you too, Rafael," the man said and took a chair across from him.

"Allow me to get to the point. I need a favor. There is a lady and her daughter living in your building. It's in condo unit Number 602. I want a passkey to their door. I'm willing to give you one year's supply of cocaine for your efforts."

"Why?" the manager asked.

"No questions!" Rafael reminded the manager. "This remains between you and me."

The condo manager nodded in agreement.

"You know what will happen to you if you tell anyone about this arrangement?" Rafael's dark brooding eyes seemed to burn into the other man.

"Yes, I do," the manager said. "When?"

He was growing impatient. "I said no questions," Rafael repeated.

The man recoiled, stood up quickly, and left the restaurant.

Rafael was certain the manager would do as he was told because of the cocaine. He was right: the key was handed to him later that day.

Rafael waited for the right time to enter condo Number 602. The rooms were neat and tidy. The woman who lived there must have maid service. She was certainly not like anyone he thought might have been involved with Hector Campos. Slipping on latex gloves, he went about his business.

The back balcony had a great view of the city and hillside. In the living room was a photo album on the end table with family pictures of the mother and daughter. It was too bad they were part of Hector's second family, because they were going to pay the price, along with Hector. Rafael stood on a kitchen chair to reach the air vents where he placed the vials. He replaced the vent screens back in their original position.

This part of Miguel's plan was finished. No one knew for certain when Hector would make his next three-hour visit, so a sentry was assigned to watch the building at all times. When Rafael was notified that Hector was in the condo, he would take the burner phone to the building and set off the vials. Fifteen days passed before Rafael received a call from the sentry: Hector was in the condo. He informed Miguel when he was on his way to use the burner phone and set off the poisonous vials.

"Let me know the *exact* time you release the Peruvian Mist," Miguel said.

Hector would stay for only three hours and then begin the two-hour trip back to his camp.

Miguel waited until Rafael called him; the first step was completed. He punched in Hector's landline number.

Lorenzo Batista, Hector's second in command, would answer in the absence of his boss.

"Good afternoon, Lorenzo. This is Miguel Vargas. I want you to listen. Please do not interrupt me. What you are about to hear is very serious and may keep you alive." There was total silence on the other end: he had Lorenzo's complete attention.

"Your boss has been poisoned and will die within hours. There is no antidote. At this time there are over three hundred armed men surrounding your compound, set to charge in and kill everyone. If you decide to fight, you will be our number one target. I'm giving you the chance to leave and become wealthy. When I have complete control of the new cartel, you may return and join my business if you wish. That will be your choice."

"I don't believe you!" Lorenzo shouted into the phone.

"Calm down. Think for a moment. Would I make this call and warn you ahead of time if I were lying to you? I don't want a bloodbath. You must kill the two other top lieutenants. Then gather up as much cocaine and money as you can carry in the next hour and leave immediately." Miguel paused only a moment, allowing Lorenzo to process what he was telling him.

"What about your men—won't they try to stop me?"

"Our men will let you through, without harm, if you travel by land. If you decide to leave by air, only the pilot may go with you. Hector won't know where you've gone. He won't live long enough to go after you. Without leadership, the others will run away." Miguel could hear Lorenzo gulping and taking a deep breath at the other end of the phone. "What's your choice?"

"In one hour the two men will be dead and I will be gone!" Lorenzo said. The phone went silent.

Miguel didn't have three hundred men. He didn't even have one man outside Hector's compound, but the bluff had worked. Hector would return to find his top men murdered and a large amount of money and cocaine missing. Lorenzo and the pilot of his plane would have disappeared. That should shake up the place into utter chaos.

Miguel laughed. "Now, I'm the King of Cocaine!" His new cartel would be larger and more powerful than ever.

The next day ten heavy trucks, each carrying eight men and lead by Jake Zapata, left Bogotá on their way to Hector's old Rio Vista compound. His orders were to approach with one truck to make sure it was safe for the others to enter. He would take charge of the area and then call Miguel to tell him what he'd found. Based on Jake's report, Miguel would follow in another vehicle, leaving Rafael in charge in Bogotá.

"Señor Vargas, all is well," Jake said when he called. "Hector is dead, as are several others. When he saw his top men were killed or missing, He must have gone crazy before he died. We found him at the entrance to his underground vault clutching gold bars, as if he were trying to take them with him in death."

"Anything else?"

"Yes, we also found his chemist hiding under a bed and begging for his life. The rest must be in the jungle or in the river trying to get away. Everything seems to be intact," Jake was saying when there was a sudden explosion in the jungle.

"What was that?" Miguel demanded.

"Must have been a landmine," Jake said.

"Drive up and down the road by the entrance. Tell the people to stop running—because of the mines. Tell them everything's safe, but only if they stay where they are. They won't be harmed and may return to the compound, if they're unarmed. We'll even give them back their jobs with higher pay, those who want to stay," Miguel told him.

Miguel had made the trip many times before, but this time the excitement was different. His bodyguards were in the trucks in front and behind his armored car making certain there wouldn't be an ambush.

After arriving, his priority was to inventory the money and the drugs left behind. Next, he ordered the residence completely gutted. All Hector's furnishings and personal effects were placed in a clearing and set afire.

The flames leapt into the sky. Slowly, people began to emerge from the jungle, their hands in the air. Jake and his men surrounded them and checked them for weapons. They found none.

"Get them some food and water and let them sit in the shade." Miguel wiped his handkerchief across his forehead. It was a lot warmer here than in Bogotá. One of Jake's men came running up, shouting and waving his arms to catch his attention.

"You must see this boat down at the river!" He was gesturing to the east. Jake and several of his men followed him back to the river.

"Holy shit!" Jake said and picked up his cell phone to call Miguel.

"What the hell's going on down there?" Miguel said.

"Boss, ya' gotta see this."

"I'm on my way," Miguel said, and motioned for the body guards to follow him.

There was a long, narrow corrugated tin building that was completely camouflaged. It would have been nearly impossible to see it from the air. Wide doors stood open to the river.

"Have you been inside?" Miguel asked.

"Just to look in," one of his men said.

They stood around and peered in, amazed.

"I'll be damned," Miguel said. "It's some kind of submarine. Don't go aboard yet. It may be booby trapped."

"I'll ask one of Hector's people to test it out."

Soon one of Hector's former team appeared and boarded the sub. The others stood watching from a safe distance. He emerged within a few minutes. "It's all okay. There's no problem."

Miguel and Jake boarded the craft and went below. It had been designed to carry a large amount of cargo. Miguel estimated it to be fifteen feet wide and sixty feet long, and it would probably need at least two or more men to operate it. He wondered whether it had been used yet. Did anyone know how to operate it? He sure as hell didn't.

27

OREGON

Morrison was brought to the courthouse wearing an orange jumpsuit and underneath it, a bulletproof vest. He was secured with cuffs and ankle chains. He moved slowly, shuffling along, his head down.

It was an overcast morning with a threat of rain, and the trial was set to begin at ten o'clock. The capacity of the courtroom gallery was limited to fifty; each day seating for the public was decided by lottery. In addition, there were family, lawyers, marshals, and court personnel. It was the largest courtroom in the building; however, no TV coverage was allowed for the trial.

Out on the street, network trucks lined up and closed down one lane, interfering with local traffic. Several witnesses were in the hallway waiting for their time to be called. It was an older building and the air conditioning struggled to keep the packed courtroom bearable. By afternoon, it would get stifling during the summer.

"All rise. The Honorable Judge Henry Rolfe presiding," the bailiff announced. Once the judge was seated, he turned to the courtroom. "You may be seated."

The judge opened the file on his desk. "Are we ready to begin?" He looked first to the prosecution and then to the defense attorney.

"Yes, your Honor," the attorneys said, and the trial began.

Henry Rolfe was a well respected judge who always kept a tight rein on courtroom proceedings. The opening statements were read and the evidence was introduced into record.

"The defense is requesting a mistrial at this time," BS Singleton said.

"Request denied," the judge said automatically.

The defense presented one objection after another, and once even requested a change of venue.

Judge Rolfe was looking weary. "Denied," he would say again and again, and then, just as often, "Overruled."

A sketch artist was making drawings of everyone in the room except the jury. It wasn't long before the room became too warm due to the old air conditioning, and people were waving hand fans or even a magazine in the effort to create any breeze.

The State called BJ Taylor to the stand. He was asked to describe and list the timeline of the investigation. The prosecution paid special attention to how he and Jumpy found the plastic trash bags behind the school. Sheriff Patterson took the stand next. He was asked to describe the chain of command and how decisions were made in his department.

BJ thought that he seemed to enjoy himself a little too much... then again, he was the sheriff. David Nightingale brought into evidence the positive DNA match, but apparently was saving Becky's testimony for last.

So far, the defense attorney's objections were met with Judge Rolfe's calm: "Overruled."

Morrison sat with his head down on the table and never looked up. The string of witnesses continued: Becky's parents, school teachers and staff, classmates, psychiatrists, social workers, doctors, and nurses from the hospital. Each told a separate part of the story.

The trial lasted three weeks. The jury took only one hour to find Morrison guilty on all counts. Judge Rolfe sentenced him to life in prison without the possibility of parole. California declined to extradite him and would let the State of Oregon's verdict stand. The Grants Pass paper covered the trial, and their articles left no doubt about the critical role BJ and Jumpy had played in solving the case.

Becky's testimony had been heart-wrenching, and her emotional scars would surely take a long time to heal. After the trial was over, she would return to school. With the help of a private tutor she was able to make up her classes and would remain in the same grade with her friends. Becky was not as outgoing as she once was. BJ hoped that with time, that too, would change.

28

OREGON

BJ and Carol drove up to their property driveway entrance and stopped. Carol had wanted to take more pictures to document the progress on their house.

Directly before them stood an eight-foot tall, six-foot in circumference, chainsaw woodcarving of a bear that stood on his hind legs, paws in the air, his mouth opened in a permanent growl. At the base, in letters that were at least ten inches tall, was carved their name: The Taylors. Attached to the bear was an envelope; inside was a note that read: *With great thanks, love, and respect. From the Hanson family.*

"What a wonderful gift." Tears were tears running down Carol's cheeks, and she hugged BJ.

Five minutes hadn't passed when BJ's cell buzzed. "It's Jumpy."

"You're not going to believe what was just delivered to our place!" Jumpy managed to say. He was bursting with excitement. After he paused to take a deep breath, he continued. "It's a chainsaw carving of a mama bear and her little cub with our name carved at the base. It's beautiful workmanship. It's from the Hansons."

"You sure it's not that bear that ate our fish?" BJ teased him. "We received a carving too. Boy, it is mighty special."

"Hey, let's get together for dinner. Our gals deserve a night out—and we do too," Jumpy said.

"Name the place, and we'll meet you," BJ said.

"How about The Brewery, about seven? It's an exciting place, I hear," Jumpy said. They both started laughing.

Although it was a weekday, The Brewery was packed. People were standing outside waiting to be seated. Apparently seven was the peak dinner hour; they should have made reservations. BJ circled the lot, but all the parking spots were taken. He finally parked on the street a half block away.

Walking up to the entrance, BJ was aware of people whispering as they passed, and then the waiting crowd erupted in applause. He really didn't want all this attention. He smiled and waved. After they entered, the folks in the lobby did the same.

"We didn't think it would be this busy during the week, so we didn't make reservations," BJ told the young girl at the podium who wrote down their names.

"It looks like about an hour wait," she said. Jumpy

and Sandy walked in and another roar went up. The people started cheering. "Put them at the front of the line," one group chanted. "They're truly heroes!" There was more applause.

"I'm a bit embarrassed," Jumpy said. Sandy nodded.

Carol was blushing. All four of them were beginning to feel embarrassed. The manager appeared and took charge of the situation. He led them to a table in the main dining room. It wasn't long before drinks began arriving at the table, and folks were coming over to shake their hands or congratulate them. The manager returned to the table with the check, with "Compliments of the House" stamped across it.

Jumpy leaned over to BJ and whispered. "If you were to run for sheriff now, you'd win in a heartbeat."

BJ smiled and shook his head. "Not a chance, buddy. I'm completely happy right where I am."

For the next two weeks, BJ and Carol worked on the property, watching as the workmen completed their home. Carol and Sandy drove to Medford to purchase new appliances. There were other decisions: the carpeting, granite countertops, interior paint colors, and new furniture.

John had brought in another crew to build the boat ramp and launch. "If the weather doesn't change, we should be done in three weeks," he said.

"What's left to do?" BJ asked. To his eyes the house looked nearly complete.

"I still have cleanup outside. We'll need to do a final grade and lay the asphalt driveway to the garage approach. That will take care of almost everything." John paused. "During the contract phase, you said you'd decide later about landscaping. Let me know and I'll hire a sub."

"I'd like to pick out the flowers and shrubs," Carol said. "I think we have enough trees for now."

BJ nodded. "Nature has done a great job landscaping everything else. I can plant the shrubs and dig the flower beds."

His long years in law enforcement made BJ feel the need to revisit the remaining cold cases the sheriff had handed him. It was as if his work was not done—like an itch he couldn't reach. He wouldn't rest until they were solved... or until he had tried everything he could possibly do to solve them. He called Jumpy.

"We can start first thing Monday, if that works for you." Jumpy had said.

When BJ drove up to Jumpy's place at eight on Monday morning, he noticed their front door had been painted a bright red. The porch railing had received a fresh coat of dark green, while the rest of the house color was still a gleaming white. He thought the colors went together nicely. Jumpy slid into the passenger seat.

"Looks like you've been busy." BJ pointed to the house.

"I'll give Sandy the credit for the painting. I've been working on some other minor repairs." As they headed into Grants Pass, Jumpy asked, "Which one of the cases should we tackle next?"

"Let's start with the murder case," BJ said. They pulled into the parking lot behind the Sheriff's Office.

29

Colombia

A man carrying a white flag was coming up the road toward Miguel's new residence and compound. Two of Miguel's armed guards followed him closely.

"Who the hell is that?" Jake shielded his eyes against the sun, straining to recognize the man.

One of the guards raised his voice. "He says his name is Lorenzo. He wants to talk to Miguel."

"Did you search him real good?" Jake asked.

"Yes, Señor Jake," the guard replied. "Very good."

Jake pulled out his walkie-talkie. "Hey boss? There's a guy out here named Lorenzo who wants to see you." Jake was watching the man closely. "Put your hands behind your back," he ordered. Lorenzo did as he was told while Jake secured his hands with a zip tie. Miguel came to the entrance and waved them in.

Lorenzo had been in Hector's place many times

before, but he must have noticed the difference immediately. All the old and ugly furniture was gone, the worn shag carpeting had been pulled up, and the crude paintings had been removed. Miguel was sitting on a crate in an empty room when they entered.

Miguel stood to greet the new arrival. "Believe it or not, I'm glad to see you, Lorenzo."

"I wasn't able to leave with the pilot. I gave him some money and told him Hector was dead and he was to wait for me. Before I could get back to the airstrip, he had taken off. I ran into the jungle and tried to hide."

"So you don't have a pot to piss in now," Jake shoved Lorenzo to his knees.

Miguel shook his head. "Let him up, Jake. What's with that big boat in the building down at the river?"

"It's a submarine made to ship cocaine to different countries and go undetected by their coast guards," Lorenzo said. "It was patterned after a World War II German sub. It can submerge up to a hundred feet and has a high-tech periscope."

"Who was going to drive it?" Miguel wondered whether "drive" was the correct word but didn't ask Lorenzo.

"A man named Captain Gomez. He was in the US Coast Guard until he killed some guy. They kicked him out. He was serving time in prison, but he escaped and came to Colombia."

"Where is he now?"

"He's staying in Bogotá."

"Can you get in touch with him?"

"No. He was coming back next week for the first trip to the United States in the submarine."

"What does it use for fuel?"

"Diesel. There's a stockpile in 200-liter drums, under tarps, down by the river."

Miguel looked hard into Lorenzo's eyes. "Do you want to work for me?"

"Yes, Señor Vargas, I do. You can trust me."

Lorenzo looked serious, like he meant his promise. They all did. "Very good. Jake will be your boss," Miguel said. "Jake, cut the zip tie.

Miguel hit speed dial; Allison's number was always first. "Sweetheart, it's so nice to hear your voice. How is everything going in Oregon?"

"Just as we planned," Allison said. "I've set up the bank accounts and rented a unit in Medford."

"Great, when will you be purchasing the houses in Cave Junction?"

"I'll start house hunting tomorrow with a realtor," she said.

"I miss you already," Miguel said.

"I miss you too," she said softly.

"We've taken over Hector's cartel, and we're already making changes." He was laughing, glad to share his news with someone other than his men.

"Jake will be staying here and running things while I'm in the United States. It won't be long now. I still have some business to take care of. I'll see you very soon. Goodbye, my love."

"Jake, you get things organized here. I don't want any decrease in the production of cocaine or marijuana. We have to let our contacts know they can depend on us." Miguel was like a general, barking orders to his army. "I'll let them know that the quality will be improved, without any increase in price—for now. Round up Hector's people and get them back to work." He stood by and listened as Jake delivered his message.

The workers were gathered, standing about in a large group, probably wondering what their fate would be. Jake was standing in the bed of a pickup, an AK-47 braced on his hip, while he addressed the crowd. "Señor Vargas is now in control of the cartel. You will have your jobs back." A murmur of disbelief rippled through the group. "If you work and if you are loyal, you will receive double wages. If anyone of you steals or hides drugs, you and your family will be killed." Jake waved the rifle for emphasis.

Miguel contacted Rafael. He would need to redecorate and refurnish the house. There were interior designers they had trusted before. He faxed Rafael plans of the house and asked him to hire a design firm. Soon, it was as though there had never been any interruption of business. Miguel would stay until Captain Gomez arrived.

"I shall rename this place too. Now it will be called Nieve del Diablo!" Miguel chuckled at the play on words. The "devil's snow" was a good name, much better than Rio Vista. He'd discovered there was no view of the river, as the old name indicated, and much of the river couldn't even be seen from the air.

Three days later a delivery van arrived, followed by several trucks carrying more of Miguel's men. They were assigned the work of painting the inside and outside of the main house. Tile was laid in place of the old carpet; new, elegant furnishings were arranged throughout the house. It was a complete metamorphosis. Jake would now be living in luxury compared to his small apartment over the garage in the original compound in Bogotá. The master bedroom was reserved for Miguel when he was in residence.

Miguel sent word to the guerrillas that he had taken over the cartel and wanted to maintain a positive relationship, one in which they would both prosper and benefit. His contacts within the military would keep him informed of any pending raid or interferences. Payoffs would still be made to the politicians and police in Bogotá.

With Jake running operations here, and Rafael controlling the office in Bogotá, Miguel could become a ghost. The second part of his overall plan was nearly complete.

Guards escorted Captain Gomez into the main house. Gomez was a tall, lanky man with sharp features. He stood straight, his chin lifted slightly, his hands clasped behind his back, and his stance a neat one-foot apart; he definitely looked like a military man.

Miguel motioned for him to sit down. "Good afternoon, Captain."

The Captain took the seat across from Miguel. "A good day to you, sir."

"Tell me about the big iron boat down by the river. Is it really a submarine? Who built it?"

"Ah... yes, sir. It is indeed a submarine. The late Señor Campos had commissioned it to be built in Mexico out of scrap metal from a shipyard," the captain explained. "I have sailed it already and it performs well. We have used bags of sand to equal the weight of cocaine that would be shipped."

"What is its sailing range? How many men do you need to operate it?"

"The estimate is two thousand nautical miles, with a crew of two men." Gomez seemed to hesitate. "However, I will need to train another one."

"Why is that?" Miguel demanded.

"Lorenzo killed the man I was training. He was one of Hector's lieutenants," Gomez finally answered.

Miguel nodded and shrugged. Lorenzo had carried out his orders. "The destination I have in mind is... hmm... approximately three thousand miles."

"A voyage of that length...." Gomez considered for a moment. "I would certainly need to stop for fuel at least twice."

"How long would such a trip take?" Miguel asked. He had never confided this to anyone, but he disliked being in cramped quarters, where he could not see daylight or the sky.

"Depending on the weather and the current," Gomez said, "I estimate the voyage would be ten—or as much as twelve—days."

"Of course." Miguel smiled. "Welcome aboard, Captain. I will provide another man for you to train. You will be well paid."

The Captain smiled and raised his hand in a salute. "Aye, aye, sir."

Miguel began sending the men who had been educated to speak English into America; they entered in small groups, through California, Arizona, and Texas. They were well mannered and well dressed; they spoke excellent American English, and they had money. They certainly didn't look or act like typical illegals. They were to arrange travel to Oregon, meet with Allison and put together the grow houses.

30

Oregon

At six in the morning, BJ walked into the Sheriff's Office and headed straight for the coffee machine. The office was unusually quiet. The night shift was struggling to stay awake; it had apparently been a quiet night. He had hoped for relative peace, so he could concentrate on their next cold case—a murder that had taken place three years ago.

The file was thick with paperwork, photographs, and notes. For the next three hours, BJ pored over the contents, trying to establish a timeline. His cell phone buzzed, bringing him back to the present.

"Hey, Jumpy!"

"I called your house. Carol said you left for the office hours ago. Just checking in."

"I've been reading everything I can about the murder of Roxy Moran."

"Anything to go on yet?" Jumpy asked.

"Not so far."

"I'll be there in fifteen minutes."

"Maybe a fresh pair of eyes will help. I'm counting on it."

By the time Jumpy arrived, BJ had pulled the file apart. Papers were spread across the desk. "Wow! Looks like there's more to go on this time," he said.

"Not really."

"Had breakfast yet?"

"No, just coffee. Lots of bad coffee."

Jumpy stared at the piles of paper. "Let's walk down to the Tee Time Coffee Shop and grab something,"

"Okay," BJ said. "I'll put this together first."

The coffee shop wasn't crowded since most of the early breakfast crowd had already come and gone. They chose a booth toward the back and ordered automatically, without looking at the menu.

Jumpy had already read through the file, but he'd also brought it with him. He leaned back against the booth, chin cupped in his hand. "It's strange. There hadn't been an entry in over two years. We know she was shot in the back of her head with a .38 caliber hand gun and dumped in the Rogue River, close to Hellgate Bridge."

BJ nodded. "That's where the river's wild and scenic area begins, at that overlook. Beyond that point the river narrows, with steep cliffs on both sides. The rapids are treacherous and require a permit to travel. Most people need a guide to make it through."

"It says that her body had been in the water at least a week and was found by hikers. Look at this picture. She was so damned bloated no one could recognize her. A bullet was also found in her torso from a .38 Smith & Wesson. She was finally identified by fingerprints," Jumpy said.

"How the hell can you look at that and then eat breakfast?" BJ asked. The waitress had arrived with their food.

Jumpy closed the file before she could see the pictures. He was laughing at BJ. "Don't tell me that bothers you."

"Not really, but I don't usually look at that kind of stuff just before I sit down to a nice meal." BJ took a bite of the hash browns.

When they'd finished eating, BJ opened the file again and began reading from the report that included a rap sheet showing several arrests, mostly for petty crimes:

Roxanne Moran
Born: May 5, 1965
Height: 5' 5"; Weight: 110 lbs
Hair: Light Brown; Eyes: Green
Prior arrests:
1999 Drunk in public: Lockup overnight. Issued a warning.
2000 DUI, with no auto insurance. Court fine of $1,000 and proof of insurance.
2001 Petty theft: Stole clothes from Walmart.

Received forty hours of community service.

2001 Disorderly conduct and resisting arrest. Anger management classes.

2001 Possession of a loaded firearm in a motor vehicle; Three months probation.

2003 Assault and battery; hit husband in the head with cast iron frying pan. Husband dropped charges.

2003 Smoking pot in a public park: 30 days in jail.

"She had some minor issues, but nothing big enough to kill her over." BJ continued to flip through the pages.

The file had been put together by Deputy Stewart Miller, who had also started the Hanson case. His notes indicated he suspected the husband, but Tommy Moran had had a solid alibi.

"Says here he was a lumberjack and was out of town with his crew clear-cutting. The crew testified he was with them the whole time. It seems they lived with his father in Wilderville."

Jumpy looked puzzled. "Where the hell is that?"

"A small community just west of Grants Pass—not big enough to call a village."

"Maybe we should pay Tommy a visit," Jumpy suggested.

BJ looked thoughtful. "Sounds good, but let's run it by the sheriff first."

"This case is strange. It's like she just fell off the earth. There were no clues, no murder weapon, and no witnesses. Good luck, guys," Sheriff Patterson said, and was off to another meeting with the mayor.

Wilderville's lone street boasted a combination gas station and grocery store, a good place to start asking questions.

"Good afternoon," BJ said as he stepped up to the check out.

"Howdy, neighbor," the lady at the cash register greeted him. "What can I do for ya'?"

"We're from the Josephine County Sheriff's Office." He displayed his badge. "Would you mind if we asked you a few questions?"

"Hope I can be of help to you."

"Do you know Tommy Moran and where he might be living now?"

"Sure do. He's still at his dad's place, but don't see much of him nowadays. He keeps to himself, I guess."

"Thanks for your help," BJ said, and they left the store.

"I show his address as 1557 Birch Creek Road." Jumpy was entering the data in the GPS.

The Moran place was a rundown, sorry place. There was junk piled around the yard and two old pickups looked like they had died in the driveway. BJ glanced around: the grass and weeds hadn't been mowed in recent memory.

Tommy must have heard their unit pull up and stepped out on the front porch. "What do you guys want?"

"We're from the Sheriff's Office," Jumpy announced.

"Yeah, I know. Mable, down at the store, said you were looking for me. Like I said, what do you want?"

"We're looking into your wife's murder and want to talk with you to familiarize ourselves with the facts." BJ was walking slowly toward the young man.

"I've told the cops everything I know," Tommy said. "Just let it be."

Jumpy tilted his head in the direction of the house. "Anyone else in the house?"

"No, I'm the only one living here," the man answered. "Why?"

"The lady at the store said it's your dad's place," BJ said. "Does he live here with you?"

"No. He died about a week before my wife disappeared." Tommy was starting to look nervous. "He ran into a bees nest. He was allergic to bee stings."

"It's been almost three years since your wife was killed." Jumpy was trying to refocus the conversation. "Any idea why anyone could have wanted to kill her?"

"She pissed off a lot of people with her wild drunkenness. Maybe it was one of them."

BJ shook Tommy's hand and concluded their visit. "Thanks for your time."

"The only thing we learned there was that he lost his dad and his wife at nearly the same time," BJ said as they left the rundown yard. They next drove to Hellgate Bridge and clocked it from Tommy's house. It was twenty-three miles, exactly.

Jumpy peered down over the railing at the center of the bridge. "Damn, that river current is fast."

"That bridge is only one lane each way, so I doubt that someone would stop in the middle, get out, unload a body, and toss it over. They would have had to park at the end and carry the body to the center. Both banks have too many rocks and the body could get snagged up there." BJ raised his voice so Jumpy could hear him over the raging river.

"There's a fair amount of traffic during the day, so it must have been done at night," Jumpy said.

"I think you're right." They climbed back in the unit and headed for Grants Pass.

"I've been looking at a bass boat at Charlie's Marine," BJ said. "Would you like to stop there on our way back? I'd like your opinion."

"Lead the way, partner." Later, as Jumpy walked around the boat, he whistled softly. "Man, that's one beautiful boat."

"It's been here only a few days. Charlie took it on consignment—from a lady in town whose husband passed away recently."

"Damn, it's fully loaded. Two high-swivel seats, great navigation equipment, a ninety-horse motor, electric trolling motor, new life vests, dual anchors, a live fish well, rod holders, and a tilt trailer—we could do some serious fishing in that rig."

BJ grinned. "I think I'll talk it over with Carol. You

know, she sometimes enjoys fishing too. If she agrees, I'll make an offer tomorrow."

The next day the first crisp touch of fall was in the air. An early morning fog lasted until shortly after eight and then burned off. Hints of color on the deciduous trees were starting to appear.

"Isn't this weather great?" Carol said. They were standing on the deck, sipping coffee on the pleasantly cool morning.

"Yes, but let's hope it holds like this," BJ said. They were hoping to be in their new home before the rainy season started. BJ made an offer on the boat, and Charlie's client accepted.

Excited to share the news, he had punched in Jumpy's number on his cell. "Jumpy! I've bought the boat! But I have a favor. Would you have some room at your place where I can store it, just until our home is finished?"

"You bet," Jumpy had assured him that day. "There's at least a month before the end of Steelhead season. Now we can reach that fishing spot without running into my bear."

"If you and Sandy are free Saturday, the Car Club is going over to Coos Bay for a cruise night through town," BJ had continued. "We'll end the day with a picnic on the beach. There'll be over a hundred classic cars from their club, plus ours. It should be fun."

"Count us in," Jumpy said.

"We'll pick you up early Saturday morning. Bring a jacket, because in the evening it's cool at the ocean. The host club is providing everything else."

At Coos Bay there were cars from the '30s through the '70s. There was every conceivable color and all makes and models, from stock to complete customs. Several special prizes were awarded. BJ received one for the best '56 Chevy. Coos Bay had blocked off streets that ran through the center of town. Crowds had gathered along the way to cheer as the cars traveled the three-mile course. People were waving and singing; many of the cars had outside speakers playing music from the '50s.

"This is great!" Jumpy said.

"I don't know when I've had so much fun," Sandy told BJ and Carol.

Monday they met at the office at ten o'clock and drew up a list of people they wanted to interview: neighbors, Tommy's work crew, and people at the bar where the Morans did most of their drinking. The Wonder Bar was close by, so they decided to start there.

"'Wonder Bar,'" BJ muttered. "Who would dream up a name like *that?*" It was eleven thirty, but several patrons were there already "drinking" their breakfast. BJ and Jumpy approached the bar and asked to speak to the owner or manager.

"He's in the back room working on the books. I'll tell him you're here."

A few moments later, a short, middle-aged balding man smoking a cigar walked out and extended his hand. "Good morning, gentlemen. My name is Stephen Wonder." He drew several times on his cigar. "Most people call me Little Stevie. I own this place. How may I help you?"

Oh God, BJ thought. *Little Stevie Wonder—who would have guessed?* He was struggling to keep from laughing. "We're investigating the murder of Roxy Moran. We understand she and Tommy frequented your business quite often."

"Yes, sir, they did. Tommy's old man too. The three of them drank, danced, and closed the place up almost every Saturday night," Little Stevie stated, sounding rather proud.

"Did they ever get into an argument or fight with anyone?" Jumpy asked.

"Not that I can remember," Stevie said.

"Is there anything else you can recall about her?" BJ asked.

"She was a wild one, all right. She would pay as much attention to the old man as she did to Tommy— like sitting on his lap and kissing him playfully. I think it was all in fun. Tommy didn't seem like the jealous type," Stevie said.

The conversations around the bar had stopped; the early patrons were listening to closely to their discussion with Little Stevie.

BJ thanked Little Stevie and they left. They drove out

to Wilderville to begin interviewing Tommy's neighbors. One had died of old age, one had moved away, and the others were no help at all.

Jumpy picked up the file and flipped through it as they drove. "We're not making any progress on this case at all."

"Let's check on the death of Tommy's father. We can head over to the hospital and look up his record." BJ turned onto Highway 99.

"We're investigating a case involving Chester Moran who was admitted to this hospital a couple of years ago for bee stings," BJ explained when they finally reached the hospital and the Medical Records department. The young woman checked their IDs and entered Chester Moran's name into her computer.

"Yes, Mr. Moran was admitted with multiple bee stings over his entire body and was unconscious when he arrived. He was accompanied by his son who stated they had been picking blueberries when Mr. Moran was attacked. He expired before he was seen by the medical staff. It was determined that he was severely allergic to bee venom." BJ thanked her, and they left.

"Even though Tommy seems to have an airtight alibi, I'm still looking at him for Roxy's murder. It's just a gut feeling," BJ said and gestured emphatically, hoping to make a point and convince someone, even if it was Jumpy.

"I know, but we just keep coming up with dead ends."

"Let's take another run at his logging crew and see where that leads."

There were five names in the file, complete with addresses and phone numbers. None of them were living in the immediate area, and all the information was three years old. Some of them lived in the little community of Wolf Creek. It was a wilderness area, sparsely populated, about twenty miles north of Grants Pass. The residents in general seemed to be tight-lipped and uncooperative. They preferred to be left alone, and let it be known that strangers were not welcome.

One by one, they checked out the crew. Tommy Moran was living on Birch Creek Road in Wilderville, Oregon. They'd already met with him. Then it seemed that their luck ran out. Mickey Benson had died in a logging accident, Samuel Waters was on death row for killing a police officer, and Harold Beatty had died from an overdose of heroin. One witness was still accessible: Casey Overby, who lived on Azalea Road in Wolf Creek, Oregon.

"I think we need to contact Mr. Overby," Jumpy said.

"Let's give him a call and make an appointment." BJ dialed Casey's number, and, after four rings, a recorded voice came on the line: "The number you dialed is no longer in service." BJ put his phone back in his pocket. "Looks like we'll be visiting Wolf Creek instead."

The drive from Grants Pass to Wolf Creek on I-5 was through gently rolling hills of dense, evergreen forest.

Taking the exit marked for Wolf Creek, there was only a small arrow at the end, pointing left. Two miles later, they arrived at a small village that was about a city block long: there was a gas station, an IGA market, and a lumber yard. A sheriff's unit cruising through town would definitely catch someone's attention.

BJ chuckled. "I might as well have switched on the lights and sirens!"

They could sense the word going out, as if there were a four-alarm warning for anyone doing anything illegal. They would know the cops were in town within ninety seconds. When BJ turned left off the main street, the road became narrow and full of potholes, twisting and turning.

"Thank God for GPS," Jumpy said. "Otherwise we'd be so damned turned around!" They followed the directions on the GPS to Casey Overby's house where a sign at the driveway read: *Trespassers Will Be Shot.*

BJ switched the radio to outside speaker and grabbed the mike. "You, in the house! We need to speak with Casey Overby. Please step out and walk out to the driveway entrance. We are not here to arrest anyone."

The speaker seemed to echo off the surrounding hills. Two large dogs that must have been behind the house came running around to the front, barking and heading for the sheriff's unit. The front door opened and a man shouted something at the dogs. They stopped barking instantly and came to a halt yards from the unit.

"What do you guys want with me?" The man spoke with a slight southern drawl.

"We would like to talk with you about Roxy Moran," BJ said into the mike. "Are you Casey Overby?"

"Yeah," the man said. "Ya'll could have driven up to the house." He was walking out toward BJ and Jumpy

"We took your sign to heart. Earlier, we tried to reach you by phone." Jumpy said. He stepped out of the unit and shook Casey's hand. He was keeping a close eye on the dogs.

"Hell, I hardly knew that crazy bitch. I haven't talked to Tommy in over two years," Casey said. Two pickups, each with two men, roared up the drive and came screeching to a stop behind the sheriff's unit.

"Everything's all right, Clyde. Thanks for checking." Casey waved them away. The trucks pulled out slowly; as they drove away, the men in them turned and glared at BJ and Jumpy.

"Great neighborhood watch program you have here." Jumpy watched the trucks disappear down the road.

"Yeah, works pretty good, don't it?" Casey laughed at his witty remark.

"Do you own a .38 caliber Smith & Wesson hand gun?" BJ asked.

"No, sir, I don't... but I used to," Casey said.

"What happened to it?"

"A bunch of us were doing some target practice. Afterwards, we did us some heavy drinking. A day or so later, I went looking for it. It was nowhere to be found. I was sure I put it under the driver's seat of my truck." Casey looked thoughtful and shrugged. "I thought it must have fallen out someplace, so I back-tracked to all the places I had gone. I never did find it."

"Where did you acquire the gun?"

"At a swap meet, about five years ago."

"Did you register it?"

"No, sir, but I might still have the bill of sale."

"Was Tommy with you the day you went target shooting?"

"Yes, sir, he was."

The three of them trailed back to the house. The dogs followed but seemed perfectly content to sniff at their heels.

Casey came out holding a sheet of paper. "Yup, I found it." He waved it in the air triumphantly.

BJ looked at it closely. "Damn," he whispered, "I can't believe it!" It was just what they were hoping for—the serial number was there, appearing in bold print. He hurriedly copied it down; now the entire history of the weapon could be traced.

"Hey man, do you think I'm in any kind of trouble?" Casey asked.

"None that I can tell, at the moment. I would like to ask you one more question."

"Shoot.... Ah, I mean, go ahead."

"Was Tommy Moran with you and your crew the day Roxy went missing?"

"The honest to God truth is this. I was there that day, and the other guys told me Tommy was working in a different area. I personally never seen him."

"We want to thank you for your cooperation," BJ said as they left. *How many times had he said those exact same words in all his years as a cop?* He turned to Jumpy. "What do you think? Could Tommy have swiped Casey's .38 and used it on Roxy?"

"Maybe he never got rid of it... or it's hidden someplace," Jumpy added.

When they arrived back at the Sheriff's Office, one of the ladies who worked the front desk told BJ that a lady from Wilderville had called. "She left her name and number and wants you to call ASAP."

Meanwhile, the history of the gun showed it had traveled from the manufacturer to a dealer and several other owners, but no crimes were linked to that weapon. "Not to date, at least," BJ said softly.

It was late in the afternoon, and Sheriff Patterson was just returning to the office. He walked by them and did not acknowledge their presence.

Jumpy lowered his voice. "Wonder what's eating him."

"Probably his main concern—politics," BJ answered.

"You gonna call that lady?" Jumpy asked.

"Yeah, I wonder if someone else in Wilderville has information on Roxy Moran," BJ said as he dialed the number. "Hello, ma'am, this is BJ Taylor from the Sheriff's

Office. I was told to call this number."

"Yes, Mr. Taylor, I called earlier. I'm Mrs. Delores Knapp. My late husband was Pastor Ralph Knapp of the church in Wilderville. He died last week."

"I'm very sorry for your loss, Mrs. Knapp," BJ said, rather bewildered what he was supposed to do about her husband's death.

"I was going through his things at the church. That was when I found a note with a sealed letter attached to it. The note said to give this to the Sheriff's Office upon his death. On the outside of the envelope there's the handwritten name Roxy Moran. Should I open it?"

"No!" BJ said, probably more forcefully than he meant to. "Please let it be. Leave it where you found it. We'll be right there. Are you at home or at the church?"

"At home," she said and repeated the address.

"We're on our way, Mrs. Knapp."

They pulled in at the Knapps' home address and walked up to the front door. Mrs. Knapp was waiting for them. She was holding a sealed letter; there was note stapled to it. She held it out for BJ to take.

Jumpy stepped forward, a clear plastic envelope held open before him. "Thank you, ma'am." She dropped the letters into the evidence bag.

"Can you tell us any more about this letter, Mrs. Knapp?"

"No, sir. It was like I told you on the phone. I was going through my husband's things in his office at the church when I found it. And I called you right away."

"Did the Moran family belong to your church?"

"Not that I know of. I believe Tommy came to see my husband at our home a couple times. I think it might have been after they had found his wife's body. They talked in private for a while. I couldn't hear what they were saying, of course, but Tommy seemed upset and my husband was trying to console him." She paused and looked thoughtful for a moment. "There's one other thing I recall. On his way out of our house, the last time he was here, I remember my husband telling Tommy: 'Your secret's safe with me. Go with God.'"

BJ sighed and shook his head. *Damn, what next?* As always, he remembered police courtesy. "Thank you very much, Mrs. Knapp. You've been most helpful."

"We'll take the letter into Captain Smith and see if he can have a fingerprint expert dust it. It's a long shot, but it's the only shot we've got," Jumpy said.

When they returned, Sheriff Patterson was calling a special meeting of his staff and key personnel. BJ and Jumpy were told to attend.

"Ladies and gentlemen, may I have your attention please. I have met with the Grants Pass Police Chief and I need to pass along that there have been numerous reports of gang sightings in and around Grants Pass. This includes the motorcycle group known as 'The Outlaws.'" He paused and glanced around the packed meeting room, making certain he had everyone's attention.

Patterson continued, "They haven't caused any trouble as far as we know, but we're not sure why they're suddenly here. We've had very few problems with gangs in the past... we sure as hell don't want any now. You're to pass this information on to the rest of the deputies. There'll be an urgent memo on the staff bulletin board. Everyone must read it and sign it by 2400 hours tomorrow. I'm instructing all deputies to find 'probable cause,' pull any biker over, cite him—remember, find *any* reason—and let them know they're not welcome here. The city cops will be doing the same."

One of the deputies raised his hand.

"Yes, Davis? You have a question?"

"Sir? What if they're not really doing anything wrong?" the newly hired, young deputy asked.

"I don't give a damn. Read the law, the fine print. Find something—I don't care if it's that the guy's nose hair needs trimming. Make sure your citations are in order."

"Geez. Maybe that's what's been under his skin," Jumpy said.

"Right now, we have our own business," BJ replied. Could the contents of the letter Mrs. Knapp had given them be a lead to Roxy's killer?

31

OREGON

Over the next week, Miguel's twenty men had arrived in Medford and assembled at the warehouse. None of them had had any contact with the DEA or any other law enforcement agency during their trip. They had traveled separately, using slightly different routes whenever possible.

Allison insisted they speak only English, during their journey and upon arrival in Medford. She was pleased with their progress. Most of them had lost all traces of an accent; if she hadn't known them before, she could have been completely fooled by their cover. She had provided cots and food for them until they left for Cave Junction. Accustomed to luxury while living in Miguel's Bogotá compound, some complained about the primitive conditions in the warehouse.

"Tell it to Miguel," she told the complainers. "Your comfort is not my concern. You know why you're here.

You'll soon be living and working in a home, two of you to each house."

She had purchased twelve of the fifteen houses in that area, careful to select rural properties distant from nosy neighbors and busy roads. The plan was to place two men in each house and have them prepare the house for the plant growing operation.

The house would appear, smell, and sound like any other rural home. It was critical that outward appearances should not raise suspicions. Marijuana had a strong, distinctive odor; hundreds of plants would smell even stronger. They would use charcoal filters in the air circulation systems to absorb and decrease any odor that might leak from the house. Law enforcement looked for two clues in a grow house: excessively high water usage and electric consumption. For Allison's houses, water was not a problem, because each had its own high-producing well.

After the houses were ready, she would deliver the supplies, and the men would complete the setup. It would take from two to six months for seeds to mature to a full grown plant, depending on conditions. In the meantime, Miguel would be shipping her bundles through his already well-established routes in the United States.

Miguel had made contact with two of the largest, most brutal gangs in Portland to handle his drugs: the Rollin 60s Crips and the Outlaws motorcycle gangs. They agreed to split the city and outlying areas. They would come to Grants Pass at a designated time and pick up their orders. He had assured them the quality and price would be better than their current suppliers.

In the past two months, all fifteen of the houses had been completed and were growing thousands of marijuana plants. Allison shifted the men among the houses and was busy constantly. She talked with Miguel almost every day, but she missed him terribly. When would they be married? She held onto that hope. His business was flourishing and money was pouring in. Allison bought a forty-eight foot fishing trawler that was docked in Bandon, Oregon. Their plan would be to meet the sub in open water at night and transfer the cargo.

Her business with the gangs was increasing every week. Miguel's men would transport the drugs to a location near Grants Pass, meet the gang, make the exchange, and return to her with the money. Her biggest concern was safely storing large amounts of cash until the sub arrived with more drugs. Allison would meticulously record the exact amount of money from each sale, then bundle and seal it in heavy plastic wrap. She stored the bundles in the basement of the largest home, locked in the safest place she could find.

She would then call Miguel with the total amount. He would record it, then recount it when he arrived in Oregon. She knew his rules well: the total had better be the exactly the same or someone would face a slow, agonizing death. If anyone stole from him, he would first cut off his hands. If someone lied to him, he would cut out his tongue.

Allison regularly delivered Miguel's instructions to the men. It had become her job to arrange dates, times, and places for the drops to the gangs. Miguel confided that he planned to expand into other sites in Oregon. They would need to incorporate more gangs to cover the state. His plans would take him into Northern California and then south to Modesto. The DEA would be watching for traffic moving south to north, not the other way around. The demand for his drugs would be substantial and growing, but he'd already made plans to handle the volume.

Allison had rented a small house on Lake Selmac, a few miles east of Cave Junction. The lake was scenic and peaceful. There were fewer than a hundred homes and cabins throughout the surrounding countryside. A small country store with gas pumps was a gathering place for the community and the latest gossip. As time went by and her work was mostly completed, she had more time to relax by the water and read or swim. She couldn't wait for Miguel to join her and be in his arms again. She longed to show him this place: it was made for lovers.

It was late morning on another Chamber of Commerce day at the lake. Allison had just finished breakfast when there was a knock on the door. She peered through the window: an elderly lady was on the doorstep, holding something in her hands.

Allison opened the door and smiled. "Hello. May I help you?"

"Good morning, dear. My name is Fran—Fran Doyle. I'm one of your neighbors." She gestured down the road. "I'd like to welcome you to the lake. Here's some of my banana bread, fresh from the oven."

Allison took the still warm loaf from the woman; it felt good and comforting in her hands. "Thank you so much. Would you like to come in? I'm Allison." She never mentioned her last name unless it was absolutely necessary, and then she used one of the forged IDs Miguel's counterfeiter had created.

"No, thank you, dear. I would like to invite you to the lake's annual potluck picnic this Saturday at ten. Bring a dish to pass. We're expecting about seventy people this year. The park is at the south end of the lake. You'll see the posted signs." Fran waved goodbye and she stepped out onto dirt road, headed back to her house.

"See you there!" Allison called. She entered the date in her cell phone calendar. Since the date and time didn't interfere with any of her work plans, she planned to attend. She would make a bowl of potato salad, one of her few specialties. During her time with Juan and Carmela, and then with Miguel, she had rarely cooked. It was nice to do something that was honest, simple, and fun.

It was a gorgeous Saturday morning, and the annual potluck was about to start. Allison had loaded everything for the picnic into a cooler and placed it on the passenger seat of her truck. She'd decided to wear navy blue shorts; a white, sleeveless blouse pulled up and tied around her waist and showing only a little skin; and a pair of sandals. Her hair was pulled back into a ponytail, and she still had a nice tan. She knew she looked good and would always stand out wherever she went, but she must be careful not to overdress. In the country, fashion was quite different than what she was used to.

Driving around the lake, she noticed a county crew working on a project at the edge of the road. They were digging and had placed flashing caution signs to warn oncoming traffic. As she drove by slowly, she noticed one of the men leaning on his shovel. He was at least six foot two, and he had blond, wavy hair. He wasn't wearing a shirt. His shoulders were broad and muscular, and his chest narrowed down to a trim waist. Working in the heat he glistened in the sunlight. *That's one handsome hunk,* Allison thought as the line of one-way traffic eased around the construction. *Had he read her mind?* He winked as she drove past, and she winked back.

She was one of the last to arrive at the picnic. It seemed as though all the people stopped what they were doing and stared directly at her. Several of the men came over to introduce themselves, receiving disapproving stares from the women, who were probably their wives. Within a few minutes, the ladies had gathered around her and were welcoming her to the group, asking all sorts of questions. She'd anticipated this and had prepared a cover story.

A tall, thin man said a prayer and then lunch was served. There was much laughing and joking. After they'd finished eating, several men set up a volley ball net and chose teams. Some of the older men were playing horseshoes. Occasionally, Allison would glance down the road to see whether the workmen were still there.

It had been several months since she had enjoyed making love with Miguel. She had gone through multiple sets of batteries for her vibrator, but even that wasn't the same. It never was. How she longed to feel the warmth of a man's body next to her. The next time she looked, the work crew had packed up and left. Perhaps they would be back, because the flashing barriers were still there beside the mound of dirt. If they returned Monday, she could bring them some nice, cold lemonade. She smiled at the thought.

The potluck was over, so she headed back to the house, still thinking about the handsome stranger. Her vibrator would get a good workout tonight. It would be playing with fire to get involved with anyone. Miguel would be coming to Oregon soon; and if he found out she had messed around with any other man, he would probably kill him and her. She would keep the handsome hunk at arm's length… at least, until the time was right.

On Monday, she waited until noon. She loaded two jugs, one with lemonade and one with iced tea, and added a bag of ice to her cooler. She drove up to the crew and handed out the two jugs. "Here's some ice and plastic drinking cups."

"Thanks, lady!" Some of the men called.

"Break time!" someone else said. The men crossed to a shady area and sat down to enjoy their refreshment.

The blond hunk stayed close to her SUV. "What's your name? I saw you pass by yesterday."

"Allison," she replied.

"I'm Steve. You live around here?"

She pointed to her house across the lake. "Yes.

"Are you married?" he asked.

"Not yet, but I'm engaged. You?"

He looked deep into her eyes. "No, never been. Never will be."

Allison laughed. "You just haven't found the right woman yet." She drove away slowly, waving goodbye.

———

Steve picked up his shovel. He was completely confused by the blond dame. She was flirting with him, toying with him, and yet made it a point to tell him she was promised to another man. He never had had trouble getting a woman. If anything, he usually had trouble getting rid of them. He vowed to teach the cute little cock-teaser a lesson.

The moon was casting an eerie light across the lake. It was eleven at night, when Steve's shadowy figure moved among the trees, creeping closer to Allison's cottage. He was wearing a hoodie, dark clothes, and latex gloves. In his pockets, he carried a camera, duct tape, a thin nylon rope, and a knife. He had done this before and had never been caught: he was more sure of himself than ever.

God, how he loved intimidating women. They were all such bitches. Carefully, he removed the screen to the open window and crawled inside. He stood there waiting for his eyes to adjust to the darkness. He removed his shoes and silently crept into the bedroom. The door was wide open. She was lying on her side, dressed in a short nightgown, and sleeping soundly. He drew his knife and pounced on her, using the full weight of his body to keep her from struggling, and pressed his hand over her mouth. She couldn't move or cry. *Good, the bitch is scared shitless,* he thought.

"Not a peep out of you, or I'll cut you from ear to ear," he whispered. He slapped a piece of duct tape over her month, rolled her onto her stomach, and tied her hands behind her back.

"Don't even try to look at me. Keep your face down," he said. With the other lengths of rope, he tied her legs, spread-eagled to each end of the footboard. "You're mine now, you little cock-teasing bitch. Let's see what the rest of you looks like," he muttered. He climbed back onto the bed and slowly cut away her nightgown. "Ah... very nice," he murmured. He eased back from her to stand at the foot of the bed.

He was taking pictures of her naked body from every angle. The flash from the camera was blinding her. She sobbed and struggled harder. *She must know what's coming next.* He removed the glove of his right hand and rubbed it lightly over her breasts. He pinched one pretty pink nipple. He was in no hurry.... He let his hand rest on her pubic hair and then slid one finger high inside her. He flicked at her clitoris. "You'll do, baby. And you want me and you'll beg for more."

He stripped off his clothes and began to masturbate slowly. "We have all night to spend together, my dear. And I'm going to enjoy every minute of it." When he was ready, he crawled back on top of her and, without waiting for any lubrication, he jammed himself into her. He knew he was hurting her, and deliberately tore at her flesh.

He whispered, "I know you like it, baby, and I'm just the guy to give it to you."

An edge of the duct tape had caught on the pillowcase, and Allison was able to free the seal from her mouth. "You're tearing me up. Please use the KY in the nightstand," she managed to say.

Her voice must have startled him. However, she wasn't screaming. He decided to let her talk. "If you let out even one scream, I'll bash your head in."

She nodded in agreement, and he reached into the nightstand for the jelly and rubbed it sloppily deep into her crotch and up high into her butt. Then he returned to business and pushed himself back into her, this time with ease, pushing deeper, still wanting to hurt her. His thrust became more rapid and harder, his breathing labored, and he exploded within her.

"Now that you've finished, please leave me alone," she sobbed.

"Oh, I'm not done with you yet, bitch." He was laughing. "We've just begun to play." He took another piece of rope and tied it around her neck and tied the other end to the headboard. "I'm going back to my truck to get a beer. Do you want one?" He was laughing again as he replaced the duct tape on her mouth. Three minutes later he returned, smelling of beer. It had been over twenty minutes since he had climaxed, but he was ready again.

"This time, sweetie, I'm going to do you up the ass." He rolled her over and raised her until her butt was in the air. She was trying to scream as he pushed himself inside her, but the sound was muffled by the tape. After he had finished, he put his clothes back on and cut the rope binding her hands.

———

There had been nothing sensual about his touch — never in all the time he had spent with her: it was violating and disgusting. All the while she had endured him, she kept asking herself: *Why is this happening to me? What have I done to deserve this?* There were no answers.

When he had spoken, there was a grit of evil to his voice. *I've heard that voice before,* she thought. She was glad he hadn't covered her eyes. Once her eyes had become accustomed to the darkness, after the stunning flash of the camera, she had turned her head just enough to see his image in the mirror on her dresser. What little moonlight there was filtered in through the window. She could make out the image of a tall, muscular man with something covering his head. He had a musky smell, like he was perspiring. His hands were strong, rough, and calloused.

The pain when he'd forced himself into her had been unbearable. Then, when she knew he was about to come, she was certain he wasn't wearing a condom. Her rage and pain was joined with fear: what if he got her pregnant? Then he had exploded inside her, and she thought it was over, but it hadn't been.

She felt so violated and ashamed, but she knew that Miguel would find him and kill him in a slow and painful way. She had figured out that her rapist was Steve, the guy she had thought was a hunk. *No matter what he else does, I'll never let him know I've recognized him,* she vowed.

"Count to one hundred before taking the other ropes off," he'd said as he left, this time using the front door.

Allison had known that was bullshit and immediately began untying herself. She couldn't get into the shower fast enough to cleanse herself inside and out. She wouldn't worry about evidence of rape, because she had no intention of going to the authorities. Miguel would handle justice. Her greatest fear at the moment was getting pregnant. Standing in the shower, she was overcome with rage.

"That slimy son-of-a-bitch will pay for this!" she screamed to the silent cottage.

From then on, she instructed Miguel's men to watch her house at night, in case Steve tried to return. She was no longer comfortable living alone and kept a knife from the kitchen under her pillow. She would use it if she needed to.

32

Oregon

The State lab confirmed that Pastor Knapp's prints appeared on both the envelope and the letter. Mrs. Knapp's prints showed up only on the envelope. The letter read:

June 4, 2011

To whom it may it concern:

I, Ralph W. Knapp, Pastor of Wilderville Community Church, do hereby swear that Mr. Thomas Moran, husband of Roxanne Moran, confessed to me that he alone was responsible for the death of his wife. Tommy Moran said he learned that his father and Roxy had an ongoing sexual affair and that she refused to stop. Tommy has said further that he knew his father was allergic to bees; his father was as much of the problem as Roxy. He had planned to take his father to a place he knew of where there was a large beehive in the blueberry bushes. When his dad got close enough, Tommy pushed his father into the hive. Tommy said he had sprayed himself with repellant and only received a couple of stings. Tommy said he let his father lie there until he was unconscious and the bees were gone, and then he took him to the hospital. A few days later he shot Roxy in the back of the head with a gun he had stolen and dumped her body in the river at Hellgate Bridge. Tommy also told me that the gun he used was buried, inside a plastic bag, and is under Roxy's headstone at the cemetery.

I felt bound and obligated as clergy not to reveal this information.

Sincerely,

Ralph W. Knapp, Pastor

P.S. My wife had no knowledge of this.

"Holy crap, this is incredible! Find out where the hell she was buried and go check for the weapon," Captain Smith said, gesturing toward the door. "Make sure you've got enough evidence kits."

BJ and Jumpy called the three cemeteries in Grants Pass with no results.

"Is there one in Wilderville?" Jumpy asked.

"I'm not sure." BJ reached for the phone. It seemed that he spent one hell of a lot of time on that phone.

"Hello, Mrs. Knapp, this is BJ Taylor from the Sheriff's Office. Can you tell me if there's a cemetery in Wilderville?"

"Oh, yes, Mr. Taylor. There's a small one behind our church," she said softly. "You know, I believe Roxy Moran was the last person buried there."

It took them only fifteen minutes to get there. "Let's park behind the church," Jumpy suggested.

BJ nodded in agreement. "We don't want to draw any unwanted attention."

It was an old cemetery and not well maintained. Some of the headstones were tipped over and the grass needed mowing badly. There remained a couple hours of daylight, and with less than a hundred headstones, it shouldn't take them long to find Roxy's. They divided up, starting at opposite ends, and planned to meet somewhere in the middle.

"Here it is!" Jumpy pointed to a flat granite stone no more than eight inches wide and eighteen inches long. Only her name and the dates of her birth and death were inscribed on it.

BJ carefully snapped photos of the site before they disturbed anything. He used a knife to cut away the grass and loosen the dirt around the stone. They pressed down, using their fingers on either end, digging until they reached the bottom edge of the slab. Slowly and carefully, they lifted the headstone from its resting place. They laid it aside on the grass and took several more photos. Underneath was a hollowed-out spot in the dirt. Deeper was a simple, plastic shopping bag, wrapped around an object that definitely appeared to be a gun.

"Jumpy, grab one of the large evidence bags from the unit," BJ said. "We sure as hell need to preserve this for the forensic team."

After sealing the plastic bag in a larger evidence bag, they carefully replaced the grave marker.

Jumpy surveyed their work. "You could never tell it's been moved," he said to BJ. "You been doing this a long time?"

"God, I hope not!" BJ said and they both laughed. "Let's head back to the office and find out if this is the weapon used to kill Roxy—we can hope there're some prints on it." BJ was feeling pleased; there was progress at last.

One of the two slugs recovered from Roxy's body was in good enough condition to be used for comparison: the rifling was an exact match. Tommy's prints were on the gun and the bullets that remained in the cylinder of the .38.

Sheriff Patterson personally arrested Tommy Moran for the murder of his wife Roxanne Moran. Tommy put up no resistance whatsoever. Instead, he walked with his head down into the jail. He looked like a defeated man, as though he was relieved it was over.

After several hours of intense questioning, Tommy confessed to killing his wife Roxy and his father. He willingly gave the detectives a full account of his involvement. The court offered to appoint legal counsel for him, but he declined, "I just want to plead guilty."

The sheriff called a news conference, and to BJ's surprise, Patterson actually gave him and Jumpy credit for solving the case. Now it seemed that the entire town considered BJ a super cop. Whenever he met the townspeople in passing, inevitably someone would stop to shake his hand. "How the hell do you do it?" was always the question. He'd laugh. "Just getting my second wind, I guess" was his standard answer.

Tommy was sentenced to life in prison, without possibility of parole. He seemed strangely content, knowing he had to pay for the crimes he had committed. The following year, BJ would learn, Tommy Moran was killed by another inmate: they were fighting over a pack of cigarettes.

BJ and Carol's home was completed at last; they were more than ready to move in. Rogue Lea had been a fine place to live in the interim, but there was no place like home. Hand in hand they strolled through their new, empty house.

Carol was crying. "Oh, don't mind me, dear. They're happy tears."

"We're home, honey," BJ said softly; he took her in his arms and kissed her.

BJ rented a truck and, with Jumpy's help, they emptied the storage unit and drove the truck to their new home. Carol phoned the stores where she'd ordered the rest of the furniture and appliances to set a delivery date. Soon everything was in place.

Carol settled to the chore of making draperies. "This is my last stand as a domestic goddess," she declared. "I'm more comfortable with a suture needle."

BJ laughed, but he understood: she missed her career as a registered nurse.

BJ and Jumpy had launched the boat and taken her on a test run. She was all he had expected. However, BJ was warned that he should learn the river well to avoid the dangerous shallows where he could easily damage a prop. Earlier, he had gone to the fire rescue group and bought a map that marked the river depths from the dam to Hellgate Bridge.

He learned he could also launch the boat at the coastal town of Gold Beach where the Rogue River emptied into the Pacific Ocean. From there, he could come back upstream, but sailing against the current. Local fishermen would often take this route, especially when the Pacific King salmon were running in the fall.

BJ had discovered that he actually enjoyed helping others in his part-time work for the sheriff. It gave him a sense of pride and accomplishment, although he and Jumpy never received any monetary compensation. He was happy to do the work. It was even better being in their new house, enjoying life together in a home that was truly theirs. For now, the house, the landscaping, the land, and his boat would require more of his time. BJ also longed to be more involved with the Grants Pass Classic Car Club.

For the next two days, a rain storm came in from the west, high winds causing most of the dead leaves on the trees to fall. He hadn't counted on that, something he'd never had to deal with much in Riverside. He discovered that if he wanted to burn anything on his property, he would need to check with the fire department to see whether it was a safe "burn day." A spark could float away, spreading fire or causing a major conflagration across the countryside and into the forests. Meanwhile, he raked the leaves into large piles. The fire marshal would have to give the okay before he could touch a match to them, even to legally use a burn barrel.

"The boys are coming in next weekend, so put together a list of any jobs you want them to help with," Carol reminded him and looked up from the book she was reading.

"How long will they be home, honey?"

"Friday afternoon until Monday evening," she said.

"You know they'll probably bring a pile of dirty clothes, don't you?"

Carol laughed. "Of course. I'm ready for that, but they should know how to do it themselves by now. This is a courtesy."

"I have a meeting at the Sheriff's Office on Friday morning," BJ said, "but I plan to spend Saturday with the boys."

33

COLOMBIA

Miguel's cartel had expanded to include the south-east coast of America through Miami, Florida. Supplies were transported by freighters and then transferred to what were called "Fast Boats." About 70 percent were making it past the DEA and the Coast Guard. To Miguel, the 30 percent loss of product, boats, and men was expendable. His profits were such that he considered the loss a cost of doing business. Even after spending several million dollars on equipment and payoffs, his vaults at both compounds still overflowed with cash.

The Mexican cartels near the borders of California, Arizona, and Texas were his main competition, and again he had a plan to deal with them without any bloodshed. It would take a while to plant someone inside their organizations. That person's sole objective would be to inject a deadly poison into the bundles of weed and cocaine, thereby killing the end users. The buyers would no longer trust the Mexican dealers and would look for new suppliers. His men would just so happen to be there, ready to accept the orders.

He had two more submarines built at a cost of $20,000,000 each. They would be operating off the eastern coast of Colombia near the small town of Necoclí. Miguel had purchased three thousand acres of heavily forested jungle where a navigable river emptied into the Caribbean. The trip from this point to the panhandle of Florida was less than nine hundred nautical miles and could be made without refueling. Captain Gomez would train two new crews to operate the subs.

The time for Miguel's trip to the United States was near; all his operations were running smoothly. Jake proved capable of running the day-to-day operations of the cartel's compound, and Rafael completely controlled the business in Bogotá. The trip was scheduled to take three weeks, including the time spent in the submarine. He would evaluate the business operation in Oregon and still have time to spend with Allison.

The sub was carefully loaded with cocaine worth $160,000,000 and marijuana worth several million dollars. There were provisions of food and water for six people; Miguel and the crew would pack minimally. The plan was to surface each morning before daylight and wash topside using sea water and soap, but use fresh water to rinse off the soap. Miguel's orders were no smoking and no use of alcohol on board. The only one aware of their destination was Miguel; he would inform the captain once they had submerged.

The night before they were to leave, Miguel called Rafael. "Bring me six young ladies from one of your houses for a Bon Voyage party," he instructed him. "One will be for me, so make sure she is young, very pretty, and make certain she's a virgin. I want to be the one she'll remember for the rest of her life." Eyes half-closed he could picture her: soft brown eyes, a sweet smile, tender flesh.... He knew he was a great lover.

Within a few hours, a stretch limo had pulled into the compound and parked in front of the main house. A chauffeur stepped out, walked around to the other side, and opened the back passenger door for the ladies.

"Welcome to Nieve del Diablo." Miguel smiled and beckoned them to follow him inside. He noticed one especially pretty young girl who lingered behind; she appeared slightly afraid.

"My dear, you are in good hands. All will be well with you." He spoke softly, gently putting his arm around her, and escorted her into his house that had been decorated for a party. Music was playing, a lavish meal had been prepared, and the bar was open. Miguel had told his men to have fun; but not to drink too much. "You must be able to do your jobs tomorrow when we leave on our trip."

The four-man crew from the submarine, Lorenzo, and Miguel were ready to party.

Captain Gomez proposed a toast in English: "To a safe and profitable trip."

They all drank to his toast, even though the young ladies hadn't the slightest idea what he meant. Each of the men had picked a lady, leaving the youngest for Miguel. Everyone was eating, laughing, and dancing. Soon, it became quiet as the couples drifted off, one by one. Dessert was served: it was time for the lovemaking to begin.

Miguel took the girl to the master bedroom and turned the lights down low. "Do you know why you're here tonight, Señorita?"

Silent, she nodded. "This is my first time... with a man. I am nervous." She gulped; she was trembling. "I do not know what to do."

He was kissing her, leading her to his bed. "And so, I will be your first?" Miguel asked softly.

"Yes, I have never done more than kiss a boy before." She held her hands crossed over her heart, as though protecting herself.

"I will be slow and gentle with you, my dear." He paused to kiss her again, more deeply, and she gasped. "I'll take your clothes—" He held out one hand and watched as she slowly undressed. "I'll lay these on the chair."

In the dim light, he could see her youthful perky breasts with their large, brown nipples. He was immediately aroused and leaned in to softly kiss her. He touched her breasts, and the girl gasped in surprise. He had let her drink enough to help her relax, but not enough to get drunk.

He picked her up and laid her on the bed, then bent to kiss her breasts once more. Her nipples rose up, hard and firm, responding to his tongue, and he was pleased with the girl. He reached between her legs, caressing back and forth until he felt her open to him, moistening in response to his touch. *No woman can resist Miguel,* he thought, *not even an innocent virgin like this one.* Soon, she was slick and damp, panting and moaning with pleasure. She had completely surrendered to him and put her arms around his neck, pulling him closer. Miguel was absolutely certain that she'd never experienced oral sex or given it, so he decided not to try to teach her. He pressed one leg between her legs, slowly pushing them apart.

"Please don't hurt me," she begged.

"You need to relax," he said.

"I've never done this before," she repeated.

"I know," he murmured reassuringly. "That is why I want to be your first and teach you the right way to make love. It is most important. You will have other men in your life, and some won't care about your feelings the way I do." He was straddling her for a moment, his erection full and swollen. He rubbed himself against her clitoris, like a promise.

"But I don't want to have a baby!" She was starting to cry. "I'm too young."

"There, there, sweetheart, there will be no baby. I

promise." Yet, he had not even considered wearing a condom. He wanted to feel the sweet softness of her young body against his and experience breaking her hymen. He reached under the pillow and grabbed the tube of lubricant he'd placed there earlier and applied it to her, even though she probably didn't need it. She was sweating with her own desire, a response beyond her control. Miguel raised her legs and rested them on his shoulders. With the lightest pressure, he began easing into her. She was very tight; for a moment she looked as if she were in pain.

"Relax, sweetie," he whispered. "It will feel better, much better." He continued, using short, slow strokes, caressing her breasts, and then he was totally inside her.

"Better?" he asked.

"*Sí,*" she said, "the pain... it is gone now."

It had been a long time since he had made love to Allison. This was different: he was ready to unload into this young thing and within a few strokes, he quickly did. *I couldn't care less if you get pregnant,* he thought. Sometime later, when he had had his fill of her, he told her to get up and get out of his bed. He studied the bloodied sheet that had been underneath her. He had had the maid place a protective layer underneath so the little girl wouldn't ruin his mattress.

"Thank you, Señor. You were very kind to me. I am glad that you were my first. Will I see you again soon?"

"No, my dear, I don't think that will happen. I'm getting married soon. You were just someone to relieve my tension." His earlier gentle tone of voice had vanished. "Get dressed and get out." He had never bothered to learn her name.

The party was over.

The chauffeur helped the ladies into the limo and drove away.

Before dawn the next morning, Miguel was packed. Jake drove him down to where the sub was docked. Captain Gomez and the crew were already there, loading the last of the supplies. Lorenzo was acting nervous about getting into the sub.

"What's the matter, Lorenzo?" Miguel asked.

"I don't trust that thing. If it sinks, I can't swim." he said. The men burst out laughing.

"We'll be so far out to sea, that if we sink, none of us could swim to shore." The captain laughed heartily. "We'd all sink to the bottom. If anyone escaped he'd be eaten by sharks."

It was important for them to enter the ocean from the river at high tide, especially because of the cargo's extra weight. The captain maneuvered the sub into the ocean, and within a few minutes she was completely submerged. They descended to fifty feet and then to one hundred feet without any complications. There were a few moans, creaks, and groans from the sub.

"Are those sounds normal?" Lorenzo asked. He would remain uncomfortable and nervous throughout the voyage.

Captain Gomez came up to periscope depth and checked around them in all directions. "All systems are A-okay," he reported.

There wasn't much for them to do now but eat, read, play cards, or sleep.

At night, they took on fuel three miles off the coast of Mexico. A larger ship pulled alongside the sub. The sea was calm and the moon was bright. The ship's crew efficiently completed filling the diesel tanks. Captain Gomez made their payment in cocaine. Shortly, they were on their way again.

Miguel was impatient with the process. It was the slowest, most boring, and uncomfortable trip he had ever taken. It was also the most costly, but it would be the most profitable in the end.

34

COLOMBIA

On the third floor of a commercial building in the heart of Bogotá there was a small group of American DEA agents stationed in Colombia. They huddled around a desk, watching a computer monitor on which a blinking red dot in the Pacific Ocean was moving northerly, at a slow but steady speed. They were listening to a transmitter beep as the dot moved.

Dawn Hogan was the field agent in charge. For the last seven years, she had worked her way up through the agency. She was known for her hard work and businesslike approach. She had received several promotions during her years in Colombia.

"Looks like Captain Gomez is on his way. To where, we're not sure yet. The sub stopped briefly along the Mexican coast, then has continued north." She sighed and took a deep breath. "So far, the tracking device is working fine."

Captain Gomez was actually Alex Cruz, an undercover DEA agent. Dawn had put together his counterfeit papers and background information to get him into Hector Campos's cartel. It had taken months of preparation and countless man-hours to build his identity. The DEA had heard rumors about a submarine being built in Mexico for a cartel in Colombia. After it was completed, they traced it to the compound run by Campos. They were sure that he would be in need of a navigator — something not available from just any city's *Help Wanted* ads — so they had created Captain Gomez.

Just prior to leaving, the captain was able to get a message to the DEA in the code they had agreed upon. "We leave in the morning. Tracking bug is in place. The new leader of the cartel, name Miguel Vargas, will be aboard for the trip. Exact destination unknown." The captain always sent short messages. Any communication was risky. "We may be headed to the west coast of North America. Note: whenever Miguel speaks to me he does so in perfect English." In another coded message he told Agent Hogan that two more subs had been built, and that he had trained their crews. However, he hadn't been told where the subs' ports were located.

The DEA had been working with the Colombian government, identifying the locations of drug manufacturing and working on how to safely to dispose of the chemicals that were used. Many of the chemicals were lethal contaminants, and the conservationists groups in Colombia were concerned.

"I'm leaving for the L.A. office. Continue tracking them and keep in touch with me on my cell." Agent Dawn Hogan closed her briefcase. "I want to catch these guys red-handed. Herb, you're in charge in my absence. Ken, call our pilot at the airport and tell him to have the jet ready in thirty minutes." She grabbed her backpack and headed for the door. During the flight, she notified the L.A. office of her arrival time and requested a car to pick her up.

When they landed, the jet taxied to a hangar on the other side of LAX, away from the commercial flights. A black SUV was waiting inside. As she stepped off the plane, she saw that her old training officer, Corbin Baker, was waiting for her. He was the ranking officer of the Western Division of the DEA.

As they headed for the L.A. office, Dawn gave him a full report about her work in Colombia. "I'm not quite sure where the sub is headed. It could be anywhere from San Diego to Seattle. I'll need a team ready for quick deployment anywhere in that area." She hoped it didn't sound like she was begging.

"I understand, Agent Hogan. This appears to be a major operation.... Hell, you don't mind if I call you Dawn—we've known each other forever."

She smiled and nodded.

"You'll have my full support for any resources you might need," he said.

"I'll make sure you're kept informed at all times. Thanks for your help." They were both watching her computer monitor: the red dot continued moving due north.

Dawn knew that her undercover captain would let her know as soon as he could where the drugs would be offloaded. The dot had already passed Los Angeles. After several hours, it had neared San Francisco.

"Where the hell are those guys going?" she muttered.

"I've assigned six men to you for as long as you need them. I have some urgent business in Long Beach that can't wait. I'll be in touch," Corbin said. "Be careful, Dawn."

"Thank you, sir," she said. "I'll try."

She dialed the pilot and told him to have the jet readied again for another long flight. She briefed her new team on their mission. "Make sure you bring enough fire power," she reminded the men. They understood what that meant. On the way back to LAX, she called the Portland and Seattle DEA Offices and informed them that her team might be coming into their areas. She would contact them at that time.

The traffic was heavy, the Lakers' game had just let out. To make things even worse, there was the inevitable accident on the freeway ahead of them.

"You want me to use the lights and siren to get us out of this mess?" the driver asked.

"No, we'll wait it out," she said as she watched the red dot creep north. Slowly, the traffic began to move, and soon they were able to see what had been causing the holdup. A car had turned over completely and its front tire was missing.

"Must have been a blowout," her driver commented.

"With all the emergency vehicles, the traffic was pinched down to one lane," one of the agents said. "A typical day in L.A."

"How much longer until we reach the hangar?" Dawn asked.

"We'll be there in about ten minutes," he answered.

The jet could normally hold up to twelve passengers. Dawn, the six agents, and their gear completely filled the cabin.

The pilot came on the intercom. "We're third in line for takeoff. We'll be in the air in fifteen minutes." Dawn was nervous; there had been too many delays. She longed to turn on the laptop to check the sub's position, but the pilot had requested that all electronics remain off until further notice.

At last, after what seemed like an eternity to Dawn, they taxied down the runway and soared into the sky. It was a clear evening, and the city lights faded into the distance as they headed north along the Pacific coast. The Learjet-31 cruised at 500 miles per hour and could easily overtake the sub. This was the first downtime she had had in the last twenty-four hours. She grabbed a pillow from the overhead and reclined the seat, hoping to relax. Her fresh, well rested crew rechecked their gear and settled in for a game of poker.

35

Oregon

Allison and four of her men arrived at the parking lot of a marina in Bandon, Oregon. It was late in the evening, and the air carried the tang of salty brine from the sea.

The fishing trawler was docked near the parking area. The moving truck she had rented pulled up near the boat, and the men unloaded empty moving boxes and carried them aboard. They would soon be filled with drugs. They offloaded the supply of diesel fuel, using the truck's automated lift gate to bring the drums within reach so they could be rolled on deck.

"Get everything below deck before anyone comes nosing around," Allison directed. "Cover anything else with a tarp and tie it down." She knew the exact time and place where the submarine was to surface, and she couldn't be late.

One of her men had been a commercial fisherman

and was experienced at handling this type of boat. He'd already started the engine.

"Shove off now!" she ordered.

The moon was bright, cascading beams across the water. The water was choppy, slapping at their hull. They cruised slowly out of the harbor, careful to obey the 5 mile per hour limit posted on the buoys.

Once outside the harbor, she ordered the man at the helm to speed up.

"Full throttle?" he asked.

She nodded. Allison was excited to be with Miguel again, but nervous they were taking drugs aboard. The timing could be off by anything from thirty minutes to three hours, depending on circumstances. Waiting out in the open seas, especially without running lights, could be dangerous. Forty-five minutes passed while they idled in the same spot.

One of the men spotted the sub on the surface: a tiny light blinked the number of times they had agreed upon: three and then two. "There she is!" he shouted. The sub was about two hundred yards away.

"Turn on the running lights and proceed slowly in their direction," she told her temporary captain.

They moved closer. Her men helped put out the bumpers and toss the lines when they were closer, and the sub tied up securely against the trawler. Miguel was first to board. Allison ran to him, and they kissed. Both crews set to transporting the bundles of drugs to the fishing boat. Allison handed the sub crew several bundles of cash from the past weeks' sales to the gangs. That would be their payment, and the transfer was complete.

"*Gracias.* A good voyage, Captain," Miguel said. "You may take the ship back to Colombia. You must return here," Miguel gestured to the sky and open ocean around them, "in five weeks to take me back."

After the diesel was transferred from the barrels to the fuel tank of the submarine—a time-consuming and tedious process—the boats cast off. The crew on the trawler watched the sub slowly submerge, then they headed back to the marina. They were three miles out to sea, but could easily see the shore lights from the city of Bandon.

Allison kept the running lights off, hoping they wouldn't be noticed heading toward shore. The man at the helm was navigating by the lights on the distant shore. When they were three hundred yards out, she turned on the lights and they puttered slowly into the marina. After docking and tying up, the crew members drove the truck back and parked it as close to the vessel as they could. The men transferred the boxes of cocaine and weed from the boat to the waiting truck.

"We'll be home in a few minutes, sweetheart. I can't wait to show you how much I've missed you." She spoke to Miguel softly, making sure the men couldn't hear.

Conversation between Miguel and his men had remained light and respectful. He would inspect their operations closely the following day. Their first stop was one of the larger homes Allison had purchased. On the property was a sturdy barn where they could secure the drugs until they were delivered. Miguel and Allison headed for Lake Selmac in her SUV. She had finally decided not to tell him about Steve raping her, not until later. Now she wanted to make love.

———

Dawn's cell phone broke the silence. It was her contact Alex Cruz, alias Captain Gomez. "Hello, Captain." She never used his name just in case their phone calls were monitored.

"Hello, Agent Hogan, this is the first chance I've had to reach you. I've surfaced off the coast of Crescent City, California. I offloaded Lorenzo and the crew into a raft—told them the sub was going to sink because of a malfunction. Alert the Coast Guard to pick them up. I dropped Miguel in Bandon, Oregon, with a sizeable load of drugs. I have several million dollars of his aboard we can use as evidence. After they pick up Lorenzo, ask them to guide me into the nearest safe port. I'll have a spotlight out blinking an SOS."

"Great job, Alex. I'm in the air not too far from you. We'll link up soon." Dawn smiled, relieved; the first part of the operation had been a success. She alerted the Coast Guard about the two very different rescues they would need to make and walked to the cockpit. "Where is the airport nearest to Bandon?" she asked the pilot.

"According to the charts, Medford," he said. "Actually, it's the only one in the area with a runway long enough to take this aircraft at night."

"Then that is where we're going." She dialed her cell again. "There'll be two SUVs waiting for us at the Medford airport, gassed and ready to go," she told her team.

"ETA's thirty minutes." the pilot spoke over the intercom.

The plane taxied to the end of the runway, far away from the terminal, and they unloaded their gear into the SUVs. It was still several hours before sunrise, and they would all need some sleep before heading to Grants Pass. They pulled into a nearby motel, two agents secured the four rooms they would need, and Dawn Hogan's small team settled in for a few hours rest. By eight the next morning, they were on their way again.

36

OREGON

It was 3:00 a.m. by the time Miguel and Allison arrived at her cottage; Miguel had slept most of the way. They agreed that making love could wait until morning.

The smell of coffee brewing filled the cottage, and Miguel opened his eyes to stare up at the unfamiliar ceiling. It took him a few moments to recall where he was. Allison stood in the doorway to the bedroom: she was wearing nothing but an apron.

She waved a spatula and giggled. "Which would you prefer first, me or breakfast?"

"Take off that silly apron and come back to bed. I'll show you what I'm hungry for." Miguel tossed aside the covers and grabbed her by the waist. She was laughing as he rolled her onto bed; then he was on top of her, kissing her. "My God, how I've missed you."

They made love for nearly an hour.

"Now," he said. "Now, I'm ready for breakfast. Then we'll see what you've put together here in Oregon." He grabbed her ass as she passed and he headed for the shower.

The weather was one of those days that Oregon would put on a tourist brochure: cool, sunny, and dry. Around the lake, the trees had begun to change colors and reflected in the smooth surface of the water. After breakfast, Allison planned to show him around the lake and then take him to his many businesses in Cave Junction.

"The menu this morning is eggs, bacon, hash browns, toast, and coffee. I need to keep your energy up." She smiled at him, hardly daring to believe he was really here at last. It seemed like forever since they'd been together. What really ate at her was the rape. She would need to tell him, but she would put it off as long as she could.

They held hands as they walked along the road that encircled the lake.

"Look at those trees and flowers!" he exclaimed. "I once thought Colombia was the most beautiful place on earth, but there are different kinds of beauty I'm learning. Because of you.... You never told me it was this beautiful." They stopped to watch children playing at the boat dock.

"What would you like to do next?" she asked.

"Let's see the grow houses first. Then show me where and how you schedule the buys with the gangs."

Instantly concerned, she turned to him. "We'll do that. Is there a problem with how I'm handling things? I've followed your instructions to the letter."

"No, of course not, sweetheart. I just want to see how the business is handled in this part of the world."

"Let's head back to the cottage," Allison said. "I'll get my ring of keys to the houses, and we can leave for Cave Junction."

Over the next three hours, Miguel inspected the twenty grow houses. "There're a few things we should attend to. We should clean up the front yards, mow the grass, and put up fences around the properties with electronic gates. Even though they're isolated, we should install surveillance—discreet surveillance that isn't obvious." He laughed for a moment. "I know it's difficult with two bachelor guys, but it must look as though someone's *really* living there."

Allison nodded. She'd considered these measures but wasn't certain whether contacting a security company might attract attention to the operations.

"We should build outbuildings, twenty by forty feet, about fifty feet away, connected by a tunnel from the house. Hmm... probably high enough for someone like me to walk through easily. It would be used for storing packaged drugs and have enough room for one car. Store the gate clicker there," he added. "It would be used in an emergency for escape. As much as possible, have our men do the work. You and I can go to different cities to purchase the electronics so no one will become suspicious. This is for each of the houses." He looked pleased with how the project had progressed.

Allison was busy taking notes. "I'll get them started on it right away."

"Now, I want to see Grants Pass." He gestured toward the SUV. "Another thing that surprises me about this country—the roads are so good. There's no litter any place."

They visited three county parks and a small village called Merlin outside the northwest city limits of Grants. "These were the areas where we've met the buyers," Allison told him.

"Good job, baby," he said. "One thing you must be careful about is that cameras are everywhere nowadays. Avoid parking lots or anywhere close to retail stores. Find locations with the least amount of traffic for the drops. Preferably always go at night."

"Yes, that's how we've been doing it," Allison assured him.

"See if you can find out how many patrol cars are on duty every night in the county and how large their beats are. Then you should call in a problem to the Sheriff's Office, so they'll respond to something at the other end of their beat. That way there's less chance of bother during a sale." Miguel always spoke as though he could visualize everything in his head. "You always change locations, don't you?"

The following day, Allison decided finally that she should tell Miguel about the awful night she was raped.

She wondered how she could possibly set the stage for such a thing. "Honey, for our lunch today, how about a nice picnic on the other side of the lake?"

"That'd be great," Miguel said.

Allison walked down to the little store and bought some of the ingredients she would need. As she left the store she saw Steve buying gas for his car at one of the pumps. He looked up and smiled—it was an evil smile—and waved. She turned away and walked faster. She started trembling, tears running down her cheeks. *Please, please! Don't let him follow me!* she thought. When she reached the wooded area, she ducked behind a tree and waited. After a few minutes, she glanced back toward the store: he was gone. *Now, I know I have to tell Miguel, but I can't let him see me like this.* She wiped her eyes and headed home.

Miguel was sprawled in a lounge chair on the porch and had fallen asleep. She slipped inside and fixed her makeup. When lunch was ready she woke him, and they drove around the lake to the picnic area. Sipping iced tea and munching deli-fresh sandwiches, they lounged on the blanket she'd brought. Miguel was stretched out, his head in her lap and staring up at the sky while she stroked his hair.

"Sweetheart, there is something I must tell you," she said softly.

"You've been crying, haven't you?" He reached up to tenderly touch her cheek but sat up quickly. "Is something wrong?"

Allison began to cry again. "Yes. Yes, there is."

"What is it, dear? How I can help?"

She held her head in her hands and for a moment said nothing. Then, she blurted out her news. "A week ago, when I was asleep here at home... a man broke in and brutally raped me!" she managed to say between sobs. She detailed every sadistic thing he had put her through.

"I can't believe what I'm hearing," Miguel muttered through clenched teeth. "I'll kill the son-of-a-bitch."

"I didn't tell the cops about it, because I didn't want them around.'

Miguel nodded. "You did the right thing, baby."

"I figured that you'd take care of him when you came here. Just tell me you still love me."

He pulled her close to him. "Of course I do."

She looked up, recognizing the anger boiling in his eyes; that was what she had hoped for.

"Do you know who did this to you?"

"I recognized his voice."

"So, you had spoken to him before?"

"I did once on my way to the community picnic. He was working on a road crew on the other side of the lake. I gave the crew a jug of iced water. They all looked so tired and hot... I thought I was being nice."

Miguel held her at arm's length, staring deep into her eyes. "Do you know his name?"

"Yes. It's Steve. That's all I know."

"Does he live around here?"

She shrugged. "I don't know... maybe."

"What makes you think so?"

"I saw him earlier today buying gas—down at our little store. He frightened me."

"Did he talk to you?"

"No, he just grinned and waved. I hurried home."

"Does he know you recognized him?"

"I don't think so."

"What does he look like?"

"He's tall and he has wavy blond hair. That's all I can tell you."

"Do you think the community might have a list of residents?"

"I don't know. Let's stop at the store on our way home and ask," she said.

The community around Lake Selmac must never have heard of not sharing private information, and Allison was relieved. The lady who owned the store handed her a list with everyone's names, addresses, and phone numbers.

"Thank you so much. It's nice to know your neighbors when you're new to an area," Allison explained. "Just in case of an emergency." She returned to the car, and Miguel studied the list. There were three men named Steve, but only one who did not list a wife's name with it.

"Let's check this guy Steve Ramsey on Pine Crest Road," Miguel said.

They drove through the roads up into the woods and

away from the lake until they found a road called Pine Crest. The forest was dense and bushes crowded in along the road. Steve Ramsey's driveway was long and narrow; halfway down it turned, so they couldn't see any residence or a car.

"What will we do now?" Allison looked to Miguel for an answer. "We can't risk his seeing my car out here."

"I have an idea. Let's go back to your place and gather up a few little items." Back at the cottage Miguel asked for matches and an old rag. He tore it into strips and knotted them together and attached a string to one end. "Do you have a large zip-lock bag?"

In the kitchen, Allison opened a drawer and handed him a box of food storage bags. "Will this do?"

"It's perfect," he replied. "Of course—just like you." He kissed her once before walking out to her car. He removed the gas cap and, holding onto the string, he let the rag slide down the filler tube into the gas tank. He pulled out the gas-soaked rag, placed it in the zip-lock bag, and secured it so a short piece of string remained outside. "Now, where do you dump your garbage around here?"

"Everyone uses a dumpster provided by the county," she said. When they arrived at the dumpster, it was overflowing. Miguel picked three bags and put them in her car.

"What in the world are you doing?" she asked.

"The list we have gives his phone number. I'll use my burner phone to call him. When he comes out to see what the hell's going on, you tell me if he's the right guy or not."

They drove back to Steve Ramsey's driveway. Miguel stepped out and placed the garbage sacks in a ditch near the entrance. He purposely put an electric utility bill in Allison's name next to the sacks. He then ripped open one of the other trash sacks, placed the gas-soaked rag in the opening, lit a match, and touched it to the rag. It flamed up immediately.

Miguel hopped back into the car, and they drove to a pullout where they could watch from a distance. He allowed the fire to smolder for a short time before calling Steve's number. "Hey, neighbor," he shouted into the cell. "You've got a raging fire in your driveway." Within seconds, Steve had driven down to the entrance. He jumped out and began stomping on the smoldering garbage.

"That's him! That's the dirty son-of-a-bitch who raped me!" Allison cried out. They watched as he extinguished the fire, then paused to sort through the bags. Miguel had counted on this: he would want to figure out whose garbage it was. Finally, he picked up the utility envelope. Allison and Miguel watched as he read the name, then wadded up the envelope and tossed it on the ground.

"That's one angry man," Miguel said softly. They watched until he got back in his car and drove back up the driveway. "I'm sure he'll pay you a visit tonight. We'll be waiting and ready."

They drove in silence for a few miles.

"Does that little store have rope and duct tape?" Miguel asked.

In spite of her anger, Allison managed to laugh. "Everyone has duct tape, as far as I know. I once knew a photographer who always carried a roll of tape with him in case of an equipment malfunction with his tripod."

"Okay. Stop there and buy the tape and some rope. The stronger the rope the better." He paused, and she could tell he was thinking. "Do you mind if I stay in the car? I don't want to be seen, not yet."

When they arrived home, Miguel started closing the shades, explaining his plans to Allison. "He's pissed off now. He'll want to settle the score and take it out on you. Later tonight he'll be paying you a visit. I'm sure of that. He's a fucking coward, and the asshole is going to pay with his life."

The moon was partially shaded by the clouds, making it darker than most nights. Headlights flashed through the trees, then a car pulled off the road and stopped. Someone stepped out and started walking through the woods toward Allison's cottage. He stopped at the edge of the clearing.

Miguel and Allison had left two lights on in the house: one in the bathroom and the other in her bedroom.

Miguel held his breath. From a darkened room he watched Steve walk quietly up to the house and peer through the bedroom window. Allison switched off the bathroom light, as they had planned, and walked into the bedroom. She let her robe fall to the floor and began combing her hair.

Outside, Steve continued watching. *Shit, what a beautiful creature she is.* He was going to have some more of that ass in a little while. He waited for the light to switch off; somewhere soft music was playing. *What was the name of that tune...? Oh, yeah. "In the Still of the Night"—that's what it was.* "Sweet dreams, baby." He sat down on the grass and lit a cigarette. Thirty minutes later, he was at the front door with a pry bar, opening the door.

As Steve stepped into the front room, Miguel hit him on the head with the butt of his gun. The intruder staggered and fell to the floor in the dark. Miguel wasn't sure he was out cold and for good measure, he kicked him hard in the ribs. Then he jumped on the man's back, feeling the satisfying crunch of ribs and vertebrae under his feet. With duct tape, he secured Steve's hands behind his back and wrapped his ankles together. Last he covered his mouth with tape. "Is this how you like it, pretty boy?" he hissed in the man's face.

"Miguel, is everything okay?" Allison cried, turning on the other lights.

"Yeah, yeah. Come on in and see big, strong lover boy now." Miguel propped him up with his head against the wall.

Steve was moaning. A trickle of blood ran from the top of his head to his cheek and down his neck.

Miguel slapped his face and ripped the tape from Steve's mouth. "Are you awake now, prick?"

"Yeah, what hit me?"

"I did," Miguel said.

"Why?" Steve asked.

"For raping my lady," Miguel answered while Allison stood there listening.

"I never raped that bitch," Steve shouted. "She wanted me to fuck her—it was her idea!"

"That's bullshit! You broke into my house and raped me!"

"You invited me here. You were all over me like stink on shit," Steve said.

Allison was trying to remain calm. "Oh, yeah, then why are you here tonight?"

"I thought you sent me a message earlier today."

"I don't believe a thing you're saying, you piece of cow-shit!" Miguel jerked him to his feet and carried him to the couch. He placed Steve on his stomach and used rope to hog-tie him, placing one loop around his ankles and the other around his neck: if he tried to straighten out his legs, he would choke himself. Miguel turned Steve's head to the side so he could breathe through his nose.

"We'll keep him here until morning," Miguel whispered to Allison. "Then we'll find a secluded spot to kill him and get rid of the body."

"It's Sunday morning. I doubt anyone will be around. I can back up the car to the side door. I think we can load him in the car without anyone noticing." Allison spoke softly, glancing disdainfully at a very nervous Steve.

"Drive Steve's car back to his house tonight, and I'll follow and pick you up there," Miguel said.

"Let's make sure he's secured first. We'll do it now."

When they returned, Allison spread a shower curtain on the floor. She and Miguel carried Steve over and laid him in the center of the sheet.

"If he pisses during the night, I don't want him ruining the carpet," she said practically.

37

OREGON

BJ and Jumpy were having coffee at the Tee Time Café in Grants Pass. The cozy eatery had become their office away from the office.

"I've been studying a map of the area around Cave Junction," BJ said after he had finished his first cup. "There's an abandoned silver mine near the Oregon Caves. It'd be a great place to hike into if you feel up to it." He held up his cup for a refill and Mitzi, who'd come to know the two of them, appeared like magic with a fresh pot.

She grinned at them and winked. "You guys, really. What are you two up to now?"

"My buddy here thinks I'm too old for a little hike," Jumpy said. "What's your opinion?"

"You're both just youngsters," she teased.

Jumpy laughed. "Yeah, sure. I'm game, BJ. When do you want to go?"

"Is Sunday morning open for you?"

"Let's do it," Jumpy replied. "Every *Monday*, I promise Sandy that we'll go to church *next* Sunday. Maybe she forgets."

BJ ignored Jumpy's other remark. With a policeman's weird shifts and Carol's odd nursing schedule they had rarely made it to church. "It's pretty rough back there from what I read. Bring your weapon, wear some really sturdy a hiking boots, and bring gloves. I'll bring water and my camera."

"Why our weapons?"

BJ laughed. "You never know when you might run across a bear. Maybe your very own bear."

"Humph!" Jumpy pretended he didn't hear. "What time are we leaving?"

"I'll pick you up at seven, and we should be up there about nine." BJ paid the bill and left a couple dollars on the table. They headed to the Sheriff's Office for a command meeting; all staff had been ordered to attend.

"Ladies and gentlemen, I would like to introduce Dawn Hogan from the DEA," the sheriff said.

A slender, attractive brunette stood, faced the group, and stepped up to the lectern. "Hello, everyone." Murmurs of "hello" and "hi" rippled through the room. "This won't take long. Your sheriff will fill in the details later. I just want to let know we will be working in your county for awhile on drug trafficking by a heavy hitter from Colombia by the name of Miguel Vargas. He is considered a *seriously flawed individual....*"

She paused a moment and glanced around the room, making eye contact with almost everyone.

She continued, "That's right: 'seriously flawed.' We don't use that term often. He is most dangerous and a violent individual. Please wear your badges and carry a weapon at all times. Who works the west end of your county?" BJ, Jumpy, and two other deputies raised their hands. "I believe that's the area we'll be working most." She handed a stack of business cards to the sheriff. "Everyone, please take one of my cards in case you need to contact me. Do not discuss this information with *anyone* outside law enforcement. Thank you for your time." She turned and left the room.

Sheriff Patterson took over the meeting and again mentioned the motorcycle gangs and black gangs that had been noticed in the area. "We've also been receiving many more bogus calls lately. Let's be careful out there," he said and the meeting was adjourned.

BJ and Jumpy were about to leave when Sheriff Patterson summoned them back to his office. "Gentlemen, I'm sure you'll be happy to hear that the missing woman—the third case you have—has turned up back here in Oregon. Her husband called me yesterday. It seems she ran off with another man and was traveling the carnival circuit with him for the last couple of years."

"No shit?" Jumpy asked.

"You're pulling my leg, aren't you, Sheriff?" BJ asked. "You figured we needed a good laugh after a meeting with the DEA."

Patterson laughed and raised his right hand. "The honest truth. The carnival guy took up with another woman, and he dumped her high and dry in Oklahoma. She found her way back here, and the husband took her back. All is forgiven—so mark that one closed." He chuckled for a moment. "But that is one of the strangest ways to solve a case!"

BJ and Jumpy went back to the cubicle they used for an office.

"There!" BJ had used the large red stamp that read *Closed* and replaced the file in the cabinet.

"It looks like we've worked ourselves out of a job," Jumpy said.

38

OREGON

Dawn Hogan pressed the numbers on her cell phone. Alex Cruz answered on the first ring. "Alex, this is Dawn Hogan. Can you meet me at the Holiday Inn at Bandon in three hours? Wait for me in the lobby, okay?"

"I'll be there," he said and switched off the phone.

Dawn Hogan and her crew had headed directly for Bandon after stopping in Grants Pass. Alex Cruz was already at the hotel when they arrived. "Hey, Alex, sorry we're late," she greeted him. "We stopped in Grants Pass to inform the local Sheriff's Office before we headed to the coast. We also got a bite to eat. I can run on adrenaline for a limited amount of time."

"I've been here just a few minutes," Alex said. "I stopped for some chow myself."

"I need you with us to ID this drug kingpin. Who's meeting him?" Dawn asked.

"He's mentioned a woman named Allison, but no last name. The trawler's named *Ride the Tide*. The name's in tall red letters on the stern, and they dock it in Bandon. We offloaded cocaine and weed with a street value of at least $150,000,000. I marked a few bundles of coke for evidence. You know, with our special black light marker."

"Let's head for the marina area," Dawn instructed her team.

At the third marina they tried they finally found a boat named *Ride the Tide*. Dawn called out, "Hello? Anyone aboard? *Hola?*" She called out again, "DEA! We're coming aboard!" Guns drawn and readied, they boarded and searched the entire ship, even behind the bulkheads and under the decking. All they found were the empty barrels that had contained the sub's diesel fuel.

"Run the ship's number with the state and get the owner's name. While you're at it, check with DMV for any other vehicles under that name," she said. "Alex, did Miguel mention anyplace else they were going?"

"It was a long trip, and we talked about all kinds of things. I believe there was a town Miguel mentioned where they had multiple grow houses. Cave Junction... that's it. But Allison lives in a place called Selmac. No... it's Lake Selmac," he said.

En route the agent who was running the title search called out, a thrill of success in his voice. "We got a hit on the name Allison Denney showing a commercial trawler, an SUV, and several trucks. I'll check with the utility companies to see if they have a customer with that name. "Yup, here it is: 112 Bedrock Lane, Lake Selmac."

"Great, we'll find a motel and set up a command post. I'll tell the manager that we're a wildlife film crew and need four rooms for a few days." She hesitated a moment, studying her team, and chuckled. "You don't really look like a film crew. No more suits, that's definitely out. Remember, guys, we can't be seen with weapons, badges, or uniforms. Tomorrow's Sunday. After breakfast, we'll check out her residence."

"Get a good night's sleep, gentlemen, because I have a feeling we're going to be busy tomorrow," Dawn said as she walked into the motel office.

The motel owner-manager was quite happy to rent four rooms. "Business has been a little slow lately," she said.

Dawn and her crew settled in for the night.

Before daylight the next morning, Allison backed the SUV to the side of the cottage. She and Miguel carried Steve, still bundled in the shower curtain, to the car. They placed him behind the rear seat and covered him with a blanket. He had pissed his pants and smelled strongly of urine.

She slid into the driver's seat. "Where should we go?"

"Just drive to any remote area."

They headed southwest toward Cave Junction. Allison drove through town until she came to Highway 46 leading up into the area near the Oregon Caves National Monument. Several miles later, she spotted an overgrown logging road that appeared abandoned and unused. She turned onto the primitive road and proceeded slowly into the woods. Ruts and rocks made the vehicle bounce around like a pinball. The overgrowth scratched at the sides of the SUV.

They had traveled about a mile before they came to a small clearing where dry slash lay about in piles, probably from trees cut down years ago. On the far edge of the clearing was a creek that she gauged was about twelve feet across, and the logging trail continued on the other side.

"This will do," Miguel said.

They pulled out the plastic sheet with Steve and dumped him on the ground. He landed with a thud. He was still alive but very weak. Miguel sliced through the hog-tie rope so they could stand him up. His hands and feet were still secured, and the tape remained on his mouth. Miguel steadied him for a moment: he was weak from being tied up in one position.

Miguel turned to Allison. "Do you remember exactly what he did to you?"

She nodded silently.

"I want you to be extremely angry with him. Mad enough to punish the creep for the sick, painful things he put you through." He sliced through Steve's clothes with a knife. Within minutes Steve stood there before them, completely naked, looking about him fearfully.

Miguel handed her the knife. "Show this asshole what your pain was like!"

Allison grabbed the knife and walked close to Steve, seething with anger. Using the blade, she cut a large X across his chest, from his shoulders to his waist, drawing blood that flowed steadily to the ground. Steve's face twisted, contorted with pain, and he fell to his knees.

Miguel rolled Steve over until he was on his back and stood back, his arms crossed across his chest. "Keep going, baby. Show me how much you hate him."

Again Allison used the knife to slice into both sides of his face and across his forehead. Tears were rolling down her face. She ripped the tape from his mouth. "I want to hear you scream and beg for me to stop! You get off hurting women—brutalizing women—don't you?" She jabbed the blade inside his nose and jerked. Blood spewed from his nostrils.

Steve bellowed in agony, screaming at the top of his lungs.

Miguel took the knife from Allison. "Good work, baby. I'll finish off the bastard." He rolled Steve onto his stomach again. "I hear you like it up the ass, right? Try this on for size, you fuck." He plunged the knife deep into Steve's rectum. "You'll never do that to another woman again!"

Steve was flopping on the ground like a fish out of water, but no fish ever gushed blood like he was bleeding. Miguel walked calmly back to the car, pulled out the shovel he'd brought from the cottage, and started digging a hole to bury what remained of Steve Ramsey.

This was not the way he wanted to start his life in America.

39

OREGON

"It's nearly nine o'clock." BJ was studying the GPS. "I think we're getting close. Look for an old mining trail that leads back to the silver mine."

"It's to the left," Jumpy said as they turned in.

"This old logging trail is nearly overgrown. I don't want those tree branches scratching the hell out of my truck. Let's park here and walk in."

"How far do you think we are from the mine?"

"At least a couple miles."

They grabbed their gear and water and set out. As they continued down the trail, BJ noticed that a vehicle had traveled through recently. "Don't you wonder who was that stupid?" he said to Jumpy.

"Someone who didn't care about the finish on his vehicle for sure!"

Walking the trail was easier than driving would have been; they were making good time.

"Listen!" Jumpy stopped. "I think I heard someone screaming. There it is again."

"It's just ahead!" They started running toward the sound. As they neared the clearing, they could see a man on the ground whose hands and feet were tied. He was covered in blood. A blond woman with blood on her hands and clothing was standing over him. Another man was there; he was digging a hole.

"Stop, police!" BJ shouted to the man. He and Jumpy stepped into the clearing, their guns drawn.

The woman dropped the knife and raised her hands above her head. The man jumped out of the hole, stepped behind her, and grabbed her around the neck. In his other hand, he held a gun pointed at her temple. "Don't move, Allison!"

"Drop the gun," BJ ordered. He and Jumpy were at least ninety feet away from them.

Allison's terror could be heard over the rush of water. "What are you doing, Miguel?"

"Saving my ass, if I have to!" The man she had called Miguel said. "You don't honestly think I believed that bullshit story about this guy raping you? You're soiled goods to me now. If I have to kill you, I will." He was still holding her, slowly edging back toward the stream.

"Stop—or I'll shoot!" BJ was shouting over the roar of the water.

"No you won't—not while I have her!" Miguel called back.

"The DEA team is the closest law enforcement," BJ said. "Get Agent Hogan on the line and tell her our situation."

Jumpy quickly dialed his cell. "We need your help now!" Jumpy shouted into the phone. He told Dawn their location and what was going down. "They're on their way!" His phone went silent.

Miguel had been backing up as BJ advanced into the clearing, but Jumpy was circling around to the right. The man on the ground lay still and was no longer screaming.

Miguel continued backward with Allison until he caught his heel on a rock. Together they fell back into the stream. His gun discharged: his aim had slipped as he fell and he'd shot Allison in the neck. When he lost his grip on her he aimed at BJ next but missed. BJ and Jumpy fired at the same time, hitting Miguel in the arm and leg.

Miguel had managed to wade almost across the stream, dragging Allison with him, her blood floating out behind them. He ducked behind two large boulders and let her go. She was floating downstream with the current.

Jumpy was struggling to reach her before she drowned, trying to stay with the trees. If he went in after her now, Miguel would have a clear shot at him.

BJ stepped back into the woods for cover. He hoped to distract Miguel long enough for Jumpy to rescue Allison. She was floating face down and had already passed where Jumpy had taken cover. BJ aimed carefully and shot a round at the edge of a large boulder. The shot at least caused Miguel to duck. Holding his cell phone high above his head, Jumpy threw himself into the water and finally reached Allison.

Each time Miguel raised up, BJ would fire another round. Relieved, he watched Jumpy pull Allison out of the water and into the trees, well out of Miguel's sight. She was unconscious but alive. The bullet had gone through her neck. They would learn later that the bullet had severed her vocal cords, but missed the major arteries. She would never be able to speak again, even if she once could speak multiple languages.

Miguel's wounds must not have been serious. He was limping as he disappeared down the trail. He was wet, wounded, and in an area that was totally unfamiliar to him. The trail was taking him deeper into the woods; soon he found he was in a valley, surrounded by hills on all sides. He left the trail and began to climb higher. His throat was parched, and he must have felt like hell. His wounds were throbbing and had started to bleed heavily. He tore a piece of his shirt and tried to bandage himself. *What good was all his wealth and power to him now,* he thought.

Jumpy's cell was buzzing. The display showed it was Agent Hogan. "Your truck is blocking the trail," she said. "We're on foot, heading your way."

"We need an ambulance!" Jumpy told her. BJ joined Jumpy and carried Allison back to where Steve now lay dead.

As Dawn and her crew broke into the clearing, Andy Cruz called out, "That's Miguel's girlfriend. Where the hell is he?"

"He's still on the loose, somewhere in the woods up ahead." BJ explained what had taken place. He tossed his truck keys to Jumpy. "Run down to the truck and move it so the ambulance can get through and get back here fast." Two men from Dawn's crew left to move their vehicles.

Dawn, BJ, and the rest of her team splashed across the stream and walked the trail, guns readied. They were searching for drops of blood to help follow Miguel's path. The splashes of were getting closer together; that meant he was moving slower.

It seemed Miguel had scaled up further; the blood splatters indicated he was stumbling on loose rocks. As the crew climbed higher, the trees were thinning, and they were nearly a thousand feet above the valley floor. Occasionally they would catch a glimpse of him and then he would disappear behind a boulder or a tree. Dawn's agents fanned out, trying to keep Miguel in sight. The DEA team carried handheld radios and were able to direct each other in their pursuit. BJ was trying to stay directly behind Miguel.

Now Miguel Vargas was a hundred yards ahead of them but he was still armed. They wanted to take him alive, but needed to be careful not to make targets of themselves. Miguel had squeezed between two large boulders and found the opening to a cave. It was large enough for him to walk in standing upright. He pressed back against the wall, staying in the shadows.

A moment later a DEA agent walked past the cave; Miguel took a shot at him. The bullet ricocheted off the boulder and hit the agent in the arm. The agent fell, hitting his head against the rock; he was knocked unconscious. Everyone stopped.

Dawn did a radio check. One agent didn't answer.

"Who was on Agent Styles' right," she asked.

"I was," Agent Johnson responded.

"Who was on his left?"

Agent Mather said, "I was."

"You two stay where you are. We're coming to your location."

The agent closest to BJ motioned to him. "Follow me." He led him to where Dawn was. The agents closed in to where Agent Styles had been when he was shot. BJ could hear him moaning and then saw him lying next to a tree. Their movements drew another round from Miguel, but the bullet missed.

"I can't see him, but I think he's between those two boulders," BJ told the agent. He circled around to where he could pull the wounded agent from the direct line of fire. Agent Styles had regained consciousness; BJ instructed him to put direct pressure on his wound with his other hand.

BJ called in the direction of the boulders. "Come out now!" There wasn't any answer.

"You might as well give it up," Dawn shouted. "We're not going anywhere and neither are you!"

They would learn that Miguel had worked back into the cave twenty feet only to find it was a dead-end. He was tired, thirsty, dirty, and still bleeding. He must have known he didn't stand a chance of getting out alive.

He walked up to the cave entrance. "I'm coming out unarmed. Don't shoot," he called down to the crew below. When he arrived at the boulders, he tossed his gun out first and then squeezed between the rocks, hands in the air. One of Dawn Hogan's agents cuffed him.

BJ used his cell phone to call the Medevac helicopter and gave their location. "ETA twenty minutes," someone in the chopper answered.

BJ and the DEA crew cautiously escorted Miguel back to the clearing. The paramedics had placed Allison on a stretcher and had covered the body of Steve Ramsey with a blanket. Two deputies from the Sheriff's CSI Unit had already arrived. They were stringing crime scene tape and marking the spots where the spent bullet casings were found.

"That was a hell of a job, BJ. How did you guys do it?" Dawn asked.

"Just got our second wind," they answered in unison. They laughed and gave each other a high five.

"Hey, are we done here?" BJ asked.

Agent Hogan nodded. "You're free to go." She shook hands with BJ hand and then with Jumpy. "Thanks, guys. Enjoy the rest of your weekend."

"All right. We're going to continue our hike to the old mine." BJ shared a grin with his friend. "You know, the reason I picked this area for my retirement is because there was very little crime. It just goes to show you nothing stays the same forever."

40

Oregon

It was late spring, and BJ and Carol had lived in Grants Pass for almost two years. They'd moved into their house fourteen months ago. There had been rain this morning, but it finally cleared, and by late afternoon sunshine glistened on the river.

BJ decided to walk down and collect the mail. Earlier, the postman had driven by in the downpour and waved to them. He figured whatever was there could wait.

Jumpy would be coming up from his house later on. Sometimes they'd sit on the deck, sipping a beer, and swap stories of old times. Often they talked about fishing. Talking was the easy part of retirement—maybe the best, he'd decided.

Later, on his way down to the mailboxes, BJ considered that, all in all, he'd been mighty lucky. This part of Oregon was the prettiest part of the world, as far as he was concerned. He had a good wife, whom he thought was still the prettiest gal in town.

Carson and Dane were doing well in college. Carson had even brought his girl friend home on spring break. She was a cute blond with blue eyes who was in her second year of the University of Oregon's nursing program. Did a boy really look for someone just like his mother? Time would tell. Dane had already changed his major: he'd decided to go into law enforcement, just like his dad.

BJ reached into the mailbox and pulled out the newspaper—only slightly damp—and a pile of catalogues he would toss into the recycle bin. He shook his head at the wastefulness of mail order companies and then noticed the letter with an official, embossed return address. It was the third letter he'd received from Dawn Hogan since that morning that seemed so long ago. What kind of news was she able to tell him now?

He tore into the envelope and stood there reading the letter, while the gentle sun of late May warmed his neck. He waved to Jumpy in his pickup, headed up the road to their house.

"It's news from Dawn Hogan!" he called. "Take me up to the house, and I'll share everything with you."

"Sounds great!"

BJ opened the door and clambered in. "Sorry about the mud on my boots, pal. You won't believe what she's got to say!"

Later, sitting on the deck, they had both read and discussed Agent Hogan's news.

"Another beer?"

"Not for now," Jumpy said.

"So, she's returned to her team in Bogotá. That's good."

"I'm always curious about the details."

Jumpy nodded.

"Yet, somehow the government of Colombia in coordination with the DEA managed to take down Miguel's compound in the city and his place in the country, Nieve del Diablo."

Dawn Hogan's letter explained that during the raids, Jake had been killed by a landmine, but Rafael had disappeared through one of the secret tunnels with some vast amount of cash. She confided that she doubted they could ever find him. Some of her other news included a promotion, with a substantial pay increase. She modestly mentioned in passing that she'd also received the agency's highest award.

Jumpy picked up the letter and glanced at the second page. "That's darn good news about Miguel."

Miguel Vargas had received a life sentence, without possibility of parole. He was serving time in a United States prison for the murder of Steve Ramsey and drug trafficking. Miguel's men were also arrested and convicted. Allison Denney had been convicted of drug manufacturing, money laundering, sale of illegal drugs, and second degree murder. She was sentenced to thirty years in a maximum security prison.

"Can you imagine, a beautiful and intelligent woman like Allison, never being able to speak again?" BJ said, but he knew there was no good answer.

"It's a matter of choices, I guess." Jumpy looked thoughtful and gazed out toward the horizon. "Are you happy with yours?"

"Look!" Two deer had wandered down to the river. BJ pointed to them and Jumpy turned to watch the young animals. "You bet. There's nothing like a quiet life of retirement for two old cops like us, is there?"

BJ heard the phone ring, but Carol had already answered it.

"Hon?" she called from the kitchen. "It's the sheriff. There's some other case...."

They didn't let her finish: they'd both burst out laughing.

Ends

Acknowledgments

Every writer works alone to some extent, but each of us depends on the support of many others, sometimes too numerous to mention. Most importantly, I wish to thank my wonderful wife Marilyn, for her unwavering love, support, and patience. The motivation and inspiration provided by a group of like-minded writers has been invaluable, especially the encouragement of author Priscilla Gazey. Many thanks to Lynn Cox for her friendship and help. Also, I'm especially grateful to Michaele Lockhart, my editor, fellow author, and friend, for her work and belief in me.

R. T. Wiley

About the Author

Former police officer and author R. T. Wiley brings over a decade's experience in law enforcement to his debut novel, *Seriously Flawed*. From an urban police department in California to a county sheriff's department in Oregon, Wiley has lived the world that he writes about. Now retired, he resides in Chandler, Arizona, with his wife Marilyn.

Made in the USA
San Bernardino, CA
02 May 2016